Gold Seekers of '49

By
Edwin L. Sabin

GOLD SEEKERS OF '49

I

THE MYSTERIOUS STRANGER

Charley Adams was trudging up to his knees in snow, on his way home from down town. It was Washington's Birthday, 1849, and winter had sent St. Louis a late valentine in shape of a big snowstorm. As this occurred seventy-five years ago, there were no street-cars in St. Louis (or in any other American city, for that matter); and even had there been street-cars they doubtless would have been tied up. At all events, Charley had walked down, and now he was trudging back with the mail.

His father was very anxious to see that mail. It contained the Eastern papers, and these probably would add to the tidings printed in the St. Louis papers, from the marvelous gold fields of California.

Since January, when President Polk's annual message to Congress had been read in St. Louis, in the papers, St. Louis people, like the whole population of the United States, had been crazy over the California gold. It was claimed that as far back as January, 1848, a man named Marshall, while digging a mill-race somewhere in interior Upper California, for a Captain Sutter of Sutter's Fort ranch, on the emigrant trail over the Sierra Nevada mountain-range down to Sacramento, had washed into plain sight an unlimited supply of gold flakes.

However, when the news first had reached Washington and New York and had filtered back to St. Louis, it was several months old and seemed scarcely worth attention, California being such a long way off. But now the President himself was authority for the fact that gold actually was lying around loose, for anybody to pick up, in this fair new land of California, and that thousands of people already were gathering it!

The President offered as proof letters from Colonel Richard B. Mason, the military governor of California, and from the Honorable Thomas O. Larkin, who had been the United States consul in California. The letters said not only that gold had been found, as before stated, but that 10,000 people (nearly all the able-bodied population of California) were out looking for more, and finding it, too! Sailors were deserting the ships and soldiers the ranks; servants were leaving the houses and merchants the stores, and the whole territory was wild. Congressmen at Washington asserted so much gold would be put on the market that gold money would lose its value, it would be so common.

These reports sounded like fairy-tales come true. Think of it! Gold, lying around on the surface of the ground, to be pocketed by the first finders! In spite of the fact that California had been a part of the United States only two years, or since the war with Mexico, and was distant 2000 miles across uninhabited desert and mountains, as soon as the word about gold was guaranteed to be really the truth a tremendous number of people here in the "States" set about dropping everything else and starting right away, to seek their fortunes.

Hundreds of St. Louis people had left, in parties large and small, a few to travel clear around Cape Horn of South America, or to cross the Isthmus of Panama and to sail up the Pacific Coast, but the majority to ride and walk, with wagon and team, across the deserts and mountains from the Missouri River 2000 miles to California. A number of neighbors and other friends of the Adamses had gone. Even Mr. Walker, Billy Walker's father, was going as soon as he could provide so that his family would not suffer in his absence; and he was talking of taking Billy. As Billy was Charley's best chum, this seemed pretty mean—for Charley, not for Billy, of course. To Charley there seemed no chance of his going, traveling across those wild plains and ranges, sleeping out of doors, and fighting Indians, perhaps, and then gathering gold in far California itself. His father was laid up, still recovering from wounds received in the war with Mexico. Charley was proud of his soldier father, who had served under General Scott all through the war, until disabled in the capture of Mexico City; but he did wish that there was some way for them to go to those gold fields.

The snow-storm had about ceased. The snow was two feet deep, in the streets, and the air was nipping chill. The streets were deserted, as evening settled down and Charley neared home. Now when he passed an open stairway, leading up into a building, he saw a huddled figure just inside the entrance.

He hurried on, but suddenly he stopped short. The figure had not stirred, as he passed — it looked odd — maybe it was only crouching there for shelter from the wind and snow — or maybe it was asleep — or maybe frozen. Jiminy! He ought not to go and leave it. Boy Scouts of America had not been organized, in 1849; but Charley was a Boy Scout at heart, so he turned back, anxious to do a good turn if possible.

When he peered into the entrance to the stairway, the huddled figure was there, just as first seen. It was that of a man, in ragged clothing, with worn boots, slouch hat, and unkempt beard visible where the face was bent forward upon the chest and folded arms. The figure did not move, and Charley spoke to it.

"Hello."

There was no response.

"Hello, there! What are you doing?"

Still no answer of any kind.

"Hey! Wake up!" bade Charley, more boldly. "You'll freeze."

Into Charley's throat welled a little tinge of fear; the figure remained so quiet and motionless. He reached in and shook the man by the shoulder. It was cold and stiff.

"Wake up! Wake up!"

Hurrah! The man was alive, anyway, for now he did stir drowsily, and mumbled as if objecting. Charley noticed that his hands were clenched tightly over the side-pockets of his old jacket, where the corners were drawn into his lap.

"Wake up! You'd better get out of here. You'll freeze. Want me to help you?"

Charley tried to lift the man, and to force him to move; but the man sat as a dead weight, and only mumbled crossly, and held back.

"Oh, crickity!" despaired Charley. "I'll have to get somebody to help. He's half frozen already. That's what's the matter with him."

Charley bolted out, to peer up and down the dusky white street. He had a notion to run to a little store about a block away, when he saw a man walking hastily along on the opposite side of the street. Out into the middle of the street floundered Charley, and hailed him.

"Hello! Can you please come over here a minute?"

"Sure, sonny." And he turned off, curiously approaching. "What is it you want, now?"

"There's a man freezing to death in the doorway, yonder," said Charley, excited. "He ought to be taken out."

"Who is he?"

"I don't know."

"What doorway, sonny?"

"That one. I'll show you." And Charley led off, the other man following him. He was a dark complexioned, sharp-faced man, with a little black moustache and a long drooping nose. He had bright black, narrow eyes, piercing but rather shifty. He wore a round fur cap and an overcoat with a cape.

The figure in the stairway entrance sat exactly as Charley had left him, except that he appeared to have gathered his coat pockets tighter.

"See?" directed Charley.

"Humph!" The long-nosed man peered in keenly. "Drunk, isn't he?" And he ordered roughly: "Come! get out o' here! Stir your stumps. This is no place to sleep."

The figure mumbled and swayed.

"I don't think he's drunk," ventured Charley. "He doesn't act like it, does he?"

"I dunno," grunted the long-nosed man, as if irritated. He reached in and, as Charley had done, but more rudely, grasped the figure by the shoulder; shook him and attempted to drag him forward; raised him a few inches and let him drop back again.

"We can't do anything. He looks like a beggar, anyhow. I'll see if I can find a watchman, on my way down town, and send him up."

That sounded inhuman, and Charley, for one, could not think of letting the figure huddle there, in the cold and the night, until the watchman should arrive. He did not like the long-nosed man.

"If you'll help, I'll take him home," volunteered Charley. "'Tisn't far."

"How far?" demanded the long-nosed man.

"Just a block and a half."

"What'll you do with him there?"

"Get him warm. My mother and father'll tend to him. They won't mind."

"Humph!" grunted the long-nosed man. "Well, let's see. But I don't intend to break my back for some no-'count trash such as this is. Come," he ordered, to the figure. "Get out o' here."

He grasped the figure by the arms and pulled him forward. Charley tried to get behind and boost. The tramp (if that was his kind) mumbled and actually resisted—hanging back and fighting feebly. His arms were wrenched from their position across his chest, and his coat corners fell back, with a thud, against the sides of the stairway.

"This fellow must be carrying a brick in each pocket," grumbled the long-nosed man. And halting his operations, despite the other man's resistance he roughly felt of the coat corners. But when he would have thrust in his hand, to investigate further, the other clutched the pockets so tightly and moaned "No! No!" so imploringly, that much to Charley's relief the long-nosed man quit.

Supporting their charge between them, and wading through the snow, they proceeded up the street. The "tramp" half shambled, half slid; darkness had gathered, stars were peeping out in the blue-black sky, the way seemed hard and lonesome, and Charley was glad indeed that they were bound to a place of warmth and shelter: home.

"It's right in the middle of this next block," panted Charley to the long-nosed man. "Where that horse-step is, under the big old oak."

The gate was ajar, and they turned through, dragging their awkwardly shambling burden. As they gained the front porch the front door was flung wide, and Mrs. Adams stood there, peering out, to find what was the meaning of this scuffling and grunting. Charley was glad to see her, framed in the lamp-light.

"Why, Charley!" she exclaimed. "What's the matter?"

"Please, mother, let us in," answered Charley. "We've got a man who was freezing in a stairway. Where'll we put him?"

"Gracious goodness! Take him right through and put him on the sofa. Oh, George!" and she called to Mr. Adams. "Is he badly frozen, Charley?" she asked, as Charley, tugging away, passed her.

"I don't think so, ma'am," replied the long-nosed man, speaking up. "No, ma'am. Not yet. He's fairly limber." And he scolded, to the "tramp": "Come on, now! You weigh a ton, with all your ballast."

Carrying and guiding the man, both, they continued on through the hall, into the pleasant sitting-room lighted by a whale-oil lamp and heated by a large wood-stove. At the call of his wife, Mr. Adams had hastily come from the back part of the house.

"Hello," he greeted. "What's here? Who is he, Charley?"

Charley's father was a tall man (he stood six feet one inch in his stockinged feet), and before the war he had been powerfully muscled. Now he was worn thin, and was a little stooped; and because of the wound in his knee, from a copper bullet, he limped. His full beard, trimmed around, was brown, but his eyes were a bright keen blue. Charley thought him the handsomest man in the world—and about the biggest.

"Somebody they've taken out of a stairway," explained Mrs. Adams, to him. "He was freezing. I told them to put him on the sofa."

"I should say so!" ejaculated Mr. Adams, and limped forward to help. Mrs. Adams quickly rearranged the knitted spread and the pillow; and with Mr. Adams attending to the feet end of the rescued stranger and Charley and the long-nosed man attending to the body and head, on the sofa the unknown was deposited.

"He's so thinly clothed!" cried Mrs. Adams, hovering over. "I'll get some hot milk." And away she bustled, for the kitchen.

"Let's take off his coat and boots," directed Mr. Adams, with soldierly decision. "Hope his feet aren't frozen." And he worked at the boots, to haul them from the cold, stiff feet.

Charley and the long-nosed man had a harder time with the coat. The unknown resisted, as before. He had opened his eyes (they were vacant and frightened) and had roused a little more strength. He even shoved the long-nosed man back.

"You," he appealed, huskily, to Charley, whom he seemed to accept as his friend. "You—take it."

"Well, I'll be jiggered!" ejaculated the long-nosed man. "There's gratitude for you!"

But he stood back, while Charley went ahead removing the coat. The unknown grasped the pockets, for the last time, and tried to hand them on to Charley.

"Keep it. You — —" and he fell back, exhausted.

"We don't want your coat, my man," assured Mr. Adams, briskly rubbing the feet.

"He's got something in the pockets, dad," explained Charley. "Something heavy."

"Look and see, then," bade the long-nosed man. "Now's your chance."

"Shall I?" queried Charley, of his father, doubtfully, holding the coat.

"Why, yes, if you want to. Perhaps we ought to know."

"Here's the milk," announced Mrs. Adams, hurrying in bearing glass and steaming pitcher.

Charley, with the long-nosed man peering curiously, and Mr. and Mrs. Adams looking, as well, fished out the weight from the right-hand coat pocket. It was a little buckskin sack, round and heavy with its contents.

"By thunder!" exclaimed the long-nosed man. "Hooray! I suspicioned it. This fellow's from the Californy gold mines, and that sack's stuffed with gold dust, as they call it. Open her up and see. Where's the other one? He's got the mate in t'other pocket, I'll bet you."

"Hold on, Charley. Don't open it," ordered Mr. Adams, as Charley fumbled with the string tied tightly around the puckered mouth of the little sack. "It isn't yours."

"Pass it to me and I'll open it," invited the long-nosed man. "Let me feel. Yes, sirs; that's gold dust, all right; several hundred dollars' worth."

"We'll not open it, just the same," insisted Mr. Adams, firmly. "Put the sack back in the pocket, Charley, and hang coat and all away. Wait, though.

Look through the other pockets and see if there are any letters or such things to tell who he is."

Charley sought. In the other side pocket he felt another buckskin sack, round and heavy (just as the long-nosed man, who was watching closely, had predicted), but the inside pockets contained nothing at all.

The unknown murmured weakly.

"I'd better give him a little hot milk, if he can drink it, hadn't I?" proffered Mrs. Adams; she poured a few inches into the glass and held it to his bearded lips. He tried to sip — did sip, greedily, and sank back.

Charley started off with the coat, to hang it over a chair.

"Here, you!" objected the long-nosed man. "What are you going to do? Half that coat's mine, remember. I helped fetch him in. Half the plunder comes to me."

"That's no way to talk, sir," reproved Mr. Adams, sternly. "Would you rob a helpless stranger? Not in this house, sir!"

"He's not dead. He's only fainted," informed Mrs. Adams, indignant.

"But he gave the stuff away, didn't he?" demanded the long-nosed man. "Sure he did. Supposing he dies on your hands, you count on getting all he has, I reckon! But you won't."

"He told me to keep it, anyway, didn't he?" retorted Charley.

"He didn't mean you to keep it for yourself, Charley," corrected Mr. Adams. "That's foolishness. He meant that you should keep it safe until he could use it."

"Of course," nodded Mrs. Adams. "What had we better do with him, George?"

"Let him sleep, if he wants to. His feet are getting warm. He'll be all right."

"Lookee here," blustered the long-nosed man. "I come in for half, remember. I helped fetch him in. If it hadn't been for my help he'd have frozen solid where he was, or else the watchman would have picked him up and taken him off. I'm going, now. I've got business to tend to—same as before I was interrupted. I left a business errand, to help fetch him here. Understand? My time's worth money. I know where this house is, and I know your names; and I'm coming 'round again, to see what's what. Half that dust is mine, or I'll make you trouble."

"If he doesn't use it, himself, it will go to his kin, sir," returned Mr. Adams.

"Kin!" snorted the long-nosed man. "He's from the gold fields. Look at that shirt, and those whiskers and boots; and the dust itself tells the tale. As like as not he hasn't any kin, within reach; and if he has, you're a blamed fool to summon 'em. We've got things in our own hands—understand? Think it over. I'll be 'round. Good-night."

"Good-night," they answered. "Open the door for him, Charley," bade Mr. Adams.

With a grunty grumble the long-nosed man passed out into the night. Charley hastened back to look at the unknown again.

From the California gold fields! Think of that! And with two sacks of gold dust! Who could he be? Where was he going in St. Louis? What had he seen and done, in California? But here he lay, in a stupor, with Mr. Adams rubbing his arms and legs, and Mrs. Adams hovering over with the glass and pitcher.

II

HURRAH FOR THE GOLDEN WEST

As the evening wore on the stranger tossed and murmured more and more, until it was evident that he was ill with something graver than mere exposure.

"Charley, I think you'd better go for the doctor," said Mr. Adams, finally, about eight o'clock, after they all had done what they could. "This man's getting no better. He looks as though he might have a fever."

"Yes; that's what I've been thinking, too," nodded Mrs. Adams. "Hurry on, Charley. And if the doctor isn't there leave word for him to come as soon as he can."

Out into the cold again, and into the darkness as well, bolted Charley, donning cap and scarf and mittens as he went. The adventure was growing more exciting. What a shame if the man should not recover and they would have to guess all about him!

Old Doctor Paulis, the Adams family doctor, lived but three blocks away, and through the snow and the night Charley ran the whole distance. The doctor said that he'd be along immediately, or as soon as he had finished his supper; and arrive he did, when Charley had been home only a few minutes.

He examined the stranger very carefully.

"It's a case of fever—a kind probably contracted on the Isthmus or on shipboard, if he returned that way," at last pronounced the doctor. "I'm afraid, after his exposure to the cold, that I may not pull him through; but I'll do what I can. Meantime if you can get in communication with any of his relatives or friends, you'd better do so."

The doctor left a quantity of medicine, to be given at such frequent intervals that somebody must be up all night. However, Charley went to bed and slept, and dreamed that the mysterious stranger was sitting on the sofa and was telling them that in California gold dust was shaken from the trees and shoveled into flour-sacks.

But the mysterious stranger was by no means sitting up, when after breakfast Charley saw him. He was quieter, to be sure, and he seemed to be partially conscious; he even appeared to recognize Charley; still, he was terribly weak.

It was Charley's turn to stay with him. Mrs. Adams went out to do some marketing; Mr. Adams lay down, to rest. Charley sat near the sofa, to give the medicine, and keep up the fire, and between times to pick out interesting news about California, in the papers that he had brought home. Gold, gold, gold! That was it—gold! Everybody out there was finding gold, and everybody else was making ready to start.

One item told about a railroad across the Isthmus of Panama, too—that it probably would be begun soon, by Americans; and with that completed there would be an easy way to California.

The man on the sofa was making a strange sound; and looking over at him, Charley was astonished to see himself beckoned. Up he jumped, and crossed.

"Paper," whispered the man, in Charley's ear. "Paper——" and he feebly signed that he wanted to write.

Charley flew to the desk in the corner and got a writing pad and pencil. But the man was so weak that he made only a few wavy, uncertain lines, and fell back exhausted.

"You write; I sign," he whispered, to Charley. Charley obediently took pad and pencil, and the man dictated. "Date. Say 'For service rendered I give— bearer—all my rights in—Golden West mining claim—California.' I sign. Quick." And he motioned for the pencil.

Charley held the pad, and watched him feebly scrawl a "T" and what might have been an "o"—and a haggling "m"; and then the pencil dropped. He looked so strange, he scarcely breathed; and frightened, Charley darted into the other room where his father was lying resting.

"Oh, dad! Dad!"

"Hello? What's the matter?"

"Come, quick!"

Mr. Adams jumped to the floor and at rapid limp hastened for the living-room.

"He acts worse," explained Charley, pointing. "See? He talked, and started to write, and fell back."

Mr. Adams bent over the sofa and with ear down listened. He put his hand upon the stranger's forehead.

"Get the doctor as quick as you can, Charley," he bade.

Out bolted Charley, but he did not have far to go, for he met the doctor at the gate. A glance at the sofa decided Doctor Paulis. He soberly shook his head. His examination need be very short.

"I can do no more," he said.

"I feared so," confessed Charley's father. "To bad. Well, now what can we do, I wonder."

"I'll notify the coroner," proffered the old doctor. "Meanwhile, you'd better look through the clothes and see if you can find out anything more."

The doctor left. Mr. Adams gently searched the man's trouser pockets, finding nothing, not even a knife.

"Now for the coat again," he directed.

Charley brought the coat from the closet. His father handled it. It was heavy with the two little buckskin sacks; but the pockets contained nothing else—and yet Mr. Adams's fingers paused in their search, as he was about to lay the coat aside.

"There's a paper in here somewhere," he said. "I felt it. It's inside the lining." He fished out his pen-knife; and ripping a seam, extracted the paper from under the lining.

It seemed to be several pages from an old diary, and was worn so that the pencilings could scarcely be read. Charley and his father could make out names of places in California, evidently—"Sutter's," "American R.," "Coloma,"—and stray words such as "good camp," "prospects bright," "ounces," "pan," "rain," "home"; on an inside page was sketched a rough map.

But this penciled map was so worn and faint that Charley and his father, and his mother, too, puzzled over it almost in vain. Starting from the joining of two rivers, it appeared to represent an exploring trip up along one of the rivers, and through the country, with crosses scattered like camps, and the letters "G. H." set down here and there. The page was thumb-marked so badly, and so scuffed, that some of it was well-nigh rubbed out. Charley and his father and mother later puzzled a great deal over that map, which looked like this.

But now the next thing was the examination of the sacks, round and heavy.

"I suppose we'd better open them," mused Mr. Adams. He untied the worn, greasy thong about the neck of one, and loosened the mouth. He peered in; so did Charley.

"Gold dust, sure as shooting," gasped Mr. Adams. "What in the world are we to do with it? Nuggets, too. Ever see any, Charley? Here——" and with thumb and finger he fished out a smoothish lump about the size of a navy bean.

Charley saw it. He saw the dust, too—a mass of fine particles, glinting dully yellow amidst the brownish interior. Gee whiz! And the other sack held the same!

"How much do you suppose it makes?"

Mr. Adams weighed the sacks in his hand, thoughtfully.

"I judge they weigh about three pounds apiece," he mused. "Gold is selling at fourteen dollars an ounce, I hear. Humph! If each sack contains three pounds, that makes—er, twelve ounces to the pound—thirty-six ounces in each sack, at fourteen dollars—say $500 apiece, or $1000 in all. I declare!"

That seemed like a lot of money.

"He gave it to me," declared Charley, eagerly. "Really he did, dad. And he gave me his mine, too, out in California. He did. I wrote as he told me to on a piece of paper, and he started to sign, and then he quit. It's the Golden West mine. See?" and Charley, showed the writing on the pad.

"Well!" muttered his father. "I declare! 'Tom,' that looks like. Tom who, I wonder. That's the most importance. Of course we don't want his mine or his money. Didn't he tell his last name?"

"No, sir. But he gave me the money, and he gave me the mine. He——" but Charley was interrupted by a resounding knock on the front door.

"See who that is," bade his father. "I'll lay these things away."

When Charley opened the front door, the long-nosed man stood there, on the threshold.

"Hello," he greeted, brusquely. "I called around to see our friend. How is he?"

"Why," stammered Charley. "He's—he's dead."

"When?"

"Just a few moments ago."

"He is, is he? I'll have to look into that." And the long-nosed man pushed by Charley and strode through the hall. Charley could do nothing but follow. He found the man confronting Mr. Adams. The figure on the sofa had been covered by a cloth.

"The kid says our friend has passed over," rather roughly spoke the long-nosed man. "How about it?"

"Yes, sir," answered Mr. Adams. "There he is."

"Huh!" And walking across, the long-nosed man peeped in under the cloth. "All right," he said. "Now's our chance to divvy, then, isn't it?"

"Just what do you mean, sir?" demanded Mr. Adams, flushing—and Charley knew that his father was angry.

"I mean you get half and I get half, and no questions asked. Where are those sacks?"

"No, sir!" returned Mr. Adams, decidedly. "There'll be no such performance. I shall put those sacks and their contents, just as they are, on deposit with the bank or other authorities, subject to the heirs. They're neither mine nor yours."

"He gave them to me, anyway," blurted Charley, angrily, to the man. "There's $1000. And he——"

"Charley, be quiet," ordered his father, sternly. "It doesn't concern us how much there is, or what he did. He wasn't in his right mind."

"What else did he do, bub?" queried the man.

But Charley held his tongue.

"You ought to be ashamed of yourself," continued Mr. Adams, severely, to the long-nosed man, "trying to take the hard-earned gains of a poor fellow who probably has left a needy family somewhere, and was going back to them! If you think we'll be partners with you, you're highly mistaken. Understand? I've never yet taken advantage of anybody in misfortune, and I've never yet robbed a guest, most of all a dead man. Now you'll oblige me by clearing out."

The long-nosed man sneered.

"Oh, yes," he said. "I see. You've got the swag, and no doubt he's told you about some mine, and you count on getting that, too! But your high and mighty virtue doesn't down, with me. My name's Jacobs: Jasper Jacobs. I've lived on the frontier. I'm half wild hoss and half Mississippi alligator; and

I'm a bad man to cross. I'm going to watch you, and when this swag comes to light again I'll have my share. See? Put that in your pipe and smoke it."

"Look here, sir," answered Mr. Adams, standing straight and tall—and Charley never could have believed that his father could seem so fierce, except in battle. "I'm a soldier, and I've faced worse dangers than you can threaten. Clear out, or I'll throw you out. You're insulting me, and you're desecrating that unfortunate lying there. Now go!"

The long-nosed man actually shrank. But as he retreated he still blustered, "I'm not done with you. I'll watch you. Remember, I'm on your trail. This matter hasn't ended." And he slammed the door as he went outside.

"Ha!" uttered Mr. Adams, and his face calmed. "So much for him. Now we'll do just as I said, Charley; and your mother'll approve. We'll deposit the sacks and any other valuables, with the bank, after we've told the coroner; and we'll advertise for heirs. We'll use only enough of the funds to pay the doctor, and other expenses. By the way, did the poor fellow say anything else? Give any directions of any kind?"

"No, sir. He just called for paper and pencil and tried to write and couldn't, and then had me write for him, and all he signed was 'Tom.'"

"That's very indefinite. If only he had finished his name, we'd have had some clue. But the map's no good to us, in such shape. Besides, we wouldn't think of touching money or mine, as long as there's a single chance of the rightful claimants turning up."

Charley's mother entered. She agreed that this was right; and Charley, although a little disappointed, could not help but agree, too. They pored over the diary and map, but had to give up, and put them away. They told only Doctor Paulis and the coroner.

However, although they advertised at once in the papers, for the unknown's relatives (referring claimants to a lawyer's office), nobody turned up who proved to be a genuine heir. After the funeral expenses were paid, there were over $800 left, lying in the bank. The long-nosed man, Mr. Jacobs, was unable to get at this, but he bothered the Adamses considerably by hanging about, and whenever he met Charley he made insulting remarks, and threats, and insisted that there was a mine. He did not dare to say much to Mr. Adams, though. After a few weeks he seemed to have tired, and to have drawn off. He had been very annoying.

"Well, George," said old Dr. Paulis, one evening, "I guess you and Charley fall heir to that dust and mine. Nobody else appears to have any shadow of claim on them."

Charley's heart leaped; but his father shook his head.

"They're not ours, doctor," he replied. "I'd much prefer that somebody turn up who needs them and is entitled to them."

"My dear man," protested the doctor, earnestly, "you do need them. That's the point. You need them and you're to have them. I want you to take the money and go to California!"

"Oh—hurrah!" cried Charley, springing up and sitting down again.

"Why——!" gasped his father. "But look here, anyway: it wouldn't be mine; it belongs to Charley, remember. The man gave it to Charley, if he gave it to anybody."

"Humph," grunted the old doctor, eyes twinkling. "Supposing Charley lends you half, then—and he takes the other half and you and he go shares on the trip and on what you find."

"Hurrah!" again cheered Charley. "I don't want it; dad can have it all, of course. But I'd like to go, if I can."

"No arguments, now," warned the old doctor, to Mr. Adams, who sat bewildered. "Your wife and I've agreed. You need a sea voyage, and a little roughing it in the out-of-doors yonder in the California mountains. That's just what you need, to set you up again. Now's your chance. Besides, there's the mine——"

"The Golden West mine!" cheered Charley. "Sure. That's ours, too."

"There's the mine," continued the old doctor. "Somebody ought to be developing that mine. If any real heirs ever do turn up, you see, you'll have more than $800 to give them."

"They'll certainly get either the mine or their $800," asserted Mr. Adams. "I don't want pay for taking care of anybody in distress."

"By all means no," concurred the old doctor. "But according to what Charley understood (and you heard some of it, yourself), that man gave him the dust, and also wanted him to have the mine. So you and he are going out there, and you'll start just as soon as you possibly can."

"You will go, won't you, George?" urged Mrs. Adams. "I'll get along splendidly. The main thing is your health. We can't any of us be happy or contented while you're poorly—and the doctor says California is the very thing for you. It does seem as though the way had been opened by Providence. I'm just as glad as I can be!"

"So am I!" cheered Charley. "I'm going over and tell Billy."

"Hold on a bit," cautioned the doctor. "Wait till we finish up."

It required considerable more talk before Mr. Adams was fully persuaded. At last he did say that he'd go, if Mrs. Adams could be left—and if Charley would lend him the money. Lend him the money! As if Charley wouldn't gladly give him every cent—yes, and stay home himself, to boot, if necessary. But that was not necessary; Charley was to go, as partner and comrade.

Plans followed thick and fast, and Charley was chock full of news when he found Billy Walker.

"You don't know what I know!"

"What?" asked Billy.

"I'm going out to California! I'll get there before you do!"

"Aw—honest?" queried Billy. "We start day after to-morrow. How'll you beat us? When do you start? Who else is going?"

"Start next week. Dad and I."

"Why don't you come with us? We'd have a lot of fun. How are you going to beat us? What's your outfit? We've got a mighty fine team of horses."

"We are not going overland," announced Charley, triumphantly. "That's too long, and my father needs the sea air. We're going across the Isthmus and sail up the Pacific to San Francisco!"

"How long will that take?" demanded Billy.

"About a month and a half, in all."

"Oh, shucks!" said Billy. "It'll take us three months. That's what the papers say, anyhow. Maybe you will beat us, then. But I'll have twice as much fun."

"Why?" asked Charley.

"Because we'll be twice as long — see? What are you going to take? You'd better look over our stuff. Come on."

"We've bought everything we could here in St. Louis," explained Billy, as he led the way. "They say California prices are awful, there's such a rush. Our wagon's full."

And as it stood in the Walkers's back yard, it certainly was.

"We won't need such a lot of provisions," said Charley, wisely. "We get fed on the boats."

"That's so," agreed Billy. "But dad and I'll use up 150 pounds of flour and bacon apiece, just getting across. An article in the paper said people ought to carry that much, besides coffee and sugar and salt and all that. Now I'll show you my clothes."

That was more interesting. The stout flannel shirts and the jean trousers and the heavy cow-hide boots and the belt and the wide-brimmed slouch hat and the coarse knitted socks looked very business-like. Mr. Walker's clothes were about the same, except that his flannel shirts were red, while Billy's were blue. Charley resolved that he'd get red, for himself.

"You ought to have guns, too," asserted Billy. "You might need 'em. We'll need ours, I bet, for buffalo and Injuns and grizzly bears. The papers say to take a rifle and pair of pistols, five pounds of powder and ten pounds of lead. Dad's bought one of those new-kind patent revolving pistols—you can shoot it six times and take out the cylinder and put in another and shoot six times more! Guess there won't many Injuns want to tackle us! And I've got a seven-shooter rifle, all my own."

III

AN UNWELCOME COMPANION

According to an advertisement in the St. Louis papers the steamship Georgia, from New York for the Isthmus of Panama, was to arrive at New Orleans in three weeks. That would be just about the right date, decided Mr. Adams, to allow him and Charley to make their preparations, and take a steamboat down the Mississippi from St. Louis to New Orleans.

Now all was excitement, not only at the Adams home, but throughout St. Louis and the whole eastern country. Charley bid good-bye to Billy and Billy's father, when with their team and white-topped wagon they pulled out, in their party, for Westport Landing, which is now Kansas City. From Westport Landing they were to drive on to Council Grove, thirty miles west, which was the big starting point for California. The papers declared that already, in this April, 15,000 people had gathered along the Missouri River border, all the way from Independence, Missouri, to Council Bluffs of Iowa, prepared to start on their 2000-mile trip to the new gold fields, as soon as the grass began to grow. Every boat, too, to the Isthmus, was crowded — and so were the sailing vessels, bound around Cape Horn!

The lowest cabin-fare, New York to San Francisco by the Isthmus, was $395! Counting the steamboat trip down the Mississippi, the fare was about the same from St. Louis. Whew! That seemed to Charley a lot of money — but thanks to the stranger whom they had taken in, Charley and his father had it, and could leave Mrs. Adams well provided for, besides, with what Mr. Adams had in reserve. That was good. A number of men had gone off and left their families to get along as best they could, but this was not Mr. Adams's way.

Being an experienced campaigner, Charley's father knew just about what kind of an outfit they would need; and of course, as Billy had said, the papers all had published lists, for the information of the emigrants.

All the clothing should be of the toughest and hardiest material; by accounts there would not be much chance to renew it, out at the mines, unless a person was prepared to pay tremendous prices. You should have seen Charley, when his clothes came home! It had been great fun, buying at the stores, where "California garments" were going like hot cakes, but he could scarcely wait until he had tried his things on. When he looked in the glass, and saw himself in broad slouch hat, and red flannel shirt, and belted trousers tucked into cowhide boots, with a blue bandanna handkerchief about his neck, he felt like a real gold-miner. The whitish cotton suits, for wear on shipboard and on the Isthmus, in the tropics, did not amount to much in comparison with this garb of a "Forty-niner"—as the papers were beginning to call the outgoing gold seekers.

Mr. Adams bought a brand-new Colt's revolving rifle, that shot seven times, a revolving pistol (as it was termed), and two butcher-knives—one apiece, to be worn thrust through the belt. Charley donned the knife, just to see how it looked (and it looked very business-like), but his father did not allow him to put on the big pistol. Maybe out in the gold fields he might wear it, though.

Then there were two picks and two spades and two sheet-iron miners' pans. These pans were round, about six inches deep and fifteen inches across at the rims, slanting to a foot across at the bottom. They resembled a milk-pan. They were to be used for "washing out" the gold from the dirt. Charley had no idea how to do this; neither had his father—and neither had one in a hundred of the other people who were talking California. But they all expected to learn, in case it was not possible to scrape the pure gold up with spades!

"By gracious!" exclaimed Mr. Adams, at the very last moment. "We mustn't forget the skillet! That's the most important thing yet."

"Of course!" agreed Mrs. Adams. "How'll you fry your meat?"

So a new skillet was added to the outfit. The clothing packed a trunk jam full. The picks and spades and skillet and rifle and other unwieldy things were rolled in Mr. Adams's two army blankets and a couple of quilts. That made a large bundle, and with the picks and spades showing finely it told exactly where the owners were bound. Charley was proud of that bundle.

At last, one morning, he donned his miner's costume in earnest, for the day of the start had come. The trunk and bundle were sent down to the levee in a wagon. On this day, at ten o'clock, the steamboat Robert Burns would leave for New Orleans.

Mrs. Adams of course went down to the levee with her two gold seekers to see them off. Moments were growing very precious. The Robert Burns was there, waiting, the smoke welling from her tall twin stacks. The levee was crowded with passengers and their friends and relatives. Negro roustabouts were hard at work hustling freight and baggage aboard. Charley saw their trunk carried over the gangplank—and he nudged his father and pointed, for several passengers, dressed in California costume, were carrying up the gangplank rolls of bedding just like theirs!

It was high time he hunted up their roll, too. He found it, where it had been pitched from the wagon. As he was proudly inspecting it to see that all was right, he stumbled over a small cowhide trunk. Attached to the handle was a card that read: "J. Jacobs"!

"Jacobs!" That was the long-nosed man's name. Was he booked on the Robert Burns? And why? Charley grew excited at the thought, and when his father and mother strolled across, to be near the bundle, he called: "Father! Look here!"

Mr. Adams limped over (and big and fine he was in his rough clothes), to see.

"Humph!" he muttered. "Well, what of it, Charley?"

"Do you think that's his?"

"Whose?"

"Why, the long-nosed man's."

"I'm sure I don't know," answered his father, coolly.

"But that's his name," pursued Charley. "Do you think he's going on our boat?"

"We can't very well stop him, boy," smiled Mr. Adams. "It isn't 'our' boat, exactly; and he can't do us any harm, anyway. You aren't afraid of him, are you?"

"N—no, not if you aren't," asserted Charley. "But he's no business following us up as he said he would."

"Humph!" again remarked his father. "We can take care of ourselves. We'll mind our own affairs, and we'll expect him to mind his. If that's his trunk, probably he's only going down-river a way. We won't borrow trouble this early in the game, Charley."

That sounded reasonable, and Charley had a lot of trust in his soldier father. Only—if that trunk belonged to the long-nosed man, and if the long-nosed man was going down to New Orleans with them, and if he boarded the same steamer there, for California, things looked mighty peculiar. He seemed to be such a mean, obstinate fellow that there was no knowing what he might have up his sleeve.

Mrs. Adams was curious to know the cause of Charley's evident excitement over the trunk.

"Oh, it bears the name Jacobs, dear," explained Mr. Adams, easily. "Charley has the notion it means that the 'long-nosed man,' as he calls him, is going to California with us."

"Oh, George!" And Charley's mother, too, seemed alarmed. "Do you suppose he is?"

"No, I don't. But we can't stop him, anyway."

"It's queer he'd take this same boat, though. Maybe he's been watching you."

"Oh, pshaw," laughed Mr. Adams. "Don't let's rig up a scarecrow, to spoil our good-byes. Charley and I'll take care of ourselves; won't we, Charley? We'll stick by each other, and other folks can do as they please, as long as they don't interfere. Come on; let's go aboard, and you can see our state-room, and say good-bye there."

Mr. Adams picked up the bundle, and shouldering it led the way up the gangplank. Mrs. Adams followed, and Charley, in his miner's rig, with butcher-knife stuck through his belt, proudly stumped after. He wished that Billy Walker was there, to see. But other people were seeing, anyway.

When they gained the deck, and were passing around to the state-room (which was number 19), glancing back Charley saw a darky roustabout heaving the Jacobs trunk on his back, and starting with it for the gangplank. So it came aboard, but of its owner, if he was their Mr. Jacobs, there was no sign.

Presently the big bell rang vigorously, and the whistle hoarsely blew, as signal for all visitors to go ashore. Mrs. Adams gave Charley and her husband one final kiss, and Charley added to his return kiss a round hug. She was such a good woman; he wished that she was going, too. He rather wished that he could stay at home with her; he—he—and he choked. For a moment he almost hated his miner's costume. However— —

"Write often, now," she bade, her eyes dewy, as with her they hastened out on deck.

"Yes, we will. And you write often and tell us the news. Send us the papers."

"I will, dear. Now, do be careful."

"Yes. Take care of yourself, too. If you need us, we'll come straight home, won't we, Charley?"

Charley could only nod.

"Hurry, dear, or you'll be left," warned Mr. Adams, anxiously—for already the gangplank ropes had been tautened by the donkey-engine and the plank was trembling to rise. Charley rather wished that she would be left; then she'd have to come with them! Wouldn't that be great!

But she ran down the plank. Then, near the end, she stopped, and called back.

"What's that, dear?" inquired Mr. Adams, and he and Charley listened keenly.

"Have you got the quinine?"

"Yes. Hurry, dear."

"Sure?"

"It's in the trunk. Look out—jump!"

The gangplank was rising, but with a little run Mrs. Adams did jump and landed safely. Charley laughed. They didn't catch his mother—no, siree. And she was the last person to leave the boat.

Up rose the gangplank. The engine bell jangled. The negro roustabouts cast off the bow and stern hawsers from the wharf posts, and scrambled over the gunwale as the Robert Burns began to back out into the stream. Mrs. Adams waved her handkerchief. Everybody on the wharf waved—mostly handkerchiefs, which were suddenly very popular. The people on board waved back—and they, too, used handkerchiefs pretty generally. Faster and farther backed theRobert Burns, until in midcurrent, after describing a great half-circle, she was pointing down stream. The engine bell jangled to stop, and to go ahead—and she was started for New Orleans.

They were off for California!

The levee, with his mother's handkerchief now fading into the whitish blur of other handkerchiefs, drifted behind; Charley took a long breath, straightened his shoulders, stole a glance at his father, who was winking violently in queer fashion, and began to take stock of the other passengers.

Some were leaving the rail; a number of others already had left it, and were negligently strolling about or seating themselves for comfort. They mostly were men—business men, planters, and the like, traveling down-river on pleasure or errands of importance, and a few miners bound for California. There was no Mr. Jacobs, that Charley knew, among them, and he felt easier. Probably "J. Jacobs" was some other Jacobs, and not the long-nosed man.

"Let's go in and put our room to rights, Charley," proposed Mr. Adams, as the buildings of old St. Louis merged one with another, on the shore line behind.

He briskly limped across the deck, and Charley followed. This would be something to do, at any rate. But as he passed the door of the long salon, or lounging room, he glanced in and saw clear to the other end, where there was a bar for sale of liquors. And he was certain that he glimpsed the long-nosed man, just coming from the bar!

Charley's heart fairly skipped a beat. No, he would not say anything to his father, for perhaps he had been mistaken—and what was the sense in being scared? Supposing that was the long-nosed man. He was not bigger or smarter than they, and besides, as Mr. Adams had said, he had a perfect right to travel on the Mississippi River. Everybody used the river, because there were no railroads here. However, it was queer, his choosing this boat.

Charley and his father set their state-room in order, by arranging their clothes and sleeping things.

"You can go out, if you want to, Charley," spoke his father. "I've got a little more to do, yet. Then I'll come, too."

"All right," and away clumped Charley, in his heavy boots. This time he was determined to look in earnest for the long-nosed man. He hoped that he would not find him, but he feared, just the same.

He did not have far to look. The long-nosed man was standing leaning against one side of the doorway of the salon. Yes, it was he, sure enough!

He acted as if he was waiting, for when he saw Charley approaching, to pass, he smiled, and waved genially.

"Well," he greeted, halting Charley. "So proud of your new clothes that you don't recognize old friends, eh? Come here."

Charley boldly walked straight to him. The man's tone made him mad.

"How are you?" answered Charley. "Taking a trip?"

Mr. Jacobs squinted his eyes and wrinkled his long nose cunningly.

"Y—yes," he drawled. "Taking a little trip." His breath smelled of liquor. "Suppose you're going to Californy, to look for that gold mine. Thought you'd give me the slip, did you?"

"No," said Charley. "We didn't think anything about you, especial."

"Oh, you didn't!" And the long-nosed man spat tobacco juice on the clean deck. "You reckoned on giving me the slip, though. But I've been watching you. Didn't I tell you I was half wild hoss and half alligator? What's to hinder me from going out to Californy, too?"

"Nothing, I expect," replied Charley, his heart sinking. "Why? Are you?"

The long-nosed man leered.

"Maybe I am, and maybe I'm not. You go your trail and I'll go mine, but if they cross, look out. Half of that property belongs to me, remember—and half of that money you're using, too."

"It doesn't, either," snapped Charley, angry, his spunk up. "And we aren't afraid of you; not a bit. Go on out to California, if you want to, but don't you bother us. And don't you bother my mother, or you'll get in trouble."

He heard a familiar step, and the voice of his father.

"Hello! This is the man, is it, after all?"

"Hello, yourself," retorted Mr. Jacobs, glaring at him. "Maybe you think you own this boat."

"Not a bit, sir," answered Mr. Adams, good-natured.

"Maybe you think you can dictate where I travel."

"No, sir. I expect to look after myself, and not after you."

"Well said," approved the long-nosed man. "Now will you have a drink?"

"I never use liquor, sir," returned Mr. Adams — and Charley was proud to hear him say it.

"'D rather not drink with me, perhaps," sneered the long-nosed man.

"I see no reason for drinking with you or at all, sir," sharply replied Mr. Adams. "Come on, Charley. We've got better business to tend to."

"You have, have you?" called the long-nosed man, after them. "Maybe you think I don't know what it is. Maybe you think — —" but they paid no more attention to him.

Still, the meeting was not pleasant, and Charley heartily wished that the "J. Jacobs" had proved to some other Jacobs.

IV

A FRIEND IN NEED

The Robert Burns steadily churned her way down the Mississippi, yellow and swollen with the spring freshets. She stopped at towns and other landings—some of these being plantation landings—to discharge or take on passengers and freight. These stops would have been the more interesting, to Charley, were he not in a hurry. He wanted to be sure and catch the Georgia, for the Isthmus. Supposing the Robert Burns were late into New Orleans; then they might miss the Georgia. Of course, there were other boats—the Falcon and the Isthmus and the Quaker City; but with such crowds setting out for the gold fields, it behooved a fellow to get there as soon as he possibly could.

More "Forty-niners" boarded the Robert Burns. One in particular took Charley's eye. He came out in a skiff, from a small wood landing, where some steamers, but not the Robert Burns, stopped to load up with fuel. When the Robert Burns whistled and paused, floating idly, and he had clambered in, he proved to be a very tall, gaunt, black-whiskered individual, with a long, muzzle-loading squirrel rifle on his arm. A darky tossed a blanket roll up after him, and rowed away for the shore.

The man looked like a backwoodsman—and again he looked like a Californian, too, for his clothes were an old blue flannel shirt (with a rolling collar having white stars in the corners), patched buckskin trousers and heavy boots of the regulation style. Charley chanced to be crossing the salon or main cabin when the man was paying for his passage, and there witnessed something exciting that made him dart out and find his father.

"Dad!" hoarsely whispered Charley. "That was a gold miner who came aboard in a skiff! He was paying his fare with gold dust."

"Was he? How do you know?"

"I saw him at the desk, but the clerk wouldn't take any dust, so he had to pay with money. He has a buckskin sack, just like ours. Wish I could talk with him."

"Maybe he'll talk with you, if you give him the chance. You can try and see. But don't ask him any foolish questions, or seem inquisitive."

Presently the tall man (he was taller even than Mr. Adams) emerged from the cabin, to stand by the rail, leaning on his rifle and gazing at the shore line. A picturesque figure he made, with his starred shirt-collar rolled back, and his leathery trousers wrinkled down over his boot-tops.

Charley sidled around him, expectantly; and the man noticed him.

"You look as if you were going out, too," addressed the man, a twinkle under his bushy brows.

"Yes, sir," answered Charley. "To California."

"Anybody with you?"

"My father." And Charley proudly nodded toward another tall form. "Were you ever there?" he added, hesitantly.

"I should rather think so. Five years ago, and four years ago; and now I'm making another trip by a new route. The other times I crossed by the land trail."

"Oh, you must have been with Frémont!" exclaimed Charley.

The whiskered man nodded.

"I was. I was with Carson and Frémont in Forty-three—Forty-four, and again in Forty-five—Forty-six."

"I know about those travels," cried Charley. "I'm reading Colonel Frémont's reports now. I'm just finishing his last one. I guess they're about the best description of California there is. Did you fight in the war?"

The man smiled.

"See my shirt?" he queried. "All we Frémont men wore these navy shirts—some of us clear through the campaign. The sloop of war Portsmouth sent us a lot of ship's supplies, when we marched down from the mountains to Sutter's Fort, just before the uprising of the Bear War in June, Forty-six. I saved my shirt, and now I only wear it occasionally. I'm sorter proud of this shirt."

"I should think you would be," agreed Charley. "Did you mine in California?"

"Yes, sir. I started in to settle there, after the war, till the gold craze broke out. Ever see any dust?"

"Some," admitted Charley.

"There's not much in this sack now," continued the Frémont man, showing it. "But I've filled it many a time."

"I've got a sack, too," said Charley, exhibiting it.

"You've been out there?"

"No, sir. I got this in St. Louis."

"Let's see." And the man fingered it. "It's old-timer—been used plenty. Some dust sticking to it, too. Huh."

"Is there lots of gold out there?" asked Charley.

"Gold?" repeated the man; and laughed. "I found fifteen hundred dollars in two days, first thing; then I didn't find any for a month. But I cleaned up $10,000, and I'm going back after more. It's all luck, now; but after the surface has been scraped off, then it will be skill. Does your father know anything about mining?"

"No, sir. He's a soldier. He was with General Scott."

"That won't cut much figure," said the man, quickly. "Soldiers and sailors and lawyers and doctors and farmers and trappers and even Indians are all grubbing together—and none of us knows a blamed thing except that gold is soft and yellow and will pass for currency—sixteen dollars an ounce. But good luck to you. Going across the Isthmus, I reckon?"

"Yes, sir."

"That's the easier way. Well, if I see you out there and can help you along any way, you can count on me. But it's a country where every tub stands on its own bottom, and no man's any better than any other man."

So saying, he threw his rifle into the hollow of his arm and paced away, into the cabin. Charley gazed after him, and reflected that although they might have an enemy with them, they also had made a friend.

"If he was with Carson and Frémont, he's all right," declared Mr. Adams, when Charley related the conversation. "But we'll be beholden to nobody, as long as we can help ourselves. We two bunkies can paddle our own canoe, can't we?"

The Robert Burns continued on, down to New Orleans. The long-nosed man kept to the cabin, mainly, where a number of rough passengers spent their time drinking and gambling. The Frémont man was about the quietest of all the passengers, mingling little, talking little. He exchanged a few civil words with Mr. Adams, and kindly greeted Charley, when they were near one another. That was all.

Charley thought rather the more of him, that he was not the blustering, boasting kind, even though he had blazed the long trail across to California, with Frémont and Carson. He evidently was a man of deeds, not words.

New Orleans was reached in the afternoon—and a fine big city it looked to be, as the Robert Burns whistled hoarsely and swung for the levee. However, the Forty-niners aboard her had not much thought for the looks of the city; their minds were more upon whether the Georgia had arrived, and how soon they could get aboard her, for the Isthmus and California gold fields.

In the excitement of bustling ashore Charley forgot all about the long-nosed man, who disappeared with the other scattering passengers.

"Where's the dock of the Isthmus steamers?" queried Mr. Adams, of a lounger, as he and Charley landed, the roll of bedding on Mr. Adams's shoulder.

"Eet is still down the river, m'sieur," answered the man—who was a young French creole. "M'sieur would better ride than walk."

"All right. Thank you," and Mr. Adams hailed an odd carriage, drawn by one horse between a of long curved shafts. They piled in.

"To the Isthmus dock," ordered Mr. Adams.

"You want to catch the Georgia?" asked the driver,

"We do."

"She's about coming in. They're looking for her."

"Will I have time to get our tickets?"

"Plenty. She'll lie over till morning."

"All right. Go ahead."

The driver flung out his lash, and away they whirled, down a rough street, along the river.

The dock bore a large sign, which said: "Steamers for the Isthmus and California." There was an enormous pile of baggage and a crowd of people, of all kinds, waiting. But the Georgia had not come in yet. Mr. Adams left Charley there to watch their baggage and was driven away in haste to get their tickets.

Suddenly a cry arose: "There she comes! That's she!" Down the broad river—never so broad as here—welled a cloud of black smoke, and a big steamer surged into view. What a big thing she was! She could carry two or three Robert Burnses. She was a side-wheeler, of course, but her paddle boxes stood as high as houses. Across her pilot house was a gilt sign reading "Georgia"—and on her paddle box, as she swung around, appeared another "Georgia," in large black letters.

Charley gazed in dismay, for every inch of her seemed occupied by passengers. The upper deck and middle deck and lower deck appeared full of figures, with heads craning to gaze.

"That's the boat," quoth a voice at Charley's elbow. He turned and found the Frémont man by his side, leaning on his long rifle. "Do you like her looks?"

"How are we to get on?" answered Charley. "Why, she's full already, isn't she?"

The Frémont man nodded, and smiled.

"I expect she is. She's built to carry 500 and they'll put 1500 on her. 'T isn't right—but it's the way they're doing, so as to make money. We'll be lucky to find sleeping space on deck, and get enough to eat. But everything goes, in the rush to California. If you think these Atlantic steamers are big boats, you ought to see the steamers on the other side."

"Are they better?"

"Considerably. The Pacific Mail Company runs them. They are better and better managed; but those boats'll be packed, too. All we can do is to make the best of it, after we've paid our money."

"Are you going on the Georgia?" hopefully asked Charley.

The Frémont man nodded.

"I'll go if I can find a six-foot space to lie down on—and I reckon I will."

The Georgia docked. A number of passengers hustled off, and then began the rush aboard. How the gold seekers shoved and scrambled and fought! The gangway was a mass of shoulders and hats and blanket rolls.

"Coming on?" invited the Frémont man, to Charley.

Charley hesitated. He was impatient, but he didn't know — —

"I'm waiting for my father," he explained.

"We'd better find our places while we can, and have one ready for him," prompted the Frémont man.

He picked up the bed rolls, and hurried ahead, Charley at his heels. At the rail an official glanced at his ticket, and waved him to the upper deck. Charley followed. The ticket gave first-class cabin privileges, but what did these amount to, when 1500 passengers were being crowded upon a 500-passenger boat? Even standing room seemed to be valuable.

They pushed along through the mass of passengers and friends and relatives, who acted, some of them, too dazed and confused to move aside, and mounted the stairs leading to the upper decks. When they emerged into the open air, the Frémont man paused uncertainly, puffing, to survey the outlook.

"There's no chance for a berth, I suppose, is there?" he asked, of a clerk, passing.

The clerk scanned him impudently.

"No, sir. Every berth was taken before we left New York."

"Then why did the company sell us tickets?"

"That, sir," said the clerk, with an irritating smile, "is none of my business." And he hurried away.

"Well, we might as well begin to rough it now as any time," remarked the Frémont man, after a keen look at the back of the retreating clerk. "We'll have to make our own way—and I reckon we can do it. Come on."

He shouldered ahead, Charley in his wake. The emerged aft, on the upper deck.

"Wait here a moment," bade the Frémont man; and abruptly left Charley on guard over the baggage. He returned in a minute or two.

"No berths," he reported. "I wanted to find out. Now I know. We can sleep in the steerage, they tell me. Huh! Not after we've paid extra for fresh air. Let me look around."

He did, surveying the crowded deck. Suddenly picked up the baggage.

"I see a spot," he said, and led the way.

Just outside the rail, over the stern was slung a large boat—one of the ship's life-boats. It hung by ropes to the davits, and was covered with a tarpaulin, or canvas, stretched over it and tied down.

The Frémont man halted, at the rail, and pitched the baggage over upon the boat.

"There we are," he said with a smile, to Charley. "Some of us can sleep on top—and if it rains I reckon we can double under. Go get your father, now, and I'll hold the fort."

Away hurried Charley—excited, and in his mind the idea that this was to be the queerest bed that he had occupied yet. But he had faith in the big Frémont man.

He took a look from the rail, to watch the dock below. Most of the passengers up here were crowded at this rail, to survey just as he was surveying. The stern had been left comparatively free. There was his father—he recognized the tall figure, and the limp—just arrived below, gazing about anxiously. Charley yelled, and waved, but he could not make himself heard or seen. Too much else was going on. So he raced down, and rushed out upon the dock.

"Come on, quick, dad," he greeted, breathless. "We've found a place!"

"Who?"

"The Frémont man and I. He found it, though."

"Did you get a berth?" panted his father, following him. "They told me at the steamship office that every berth was taken long ago. I had to fight for the tickets, even. Never saw such a mob."

"No, not a berth. But it's a place, anyhow. You'll see."

In the short space of time the upper deck had grown more populous than ever. They worked their way through the crowd, Charley eagerly looking ahead for the Frémont man at his post.

"This is awful," spoke Mr. Adams. "The steamship company ought to be brought to law about it."

"There he is," directed Charley, gladly. "See him. We've got the life-boat!"

But perhaps they hadn't, for when they arrived, the Frémont man was calmly barring the way of three other men—among them the long-nosed man, who was doing most of the arguing on their part.

"No, gentlemen, you're too late," asserted the Frémont man, thrusting them back with his rifle-barrel held crosswise. "That boat's occupied."

Charley remembered to have seen the little gang much together, on the Georgia, drinking and gambling. They were a tough lot.

"Tell that to the marines," retorted the long-nosed man. "We'll have that boat, or we'll know a better reason than you're giving."

"Reason enough, and here's my proof," quoth the Frémont man. "The boat's pre-empted by us three. You must hunt another claim."

Mr. Adams promptly stepped forward, to the Frémont man's side.

"What's this about?" he demanded.

"Oh, it's you again, is it—you and your kid!" snarled the long-nosed man. "You're chalking up another score to settle, are you?" And, to his fellows: "What do you say, boys? Shall we throw them overboard?"

"Over they go," announced one of the other men—a thin sallow, drooping-moustached kind—with marvelous swiftness whipping from under his coat breast a fifteen-inch blade bowie-knife.

"Over they go!"

Charley's heart leaped into his throat with horror. He wanted to spring to his father's side, but his legs would not work. However, the affair was settled very easily. The Frémont man quickly handed his rifle to Mr. Adams, grabbed the long-nosed Jacobs, in bear-like grip, and fairly threw him into the man with the knife. Together the pair went down in a heap, almost knocking over several of the onlookers.

"You next," declared the Frémonter, with a jump at the third of the gang—who hastily recoiled, in alarm. So did the onlookers. So did the two men who were scrambling to their feet again. The Frémont man had proved as quick and as strong as a gorilla. Now he laughed grimly.

"Come on," he invited. "Come on with your knives or anything else that you have. But we won't go overboard just yet. We can't swim!"

The three fellows didn't "come on," worth a cent. The one with the knife hung back farthest of all. They sputtered and glared, a little uncertain just what to do with a man so energetic and fearless as the Frémont man.

"All right, boys," snarled the long-nosed man. "There's more than one way to deal with 'em. We don't want trouble. We're peaceable citizens. But if that boat doesn't belong to us, it doesn't belong to anybody." And he threatened, to the Frémont man and Charley's father: "In about five minutes we'll settle yourhash."

With that he turned, and he and his two companions shouldered their way brusquely through the crowd.

The Frémont man laughed again.

"Fists are the only weapons needed with gentry of that class," he said, contemptuously. "Bah! I think more of Digger Injuns."

Some of the onlookers nodded and murmured assent. The half circle that had been attracted by the dispute broke up. Nobody had tried to interfere, even when the knife had been drawn. Charley soon found that similar contests for sleeping places were occurring everywhere aboard. It was a grand free-for-all rush.

Mr. Adams gave Charley an assuring nod, as if to say: "Here's a man who knows what to do and how to do it"; and he remarked, quietly, to their friend: "Thanks to you, I guess we're rid of that trouble."

"And easily rid, too," answered the Frémont man; he composedly reached for his rifle, leaned it against the rail, and standing on the bench running inside the rail began to rearrange the baggage on the canvas covering of the boat.

But he was interrupted, for there came in a hurry a ship's officer, as if sent by the long-nosed man.

"Here! Take your things off that boat," he ordered. "You can't use that boat. It's a life-boat."

"Where are we to stow ourselves, then?" queried Mr. Adams, at once.

"I don't know. But you can't use that boat."

"Will you give us a berth in place of it?"

"No, sir," informed the officer, crisply.

"We've got to have some place for ourselves and our personal baggage, sir," declared Mr. Adams. "Our tickets entitle us to a berth. We're doing the best we can, to keep from littering the deck; but if you insist on imposing further we'll carry the matter to Government authority and see whether we were not sold tickets under false pretenses."

The officer hesitated. Clearly, these three passengers knew how to stand up for themselves. He decided to let well enough alone.

"You occupy the boat at your own risk, then," he snapped. "The company does not hold itself liable. Understand that?"

"Perfectly."

The officer turned on his heel, and left them in possession.

"That settles us, I reckon," quoth the Frémont man, springing lightly down. "It's our claim."

V

AN ATTACK BY THE ENEMY

The Georgia pulled out that very evening instead of lying over until morning; and it was rumored that even with this hasty start there would be barely time enough for the passengers to catch the Pacific Mail steamship at Panama, for San Francisco.

Mr. Adams and the Frémont man (whose name was Grigsby) stayed by the baggage until the steamer sailed; but Charley wandered about the decks, "seeing things." And there was plenty to see. The Georgia seemed to be a fine boat. She had three decks, all crowded. The upper deck was for the first-cabin passengers, who paid the highest fare, and were supposed to have special privileges of table and state-rooms. The pilot-house was forward, and so were the rooms of the captain and first officers. The second deck contained the large dining cabin, with state-rooms on either side of it for the other officers and the second-cabin passengers. Down below, on the first deck, where the portholes were often under water, in a large room with rude bunks in tiers along the sides were crowded the steerage passengers. Here they ate and slept, all together. On this deck, forward, were housed the crew; and some steerage passengers overflowed into the forward end of the second deck.

Dusk was settling when the Georgia emerged from the broad mouth of the Mississippi into the Gulf. At the same time a bugle blew for supper—and what a scramble there was! The first-cabin passengers were to eat first, while the second-cabin must wait. As for the steerage passengers, Charley afterwards found out that they were fed, a bunch at a time, from a board platform slung from the ceiling by ropes, behind a railed partition. Enough were admitted by the stewards to fill the enclosure; when they had eaten out of the tin dishes supplied with stew and beans, etc., from dirty kettles, another hungry company were let through.

Almost before the bugle signal had done ringing, the first-cabin tables were crowded, and passengers were standing behind the chairs, waiting impatiently for those seated to quit and get up. The long-nosed man and his two cronies had been smart, or else they had bullied their way, for they already were eating when, too late, Charley and his father arrived. Saying, good-naturedly, "I guess I'll stand guard while you fellows eat," Mr. Grigsby had remained by the boat.

"We'll wait a bit, ourselves," spoke Mr. Adams, to Charley, as they caught sight of the turbulent dining-room.

The scene was amusing, and also irritating. It seemed to Charley as though they would never find a place. Every time anybody got up, somebody immediately popped into the vacated chair. Charley began to be alarmed lest the supply of food would run short.

"Take the first chance that comes, now," bade his father. "I'll go up and send Mr. Grigsby down as soon as you're started, so you can mount guard while I eat. I'll be watching our friends the enemy."

Charley pushed forward, and presently he himself popped into a place. The long-nosed man and his two partners had leisurely finished and were strolling out—the man with the bowie-knife using it as a tooth-pick! But Charley knew that his father and Mr. Grigsby would watch them, so he pitched into the food. It was a case of everybody reaching and grabbing. Charley only wished that he had longer arms.

Just as he was midway Mr. Grigsby came down to a seat; and soon up ran Charley, to release his father. Now was he on guard, alone, ready to do his best if anybody tried to seize the boat; but nobody did try. Meanwhile he might gaze about.

He saw funny sights, for the Georgia was rolling and tossing in the waves of the Gulf. It affected the passengers very oddly. They were all kinds, these passengers, both first-cabin and second-cabin—for the second-cabin passengers were allowed on the upper deck, although not to sleep. A great many were Southerners, including a number of long, lank, dark Arkansans, Georgians, Louisianans and Mississippians. Pistols and knives were plentiful, although notices, posted about the ship, said, plainly: "The Wearing of Deadly Weapons Aboard this Ship is Forbidden." For that matter, another notice said: "Passengers Are Requested to Wear their Coats at Meals." But nobody obeyed either notice.

There were only a few women, among the first- and second-cabin passengers; the steerage contained the most women, accompanying their emigrant husbands and sons. However, Southerners and Northerners, and the men like the women, many of the passengers were beginning to act very queerly.

They clustered along the rail, leaning over and hanging to it as they leaned; they sat down, against the rail, and against the state-rooms; and soon a lot were lying sprawled, with their eyes closed. Most of these had come aboard at New Orleans, probably. The brisk ones had been aboard already, from the North. Charley was wickedly pleased to see the long-nosed man stretched limp, and greenish in the face, while his two companions meanly teased him. And then, as Charley's father and Mr. Grigsby appeared, Charley began to feel queer, himself.

The ship sank down, down, down—then she rose up, up, up; and which was the worse sensation he could not tell. Either one was the worse, while it was happening!

"I—believe—I'll—go to bed," faltered Charley.

"Pshaw! You are looking kinder green," said Mr. Grigsby, surveying him.

"Feel sick, Charley?" queried his father.

Charley's actions spoke louder than words, for suddenly he was at the rail getting rid of his hard-earned supper. When he tottered back, already his father was spreading quilt and blanket against the rail behind which hung the boat.

"I guess you had better turn in," he directed, to Charley. "You'll be more comfortable on the deck than on the boat. Besides, I suppose that Jacobs gang wouldn't hesitate to cut the boat and let it drop, if they had the chance."

Charley crawled upon the bed. He was so miserable that really he didn't care whether anybody cut the boat down or not.

"Do you think I'll get well again?" he groaned.

His father and Mr. Grigsby laughed as if this were a joke.

"Why, sure," declared the Frémont man. "But I know how you feel. When I was in California in Forty-six a lot of us Frémont men were sent down from Monterey to San Diego by boat. Every one of us was laid flat, and Kit Carson was the sickest of all! He vowed he'd rather cross the desert a hundred times than take another sea voyage."

Charley did not open his eyes again till morning. When he did open them he was feeling much better. He sat up, and decided that he was going to be all right. The ship was still pitching up and down, and was out of sight of land. The deck was littered with sick people lying in all postures, and some cattle that had been taken aboard at New Orleans, for beef, were lowing wretchedly as if they, too, were sick. No doubt they were.

There was not much difficulty in getting a seat at breakfast this morning, for some of the passengers who had come down from the North were ill a second time. When Charley was picking his way to the dining cabin he stumbled on somebody, and looking down he beheld the long-nosed man. But the long-nosed man did not even notice that he was being stepped on. Charley chuckled. Mr. Jacobs in such shape need not be feared.

That day they were not interfered with, in their possession of the boat. Charley had the fun of sleeping on its canvas covering, that night, where, all alone, he swung delightfully as in a great cradle, while the stars shone down upon him, and the spray from the paddle wheels occasionally drifted across his face. His father and Mr. Grigsby seemed to prefer the deck, against the rail.

The voyage down to the Isthmus was rated at seven days from New Orleans. By the third day most of the sea-sick passengers had recovered, and everybody settled to enjoy themselves. A number of gamblers and drinkers were aboard; these kept to the main cabin, where they sat at cards, robbing whomsoever they might, or stood at the bar and guzzled quantities of liquor. On the decks the main pastime was reading California travels like Frémont's explorations, or Richard Dana's splendid "Two Years Before the Mast"—which Charley knew almost by heart; or in speculating on "How much gold can I dig in a day?" That was the favorite question: "How much gold do you suppose a fellow can dig in a day?" The calculations ran all the way from $100 to $10,000.

An awning was stretched over the upper deck, for shade; and as the Georgia sped out of the Gulf and headed south for the Yucatan Channel under the Tropic of Cancer, between Cuba and Yucatan, the shade felt mighty good. A number of passengers got out their white suits of linen or cotton; but the majority of the Forty-niners stuck to their flannel shirts and coarse trousers and boots.

The third evening they crossed the Tropic of Cancer, and by night were entering the Yucatan Channel, which led to the famous Caribbean Sea where pirates used to lurk. The long-nosed man and his partners had not again bothered Charley and his two partners. They had kept below, most of the time, in the main cabin, with other roisterers, and it began to look as if they had decided to let the Adams party alone.

Charley continued to sleep on the boat, swinging over the stern of the steamer, between sky and sea. Here in the tropics the days were subject to sudden sharp squalls of rain; and Mr. Grigsby unfastened the edge of the canvas covering of the boat, so that he could stow the bedding underneath, when not in use. In case of rain at night, Charley could crawl under, also, and cuddled between the seats might sleep snug and dry. Mr. Grigsby had been pretty smart, to seize on that boat when he did, for the awning leaked, in spots, and many of the passengers found themselves getting wet.

From the Yucatan Channel the Georgia crossed off the mouth of the large Honduras River, which opened into the Gulf of Honduras, on the line between Mexico and Central America. The shore of Honduras could be faintly seen, on the right, and around the course cropped up wondrous coral keys with snow-white beaches, and tufty palms outlined against the blue sky. The water was a beautiful green.

That was all very nice, and now the Isthmus of Panama was only two days ahead, across the Caribbean Sea; but the report spread that the barometer was falling and a change in weather evidently was due. Toward evening the sailors tightened the awning and made things more secure, as if they were preparing for a storm. The sun set gorgeously crimson—an angry sun; the petrels, skimming the waves about the ship, twittered excitedly, and other sea-birds seemed hastening early for land.

"You'd better crawl under the canvas, to-night, Charley," bade his father. "We're liable to have rain."

"Where'll you sleep, then?" asked Charley.

"Oh, on the deck with Mr. Grigsby. We'll find a dry spot."

Mr. Adams, as a soldier, had slept out many a night before—yes, and in many a storm; but Charley was fond of his quarters in his own private nest. He liked to cuddle there and hear the rain patter on the canvas close above him, while the waves talked beneath him, and the great paddles whirred and thumped. Under the canvas covering he gladly slipped, and got in an exceedingly comfortable position there.

He fell asleep soon and soundly—and he awakened to a storm indeed. The wind was moaning and swishing, the spray was pelting the bottom of the boat like shot, the rain was pouring in a perfect deluge, with a steady, thunderous rhythm, and the boat swayed and shook as the big waves struck the steamer's sides. Underneath the canvas all was pitch dark. At first Charley was a little bewildered and frightened; but after a few minutes he settled back to enjoy himself. He rather pitied the folks trying to sleep dry on deck; and he wondered how it was faring with his father and Mr. Grigsby.

He could hear hoarse orders to the sailors, and hasty tread of feet, forward; and calls and exclamations among the passengers. Then there was a heavy weight almost on top of him, sagging the canvas, the canvas was torn aside a little way, and he struggled to sit up, in alarm. Maybe they were to launch the life-boat. But no— —

"It's all right, Charley. Lie still," spoke his father's voice. "I'm only coming in with you, out of the rain. Don't move. Whereabouts are you?"

"In the stern. Did you get wet?"

"Some. The whole awning leaks and the cabin and every other shelter are full of people. Whew, but it's dark, isn't it! No lightning, even. If you're in the stern, I'll take the bow. There. This is fine."

The canvas had been pulled snug again, and Charley could feel his father crawling to the bow.

"Where's Mr. Grigsby? There's room for him, too."

"He's found a dry spot, he says. So he'll stay out, as long as he can. Go to sleep, now."

Charley tried. He heard his father settle himself with a grunt, and presently begin to breathe in a little snore. That was good, for his father was not well, yet, and ought to be resting. But Charley himself found it hard work to go to sleep. The wind soughed, the spray pelted, the rain hammered, and the ship staggered and quivered, while over the stern swayed the boat.

Suddenly, amidst the voices outside, along the deck, Charley caught a quick outcry near at hand, and a scuffle—the scrape of feet, and the thump of a body falling. The tones were those of Mr. Grigsby.

"What are you doing? Stand back!" Hard breathing—and the sound of a short struggle. "Now, be off—none of that, or I'll put a hole through you!

You dirty scoundrels! Thought you'd catch us, did you? Keep away, after this, or I'll shoot on sight."

Charley attempted to sit up, and scraped his face on the low canvas. His movement aroused his father.

"What's the matter, Charley?"

"I don't know. Mr. Grigsby was scolding somebody."

"What's going on, Grigsby?" hallooed Mr. Adams. "Anything wrong?"

"No, not now. Go to sleep. Tell you in the morning."

"Need me?"

"Not a bit. It's all over with. Just a prowler — and he won't come again. Go to sleep."

"Well — —" assented Mr. Adams. "Are you dry?"

"Dry as powder. Good-night."

"Good-night. But you'd better come in with us. Plenty of room."

"No, thank you. I'm comfortable."

Mr. Adams settled himself. Charley, his heart beating, waited, listening. But Mr. Grigsby spoke not again. The rain was lessening, too — and although the seas continued to pound, and the wind to sough, the storm seemed to be ceasing. Presently Charley dozed off, and when he awakened, it was morning. His father already had left, for he was not in the bow under the canvas. Charley hastily crawled out, into sunshine and a wide expanse of blue under which a gray green ocean tossed its racing white-caps.

The passengers on the upper deck were astir, spreading out wet clothing and bedding, to hang them from the awning and the rails to dry. Charley's father and Mr. Grigsby were talking earnestly together, but checked themselves when they saw Charley emerge, and land on deck.

"Morning to you," greeted Mr. Grigsby. "Did you sleep well?"

"Fine," said Charley. "Did you? What was the matter in the night?"

"Yes; you can count on me to sleep in any kind of weather," answered Mr. Grigsby. And — "Shall we tell him?" he queried, of Mr. Adams.

Mr. Adams, who looked a little worried, nodded.

"Yes," he replied. "We might as well. He's one of us."

"The truth is," resumed Mr. Grigsby, to Charley, "one of those three fellows tried to cut the boat down, in the night. But I caught him. Here's his knife."

"Which one was it?" gasped Charley, cold at the thought.

"Jacobs," said his father. "And lucky for us that he didn't do it. Mr. Grigsby has a sharp ear. Why, we wouldn't have lasted a minute in that sea. Now, wasn't that a cowardly thing even to think of?"

"I'd feared it," admitted Mr. Grigsby. "But it didn't seem possible, in any human being. Last night was a good night for it — and I suppose the davits would have looked as though the boat had been torn loose by a sea. Whew! I ought to have shot the scoundrel without parleying."

"What'll we do about it?" quavered Charley, sitting down hard on the bench. He felt weak.

"It's all over with, so don't be scared, boy," encouraged his father. "A miss is as good as a mile, you know. We're safe, after this. Oh, Mr. Grigsby and I've decided there's little to be done. Of course, here's the knife for evidence, and we'll speak to the captain; but there's nothing else to do. We have to look out for ourselves."

After breakfast Mr. Adams brought aft, not the captain, but the first mate. He was the same official who had objected to their using the boat at all.

"So you think somebody was bent on cutting that boat down, do you?" he queried, brusquely, of Mr. Grigsby.

"I don't think so; I know it," returned Mr. Grigsby.

"How do you know it?"

"Because I knocked him down and took his knife."

"Do you know who it was?"

"His name is Jacobs."

"You can prove that, can you?"

"To my own satisfaction; yes."

"Well, I suppose you are aware that there are over a thousand passengers aboard this boat, and several hundred have knives just like that one. You can prove nothing. I told you in the beginning that you occupied this boat at your own risk. So don't bring your complaints forward. But if any damage is done to this boat you'll be held responsible."

So speaking, the first mate turned on his heel and left. Charley saw his father flush angrily, but Mr. Grigsby only laughed.

"Let him go," he said. "We can do our own fighting."

A passenger standing near evidently had overheard the conversation, for he asked, quietly:

"Do I understand somebody tried to cut your boat down, last night?"

"Yes, sir."

"His name was Jacobs, wasn't it?"

"Yes, sir."

"I heard that scuffle, and I've been wondering about it. So the ship won't do anything about it, according to the mate?"

"No, sir."

"Then I know who will," asserted the man—a quick, erect, middle-aged man with grayish moustache and goatee. He wore miner's costume, but he looked like a gentleman, nevertheless. "Wait a bit."

He, too, left. Gazing after him as he passed along the deck under the awning, they noted him pause and speak with several other men, who glanced back at the stern as if he was telling them about the boat. A little group of them accompanied him, and disappeared with him.

Soon they all came up on deck again, and with them was Mr. Jacobs himself. Charley thought that he looked rather frightened, as in their midst he moved aft. The group was swelled, en route, until when they halted before the Adams party they numbered about twenty — a sober, stern lot, standing in a determined manner with Mr. Jacobs pushed to the fore.

The man with the goatee acted as spokesman.

"This is the man, is it?" he asked, of Mr. Grigsby.

"I wouldn't call him a man," said Mr. Grigsby, contemptuously. "But he's the critter I referred to."

Mr. Jacobs scowled blackly at Charley, and his father, and Mr. Grigsby, and tried to brazen it out. However, 'twas plain to be seen that he was ill at ease.

"What's the meaning of this?" he demanded, all around. "What did you bring me up here for?"

"You're accused of attempting to cut that boat down, last night, along with the persons who were in it," answered the man with the goatee.

"Who accuses me?"

"I do," said Mr. Grigsby, shortly.

"It's a lie," retorted the long-nosed man, with an oath. "I wasn't up here. I was down below, keeping dry."

"Here's your knife," pursued Mr. Grigsby, holding it out.

The long-nosed man laughed sneeringly.

"Not my knife. I don't carry one. Besides, the ship's full of knives like that."

"Yes," said Mr. Grigsby. "But it isn't full of dogs like you! If you weren't up here last night, how did you get that bruised cheek, and those finger-marks on your throat? You look powerful like somebody who'd been knocked down and held for a while."

"It's a lie," repeated the long-nosed man, but rather weakly. He braced up. "Of course it's a lie," he appealed, to the group. "Isn't my word as good as his?"

The man with the goatee laughed grimly — and so did several others.

"Your word? It's about the poorest security you can offer. Why, you're nothing but a common gambler and a thug. You're one of those rascals who've been fleecing people down in the cabin. Just yesterday you robbed a man of his last cent by cheating him at cards. Faugh! Some of us have been watching you, and we know all about you. I wouldn't put it at all beyond you to cut down a boat, in the night, and drop it, with a man and a boy sleeping in it. Well, gentlemen," and he addressed the group, "soon or late we'll have to organize a little law and order committee, for protection in the gold fields, and I suppose we might as well begin right here. What'll we do with this specimen?"

"Throw him overboard!" came the angry response.

"String him up!"

"We'd better talk it over, first, hadn't we?" proposed a more cautious voice.

"All right. Somebody guard the prisoner."

"I'll watch him," proffered Mr. Grigsby, significantly handling his rifle.

The group withdrew a short distance, to confer apart, leaving the long-nosed man in a clear space before Mr. Grigsby. A number of other passengers had been attracted by the scene, but they stood at a respectful distance, saying nothing.

The long-nosed man glared alike at Charley, his father, and Mr. Grigsby, but he was afraid to move.

"You'll pay for this," he said, loudly. "It's a scheme to get rid of me, is it, and take my share in that gold mine you're making for? But it won't work.

These passengers won't see an innocent man suffer." And so forth, and so forth, while Mr. Grigsby and Mr. Adams answered never a word—and neither, of course, did Charley. He rather hoped that, after all, the group would decide not to handle the long-nosed man roughly, even though he was a dangerous person.

Mr. Jacobs evidently was nervous despite his bragging; and when the group advanced again, he turned pale.

The man with the goatee spoke, first addressing Mr. Grigsby and Mr. Adams.

"While we believe the accused guilty and deserving of being put into safe keeping, some of us don't think the evidence that he was cutting down the boat conclusive enough to warrant us in dealing with him as we'd like to. As for you," he continued, now sternly addressing the long-nosed man himself, "we give you this warning. Don't show yourself on the upper deck again, and don't sit at cards with anybody. If we catch you up here, or gambling anywhere aboard, we'll relieve the ship of your society very quickly. Now go."

Still pale, the long-nosed man hastened away, and went below. The next time Charley saw him was on the Isthmus of Panama.

VI

THE LANDING AT THE ISTHMUS

For the remainder of the voyage Charley slept on the deck instead of in the boat. He was not exactly afraid, and if anybody had dared him to he would have slept in the boat just to show that he wasn't afraid.

But the idea that the boat might be cut loose, or might break loose, was not pleasant. Ugh! Then down he would drop, boat and all, into the wash of the steamer; the steamer would go on without him—and where would he go?

Even Mr. Grigsby and his father, who were brave men, approved of his sleeping on deck, now. As Mr. Grigsby said:

"We know you aren't afraid, but it's only a fool who takes chances when they aren't necessary. Out in the Indian country the greenhorns were the fellows who played smart by sitting in the campfire light where the Injuns could get a good shot at them. Nobody ever saw Kit Carson exposing himself that way."

The Georgia was ploughing across the Caribbean Sea. Islands were constantly in view, but now no one paid much attention to these. All the passengers were on the lookout for the Isthmus of Panama; they were tremendously eager to get ashore and start across the Isthmus for the Pacific Ocean.

On the morning of the eighth day out of New Orleans a bank of rain or fog closed down on the horizon ahead. Off yonder was the Isthmus, but who could see it? However, evidently it was near; for when Charley roved about, he discovered that sailors were busy, below, hoisting out baggage from the hold. They were getting ready to land.

The news spread through the ship, and passengers immediately engaged in a wild rush to put their things together and crowd for the steps. They acted as though they expected to make a flying leap ashore as the ship passed by.

Charley was glad to help his father and Mr. Grigsby tie up their belongings also, so as to be ready.

Here on the rolling Caribbean the sun was shining brightly, tinting the choppy waves with a beautiful green. The storm ashore was moving on, evidently, for the streaks of rain were drifting around to the left and passing out to sea, leaving the mist thin and white. Suddenly voices forward cried, excitedly: "Land ho! Land ho! There she is! Isthmus in sight! Land ho!" The cries spread, with everybody on tiptoe, peering. At one end of the mist line had been uncurtained a background of rocky, surf-washed shore, with high green hills rising behind it. Next was uncovered a lower shore, indented by a large bay, and fringed with palm-trees. Next, as on sped the mist (like a swiftly rolling curtain, indeed) there came into view a lofty headland, with trees on its crest and the waves dashing against its base.

The Georgia was swinging about in her course, and pointing up the coast. This brought the lofty headland on her left. And now all the deck was rife with questions.

"Where do we land?"

"What's that big point? Porto Bello?"

"The pirates captured it, didn't they, couple of hundred years ago?"

"Can you see the old fort on it?"

"How far's the Pacific Ocean, now?"

"Do we land in that big bay?"

"Don't think so. That's Limon Bay, isn't it? Where is Colon?"

"Colon is where the railroad's going to begin. We land at Chagres."

"Where is Chagres?"

"How far across to the Pacific at Panama?"

"About four days. Three by boat and one by mule, they say."

"Anything to eat at Chagres? Any sleeping place?"

"Don't know."

"Oh, Tom! How'll we engage a canoe? Ought to make up a party and send a man ashore at once, oughtn't we?"

Accompanied by this babel of cries, the Georgia steamed up along the shore. She passed the lofty headland, which seemed to guard a fine harbor; and she passed the big bay which people said was Limon. The shore looked very tropical, with its beaches and palms and green hills and thatched huts and glimpses of bright tinted towns, while behind rose the mountain range. Charley gazed spellbound.

"Say, where is Chagres?" were asking the passengers crowding along the inshore rail.

Yes, indeed; where was Chagres? The Georgia was supposed to land at the town of Chagres, which was at the mouth of the Chagres River, and the way to California then lay up the Chagres River, by canoe, as far as possible; over the mountains by mule, down to the Pacific Ocean at Panama; and aboard the Pacific Mail Company steamship there, for San Francisco.

"According to the map," said Mr. Adams, "Chagres is about eight miles up the coast from Limon Bay. I shouldn't wonder if we were turning in for it now."

Sure enough, the Georgia was beginning to point for the shore, which rose high and steep, seamed with darker lines that proved to be ravines running down to the sea. A narrow inlet opened in the shore; no, this was the mouth of a river—the Chagres River, said several voices.

"I see a castle," cried Charley. "It looks like a castle, anyway. On top of the cliff, above the river. Or maybe it's a fort."

"San Lorenzo castle, they call it, I believe," announced Mr. Grigsby.

Closer to the river's mouth and the castle above swept the Georgia. Her whistle sounded hoarsely. Still no town appeared; and to general disappointment, when about a quarter of a mile from shore, opposite the mouth of the river, she stopped her engines, there was a rattle of chains through the hawse holes, and she had dropped anchor! Almost immediately a boat pulled away from her, for the shore. It contained the captain and two or three other officials. They soon entered the mouth of the river and disappeared. The passengers, pressed against the rails on all the decks, their hand baggage ready, murmured irritably, but no other boats were launched and evidently it was not yet time for them also to go ashore.

"If you two will look after the baggage, I'll try to get ashore among the first and hire a boat," offered Mr. Adams.

"That's the best idea," approved Mr. Grigsby. "There won't be boats enough to go 'round, and somebody'll get left."

Charley saw his father shouldering his way through the crowd, to the head of the stairs, into which he made further way. He descended from sight. Down below he would have a harder time, for the crowd at the rails of the lower decks was thicker, where people had clustered hanging close so as to be in the first of the boats. But Mr. Adams could take care of himself, all right, whether lame or not. He had been in many a battle.

For a time there was nothing to do but gaze at the shore—at the old, crumbling Castle of San Lorenzo, where through glasses a few cannon could be descried; at the clumps of palms, standing like plumes; at the rolling green hills, bordering the shore, and at the distant mountain range which was to be crossed after the river had been ascended as far as possible. Beyond the mountains lay the Pacific Ocean, where, at the city of Panama, the steamer for California would be boarded by those who got there in time. Except for the dots of soldiers, surveying the Georgia from the walls of the fort, the only signs of life ashore were the thatched roofs of some huts, back among the trees.

In the course of an hour another murmur arose from the impatient passengers, for the ship's boat reappeared, issuing from the narrow mouth of the river—and with it was a much larger boat that soon turned out to be a big canoe, manned by half a dozen natives. Both boats headed for the ship. The canoe reached it first. It was a dug-out, fashioned from the single trunk of a tree; and its crew, wielding their paddles, were black as coals, their naked bodies streaming with perspiration. On their legs they wore white cotton trousers, loose and comfortable.

They halted amidships, under the steamer's rail, where while the thousand faces stared down at them they gestured and called up. All that Charley could understand were the words: "Go ahead!" They held up their fingers, opening them and closing them to indicate twenty, evidently. But the passengers could do nothing, although some of them almost jumped overboard in their excitement.

Now the ship's boat with the second mate in it hove alongside. The mate clambered up, by the rope ladder which was lowered for him and closely guarded. He made himself heard the best he could and the word speedily traveled fore and aft, on all the decks, that the canoe would take ashore twenty people, at once.

"And he says we've just time, if we start to-day, to catch the California at Panama," was reported.

What a hubbub resulted! Of course, every party aboard ship tried to place in the canoe their man who would engage a canoe, ashore, for the river trip. The tussle looked and sounded like a free-for-all fist-fight. Down the rope-ladder swarmed the picked men, each trying to out-elbow the others, and dropped recklessly into the dug-out. Two men jumped for the dug-out from the lower deck, and fell sprawling. Another sprang overboard, and climbed in, dripping. But Charley was relieved to see, among the lucky ones worming down the rope-ladder, his father. Hurrah for dad!

Mr. Adams was none too early. The boatmen were jabbering and dodging and shouting. Already the dugout was loaded with its twenty, but the rope-ladder was as full as ever. Out from the ship's side shoved the big canoe, its captain shaking his head vigorously at the passengers above and yelling: "No! No!" while his men began to ply their paddles.

Now there was a splash in the water, and a chorus of cries and laughter. A passenger who was bound not to be left had dived overboard, after the canoe. Up he rose, to the surface, and struck out. He was the long-nosed man, Mr. Jacobs!

"Wait! Wait! Man overboard!" rang the excited shouts to the dug-out; and Mr. Jacobs himself, swimming as high as he could, waved an arm and shouted.

But the crew of the dug-out only looked back and laughed; their captain, steering, shook his head and motioned no; and faster and faster traveled the canoe. The long-nosed man swam hard for a little way, when, giving up, he turned and came back to the ship.

The passengers gave him a round of applause mixed with laughter, as he clambered aboard; but leaning over to watch, Charley saw him pause at the rail and shake his fist after the retreating dug-out. He was not a good loser.

"Well, he's left, anyhow," greeted Mr. Grigsby, when Charley hastened back to find him and tell him. Mr. Grigsby was so tall, that he had seen as well as Charley, who was little and could squeeze about under people's arms. "It's a wonder. That kind of person usually swipes the best seat."

"I'm glad, aren't you?" answered Charley. "Maybe we won't have any more trouble with him."

"Humph! Can't count on that yet," asserted Mr. Grigsby.

"My father didn't get left. He's in the boat, all right," said Charley, proudly.

"Yes. I knew he'd make it. Now as soon as we can get ashore we'll start up-river."

But nothing was done aboard the Georgia, toward landing the passengers, until another hour. Then suddenly the word spread: "Get your baggage. Everybody ashore," and the sailors began to lower the boats.

By the fight for place, that again occurred, anybody would have thought that the ship was sinking and that only those people who got into the boats at once would be saved! The parties who had no men ashore were the most determined to be first.

"Pshaw! Let 'em go," spoke Mr. Grigsby, as the shoving crowd jostled him and Charley hither and thither. "We can wait. I'm not specially anxious to be capsized and lose all our stuff."

Boat after boat, loaded to the water's edge, pulled away from the ship for the shore, canoes hastened to help, and still the passengers clamored and fought. In the confusion Charley lost all track of the long-nosed man and his partners. The main thought now was, when could he and Mr. Grigsby get ashore and find his father?

When the boats returned for their second loads there was another hurly-burly, but the decks were thinning out, and pushing to the nearest ladder Charley and the Frémonter managed to climb down, lowering their baggage, into the boat there. The boat was loaded full almost instantly, and away it pulled, for the shore again.

Standing up, because there wasn't space to sit down, Charley eagerly gazed ahead. Slowly the shore enlarged; and turning the high point on which was the Castle of San Lorenzo the boat entered the mouth of the river. A little bay unfolded, its shore high on the left, low and marshy on the right. On the left, at the foot of the thickly wooded bluffs, among bananas and plantains, appeared a little group of peak-roofed huts, all the muddy bank in front of them alive with the Georgia's passengers. Was that the town of Chagres? Well, who would want to live here!

The passengers already landed were running about like ants, every one acting as if his life again depended upon his getting away immediately.

The landing place was covered with baggage which had been dumped ashore. A number of canoes were lying in the shoal water, and a number of others had been hauled out while their owners repaired them. Amidst the baggage, and over the canoes, swarmed the Georgia's passengers, in their flannel shirts or broadcloth or muddy white, shouting and pleading and threatening, trying to hire the boatmen.

"There's your father," spoke Mr. Grigsby, suddenly, to Charley, as their boat neared the busy landing.

Charley had been anxiously searching the shore, looking for his father; and now he saw him, standing in a canoe drawn up out of the water, and beckoning.

This looked promising; maybe that was their canoe! The moment that the ship's boat grounded, its passengers tumbled out, helter-skelter, into the mud, and raced for land, lugging their bed-rolls, to swell the bevy already landed. Mr. Grigsby shouldered his own bedroll, gave Charley a hand with the other, and together they joined in the scramble.

The route across the isthmus in 1849. About forty miles by canoe from Chagres to Cruces; twenty miles by horse, mule, and bullock from Cruces to Panama. Charley's party stopped at Gatun, Dos Hermanos, Peña Blanca, and Cruces. Of course, to-day Gatun Lake covers from Gatun to Gorgona, and people start from Limon Bay, not Chagres, by canal

"Hello!" greeted Mr. Adams. He was as breathless as they, for every minute he was shoving away persons who tried to seize the canoe, and was explaining that it was taken. A black boatman was busy thatching the canopy top with dried palm leaves—and he, too, was obliged to keep shaking his head and saying: "No. No. Go 'way."

"Well, here's our boat," continued Mr. Adams, briskly. "Here's one boatman; his name's Maria. Francisco, the other, is up town buying provisions. No," called Mr. Adams, to a Georgia passenger who was thrusting money fairly into the face of Maria, "you can't hire this boat. It's taken."

"I've paid fifteen dollars apiece, for the three of us and our baggage up to Cruces, forty miles. That's as high as boats go; there we'll have to take mules across to Panama," continued Mr. Adams—the outsider having gone off disappointed. "I think we've got a good boat; but I've had a fight to keep it. If Maria hadn't have stayed, I'd have been thrown out, long ago."

"When do we start?" asked Charley.

"Whenever Francisco comes back."

"Do you reckon we'll have time to eat?" queried Mr. Grigsby.

"Yes. And that might be a good plan, too."

"You and Charley go up and see what you can find, and I'll hold the boat," directed Mr. Grigsby, climbing in.

"All right. Come along, Charley," and Mr. Adams alertly limped on up the gentle slope, to the village.

The huts were square, made of cane and roofed with palm-leaf thatch, to a peak. There were no window-panes or doors. The Chagres men and women stood in the doorways, and gazed curiously out while they puffed big black cigars and talked about the crazy Americanos.

This, then, was Chagres at the mouth of the Chagres River, the beginning of the Isthmus trip to the Pacific. (But when the great Panama Canal was built, it left the Chagres River, above the town, and cutting across a neck of land struck the ocean at Limon Bay, eight miles down the coast. The first Panama railroad also chose Limon Bay as one terminus; so that the town of Chagres soon lost its business.)

Mr. Adams spoke Spanish, because he had been a soldier in Mexico; and right speedily he bought bread and bananas and eggs and some dried meat. There was a hut bearing a sign in English: "Crescent Hotel"; but one look into it and at its mob of panting customers decided Charley and his father to eat in their canoe.

"Good! There's Francisco!" exclaimed Mr. Adams, as they returned.

"Yes; and there's that Jacobs again!" cried Charley. "He's after our canoe!"

"He won't get it," said his father. "We've paid for it, and we keep it."

VII

A RACE UP THE RIVER

The river landing was still the same scene of wild bustle, with the white people running up and down, darting hither-thither, all determined to set out at once. The dark-skinned natives were the cool ones amidst the flurry; and the boatmen were the coolest. Every canoe was constantly being pounced upon by fresh seekers who were yet without a craft, but the majority of the canoes seemed to have been engaged. However, a few boatmen evidently were holding out for higher pay.

Sure enough, the long-nosed man and one of his partners were hotly arguing with Maria at the bows, and offering him money; whereat Maria only shook his head, under its wide-brimmed braided straw hat, and scarcely paused in his work of thatching the canopy. Francisco stood looking on and listening. He was a strapping big fellow, not very black, wearing loose cotton pantaloons. In his ears were brass rings, for earrings. Just as Charley and his father arrived, the long-nosed man roughly seized Maria by the shoulder, as if to jerk him from his work and force him to take the money. At that, Francisco sprang forward like a panther, grabbed the long-nosed man by the collar, and flung him head over heels, along the mud.

Well plastered, the long-nosed man picked himself up, and glared at Francisco. By-standers laughed. Mr. Jacobs make a step forward, as if to leap while Francisco waited, panting and ready. But Mr. Jacobs's partner said, shortly: "Come along. We can't waste time here," and with a parting scowl the long-nosed man turned away with him.

Neither of them seemed to have noticed whose boat it was. All they wanted now was anybody's boat, of any kind. Charley was glad to see them go.

Francisco grinned at Mr. Adams and Charley. From the stern where he was sitting Mr. Grigsby approved, to Francisco, with a jocular sentence in

Spanish, at which Francisco grinned again. Maria spoke aside, and Mr. Adams nodded, translating to Charley:

"Maria says we have paid for the boat and it is our boat. He and Francisco want it understood that they are gentlemen and honest."

"As long as we treat them right they'll treat us right," put in Mr. Grigsby. "We're lucky. I've seen some of these boats change hands half a dozen times, already."

"Yes; when once you get to bribing there's no end to it," asserted Mr. Adams. "I don't trust anybody I can bribe."

The baggage was in the boat; the small trunk toward the stern, and bedding rolls arranged toward the bows. Francisco had dumped in a boiled ham and a sack of rice; he took the other supplies from Charley and his father, and stowed them also. A pair of broad-bladed paddles lay along the gunwales, fore and aft.

"Go ahead," spoke Maria, stepping back from the canopy. He motioned his passengers into the canoe.

"Good!" said Mr. Adams. "Get into the bows, Charley. You and I'll sit amidships, Grigsby. How many canoes ahead of us?"

"About a dozen, I reckon."

"We ketch 'em," assured Maria, confidently.

He and Gonzales seized the gunwales and bent low, shoving. The dug-out slipped down the slimy bank, through the ooze, into the water, and with final shove Maria and Francisco vaulted aboard. Maria in the stern, behind the trunk, Francisco kneeling at Charley's feet, between the bedding rolls, they grasped their paddles, and swung the canoe up-stream. With a few powerful strokes they left behind them the bank, where the white horde, crazed by the sight of another boat making start, shouted and gestured more frantically than ever.

Charley just glimpsed still another boat putting out from the landing, when his canoe swept around a curve, and landing and crowd and village all were blotted from view by a mass of foliage. Even the sounds of bargaining ceased. The canoe might have been a thousand miles into the wilderness, where nobody lived.

"All right," remarked Charley's father, settling himself comfortably. "Now 'go ahead,' as they say. There are 300 people waiting at Panama for theCalifornia, and I only hope we get there in time."

"Maria says we'll reach Cruces in three days, if we don't have accidents," spoke Mr. Grigsby. "Might as well enjoy the scenery."

The dug-out was called a cayuca. It was about twenty feet long, but very narrow, and was hollowed from a single trunk of mahogany—for mahogany was as common down here as pine up North. Charley felt quite luxurious, riding in a mahogany boat!

He never had dreamed of such scenery. The crooked river flowed between a perfect mass of solid green blotched with blazes of flowers. Bananas, plantains, cocoa and other palms, bread-fruit, gigantic teak trees, dense leaved mangoes, acacias and mangroves on stilt roots like crutches, sugar-cane, sapotes with sweet green fruit the size of one's head, sapodillas with fruit looking like russet apples, mahogany, rose-wood, and a thousand others which neither Mr. Grigsby nor Charley's father recognized, grew wild, as thick as grass—and every tree and shrub was wreathed with flowering vines trying to drag it down. Monkeys and parrots and other odd beasts and birds screamed and gamboled in the branches; and in the steeply rising jungle and in the water strange noises were continually heard. There were violent splashes and snorts from alligators—and Mr. Grigsby saw two wild boars. Now and then sluggish savannahs or swamps opened on right or left, filled with vegetation and animals.

It was the rainy season and the river was running full, about seventy-five yards wide, with a strong current in the middle. Paddling hard, Maria and Francisco zigzagged from side to side across the bends, seeking the stiller water and the eddies. Trees bent over and almost brushed the canoe—and suddenly Maria, in the stern, cried out and pointed.

"Python!" he uttered. "Mira! (Look!)"

He and Francisco backed water and stared. So did their passengers, and well it was that the canoe had been stopped. From the lower branches of a large leafy tree jutting out into the very course of the canoe was hanging a long, mottled object, swaying and weaving. Charley saw the head—a snake's head! A boa constrictor, as large around as a barrel, and with most of its body hidden in the tree!

"Ha!" exclaimed Mr. Grigsby, and raised his rifle. With single movement the two boatmen swung the canoe broadside and held it. The Frémonter sent eagle glance adown his leveled barrel—the rifle cracked and puffed a little waft of smoke. "Spat!" sounded the bullet. The huge snake began to writhe and twist, fairly shaking the tree; then fold by fold it issued, in a horrid mazy line of yellow and black (would it never end?), until with a plash the last of it fell into the water and swirling the surface the monster disappeared.

"Bueno! Bueno! Mucho culebra (Good! Good! Big snake)" exclaimed Maria; and chattering in Spanish he and Francisco hastily veered the canoe further from the bank.

"They say the snake's mate is liable to be near and we'd better stand out," explained Mr. Adams. "He was a big one, sure."

"Forty feet, I judge," answered Mr. Grigsby.

"Where'd you hit him?" asked Charley, eagerly.

"In the eye," asserted Mr. Grigsby. "You don't think a Frémont man would shoot for any other mark, do you?"

Mile after mile steadily paddled Maria and Francisco, up the magic river. Already their bronze bodies, sinewy and naked, were glistening with perspiration, for in here, between the high wooded hills, it was very hot and moist. Charley's neck was tired, from twisting his head so that he could see everything at once; and on their seat amidships his father and Mr. Grigsby were constantly craning right and left.

Abruptly Maria and Francisco ceased paddling, threw aside their plaited hats, kicked off their cotton trousers, and crying together "Bano! Bano!" plunged overboard. Charley gazed in alarm. What had happened? Another boa threatening? But his father and Mr. Grigsby read his alarmed face and laughed.

"Oh, they're just taking a swim, that's all," explained his father. "They said 'bano,' which is Spanish for bath."

Nevertheless, this struck Charley as a dangerous thing to do, in a river swarming with alligators and other reptiles; yet frisking about and blowing and ducking Maria and Francisco seemed to be enjoying themselves. They swam like seals.

"We might as well have a snack to eat, while we wait," quoth Mr. Grigsby. He threw Charley some bananas, and cut off chunks of the dried meat for the company. By the time they three had eaten a little lunch, Maria and Francisco had climbed aboard, donned their trousers and hats, and resuming their paddles were starting on again, evidently much refreshed.

In the straightaways behind and before other canoes, hurrying up-river, were sighted. One of the canoes behind crept closer and closer. Maria and Francisco occasionally glanced over their wet shoulders at it, but although they worked bravely, and Maria sang lustily:

the canoe behind was proving too much for them. Meanwhile Charley wondered how Maria had invented his "American" song.

The canoe behind held seven persons; and of course it could overhaul Charley's canoe, for four of the persons were paddlers. Charley, facing backward in the bows, had the best view of it; and as on it came, the four paddlers digging hard, he saw, as somehow he had expected, that the three passengers were the long-nosed man and two partners.

With its paddlers grunting in unison, the water spurting from the prow, and the three passengers lolling back, it surged past. One of Mr. Jacobs's cronies yelled, mockingly: "Want a tow?"—and the paddlers grinned.

"No matter," panted Maria, to his own company. "We ketch 'em. Dey pay big mooney; pay more 'fore dey get dere. You bet."

The river ran swifter, now, and Maria and Francisco worked their level best to make way against the heavy, muddy current. The sun was almost touching the high green ridge to the west, when Mr. Grigsby, who had sharp eyes, said, with a nod of his head:

"That must be Gatun, where we stop for the night."

The canoe was turning in toward the right bank; and Charley, looking, saw a cluster of thatched huts there. A number of other canoes were tied at the bank, and their boatmen and passengers were loafing among the huts. A loud dispute was going on between some boatmen and passengers. As Charley's boat glided up, and Francisco leaped ashore to hold it, the long-nosed man's angry tones sounded loud and familiar. It was he and his two partners who were threatening their boatmen.

"We want to go on. Go on—understand? We paid you extra; big money. No stop here; no stop. You savvy?"

But the boatmen shrugged their bare shoulders, and sauntered away, leaving the three men furious.

"No use, pardner," called another gold seeker. "These niggers always stop here for the night. You might as well swallow your cud."

"But we paid them one hundred dollars to take us straight through," rasped Mr. Jacobs.

"Yes, and stole another party's boat in the bargain, I understand," retorted the gold seeker. "Serves you right."

"Well, I'd like to have them up North for about ten minutes," growled the man who had drawn knife on Mr. Grigsby aboard the Georgia. "I'd tan their hides for 'em."

"Shucks! Such tall talk doesn't go down here," answered the other. "They're as free as you are, and no crookeder."

He plainly enough was somebody not afraid to speak his mind; and since they were getting the worst of the argument the three scallawags quit complaining.

"We'll have to hustle to find lodging here," spoke Mr. Adams, rather dubiously surveying the crowd and the huts.

And indeed the outlook was not promising. The village was small and dirty, squatting here amidst bananas and palms and sugar-cane, its people the same kind as at Chagres. (To-day the surface of the great Gatun Lake, formed by the famous Gatun dam which has blocked the course of the Chagres River in order to obtain water for the big canal, covers old Gatun village — and other villages besides.)

There seemed to be enough gold seekers here, now, to fill every hut to overflowing. But Maria (who appeared to have taken a fancy to his party) came pattering back from an errand, and beckoned to Mr. Adams.

"It looks as though Maria had found something for us," said Charley's father, as they followed Maria.

Maria led them beyond the village, and behind a screen of banana trees, to a little hut crouched there cosily. The owner of the hut, and his wife, stood in the doorway.

They wore a long, clean cotton shirt apiece. Half a dozen children who wore nothing at all were peeping out from behind their parents' skirts.

The man and woman bowed grandly, and Maria spoke in Spanish.

"The house is ours, he says," informed Charley's father. "Good! Now how about something to eat, I wonder?"

That was soon answered. When they filed through the doorway, to inspect, here was a cane table set with supper—fried eggs, fried bread-fruit, also real bread, baked bananas, sweet potatoes, beef dried in strips, black coffee—and in the middle of the table a baked something that looked exactly like a baked baby!

"Oh!" cried Charley, startled. "What's that?"

"A baked monkey, 'pon my word!" exclaimed his father. "Well, that's more than I can go."

"I'm no cannibal, myself," quoth Mr. Grigsby. "Fact is, I'd rather eat outside."

"No, I'll have them take it away," opposed Mr. Adams; and amidst laughter the baked monkey was removed.

They sat on the earthen floor and ate. Things tasted mighty good. The huts had no windows, and a dirt floor. A woven grass hammock swung from the poles, and a number of cowhides were laid like a couch. Maria said something about "muchacho" (which Charley knew was Spanish for boy) and pointed to the hammock.

"That's yours," translated Charley's father, to Charley. "We men sleep on those hides, I suppose."

While eating, Charley began to prickle, and shrugging his shoulders politely scratched. His partners were doing the same, and Mr. Grigsby laughed.

"Fleas!" he grunted. "That's all. Got to expect them. Otherwise we're lucky."

Fleas? There were millions of them! They hopped even over the food; but Charley was so hungry that he couldn't stop for that. He scratched and ate.

Darkness descended early in the jungle. Maria and Francisco said that they'd all start up-river again at daybreak, or five o'clock, so it behooved the party to get to bed. Charley took one stroll, after supper, into the village, sight-seeing. The village was a-riot with noise. The natives were beginning a dance, to the light of torches, on the grass, for the entertainment of the visitors. Tom-toms whanged, flutes screeched, people cheered, and a number of the gold seekers were acting like rowdies. It was a wild scene, amidst flaring torches; but Charley thought best to beat a retreat to the safety of the hut.

With his clothes on he clambered into his hammock. His father and Mr. Grigsby lay on the pile of hides. Where the family slept could not be found out; Maria and Francisco slept in the boat, to guard the baggage.

Half the night the uproar in the village continued, but this did not bother Charley as much as the fleas did. They accompanied him into his hammock, and were busy every minute, it seemed to him. And judging by the sounds from his father and Mr. Grigsby, there were fleas enough to go around, with some to spare!

Charley thought that he had just fallen asleep, when he was awakened by a tremendous roar. The hut was shaking, his hammock trembled, and the world seemed ablaze. He half sat up, staring about him. Oh, a thunder-storm! But what a storm! The storm that had caught him in the boat aboard ship was only a shower, compared with this storm in the tropical jungle. The rain was falling in a solid mass as if poured from a gigantic bucket, while the red lightning blazed without a pause. There was no wind; it was the weight of the water that made the hut tremble—of rain drumming so steadily that even the thunder was scarcely noticeable.

The interior of the hut was constantly light. He saw his father and Mr. Grigsby also sitting up—and on the floor the water was running an inch deep.

"Stay where you are, Charley," bade his father. "You're all right. We can't do better."

That was so; and so long as his father and Mr. Grigsby were not frightened, Charley determined that he need not be, either. So he lay, high and pretty dry (the rain beat through the thatch in a thin mist), and wondered where all that water came from. He also wondered how Maria and Francisco were faring. But probably they knew how to take care of themselves, because they lived down here.

The storm passed; on a sudden the rain stopped, the lightning died away; and Charley fell asleep in earnest.

When he awakened the hut was pink with morning. His father was standing in the doorway, looking out; Mr. Grigsby was gone. His father turned, as Charley stirred; and said:

"Hello. Ready to start?"

"Yes. Is it time?"

"High time. We overslept a little. You'd better tumble out. There's some coffee on the table, waiting for you. Drink it, and we'll go on and finish breakfast in the boat."

Out piled Charley, hastily swallowed a cup of coffee, and was ready—all but washing, which he determined he could do at the river. He was stiff and flea-bitten, but otherwise felt all right.

He followed his tall father out into the fresh morning. Everything was dripping and soggy, but the sun was going to shine, and dry the world off. Together they trudged through the wetness, into the village. Other gold seekers were trooping down to the river, and the villagers, yawning and weary-eyed after the dance, were watching them, and collecting money due for entertainment.

Mr. Grigsby was standing on the river bank, leaning on his rifle and gazing about rather puzzled, while canoe after canoe was pushing off.

"No hurry," he spoke, when Charley and Mr. Adams arrived in haste. "Save your breath."

"Why's that?" asked Mr. Adams, sharply.

"Our canoe's gone, and so are our boatmen!"

VIII

A TRICK — AND ITS CONSEQUENCES

That was so! Here was the very spot where the cayuca had been tethered to a pole. Charley remembered the pole, forked at the upper end. Only the forked tip was visible, for the river had risen amazingly from the rain, and was running over its bank. But the pole was sticking out — and no canoe was attached to it. Of canoe, and of Maria and Francisco, not a sign appeared.

Two thirds of the other canoes had gone; the others were rapidly leaving, as their occupants piled into them. The canoe of the long-nosed man and his companions already had started, for its place was vacant. Charley looked to see.

"It can't be that they've deserted!" exclaimed his father.

Mr. Grigsby shook his head, and smiled.

"Scarcely," he said. "See here. I've been waiting to show you."

He waded in knee deep, pulled up the pole and returned with it. A fragment of grass rope still hung to it. The rope had been cut!

"I think," said Mr. Grigsby, slowly, "that we've our three friends to thank for this. Looks to me as though somebody had cut the rope and set the canoe adrift, with our men in it."

"Then they're liable to be miles down the river!"

"Just so, baggage and all."

"We can't wait," asserted Mr. Adams. "If we wait we run a good chance of missing the steamer. I wouldn't have those three rascals get there first for a thousand dollars. How about another canoe? Have you tried?"

"Not yet. I didn't know whether you wanted to leave your baggage."

"Certainly I'll leave it. It can follow us. We can't stay here long and run the risk of cholera. If you'll look for a canoe I'll see if we can't hire passage with some of these other parties. Here, gentlemen!" he called, to a canoe about to push out, and not heavily loaded. "Got any room to spare?"

"Nary an inch, mister," responded one of the men. And away they went.

Again and again Mr. Adams tried, and he always got the same answer. Truly, this was a very selfish crowd, every man thinking only of himself and the goal ahead. They all acted as if the gold would be gone, did they not reach California at the very earliest possible minute. The fact is, Charley felt that way himself.

Back came Mr. Grigsby, hot and wet and disgusted.

"There's not a canoe to be had," he announced. "I can't get a boat for love or money. Either they're all in use, or the people claim they want to use them later. I expect we'll have to wait."

"Do you think our men will be back?"

"Yes, sir, as soon as they can. They seem honest. We can't walk, anyway."

"No, I should say not," responded Mr. Adams, surveying the jungle encompassing close. "We couldn't go a mile. The river's the only trail. Very well, we'll wait a while. I've waited before, and so have you."

"Many a time," and Mr. Grigsby composedly seated himself on the bank, his rifle between his knees.

"I'll see about some breakfast, then," volunteered Mr. Adams. And away he strode.

Charley had listened with dismay to the conversation. The last of the gold seekers' dug-outs had left in a hurry, and was disappearing up-stream. And here were he and his partners, stranded at the very beginning of their journey across to the Pacific! That had been a mean trick by the long-nosed man. Charley grew hot with anger.

"I should think Maria and Francisco would have waked up," he complained.

"They're awake by this time, and considerably surprised, too," answered Mr. Grigsby. "As like as not they were covered with their gutta-percha blankets, from the rain, and the boat drifted away without their feeling a thing."

The sun had risen. A few of the villagers squatted beside Mr. Grigsby and Charley and chatted in Spanish. They didn't appear concerned over the matter. They seemed to think that it was a joke. Presently Mr. Adams came striding back.

"Nothing new, is there?" he queried. "All right. Breakfast is ready, anyway. I don't think these people will object to having us as steady boarders, at two bits apiece."

The breakfast, in the darkened hut where they had slept, was very good: baked plantains (that looked when whole like a banana, but when served cooked looked and tasted like squash), boiled rice, butterless bread, and black coffee again. Charley enjoyed that breakfast—how could he help it when he was hungry and the food was something new? But his father rose twice to look at the river. Evidently time was of more importance than eating.

However, the river brought nothing; and when they all had finished breakfast and went out together to inspect the river again, it proved still vacant of the dug-out, and of Maria and Francisco.

"I vow!" chafed Mr. Adams. "This is too bad."

Mr. Grigsby seated himself on the bank.

"I don't wish any snake harm that doesn't deserve it," he said. "But if a big boa would swallow that long-nosed man and his two cronies I don't reckon I'd feel especially sorry, except it would be powerful hard on the snake!"

The village pursued its daily routine. Some of the women washed clothing in the shallows, although the water seemed dirtier than the garments. Men and women, both, cut plantains and bananas and breadfruit, and scratched gardens with crooked sticks. Children played about, and a few canoes pushed out, to go fishing. But nobody worked any too fast. The sun beat down hotly, the air was moist and heavy, monkeys and parrots screamed in the trees, and ever the Chagres flowed past, brown and swollen from the rain. Considerable driftwood floated down, and this was the only passing object.

After about two hours had dragged by, Mr. Grigsby suddenly uttered, in his calm manner, with a nod of his head: "There they come." He had keen eyes, had the scout and trapper who had served with Kit Carson and Colonel Frémont, for Charley, peering down stream, saw only a small speck appearing around the bend. His father wasn't quite convinced, and squinting earnestly he said: "I hope so, but it may be some other canoe, after all."

"Not a bit," assured Mr. Grigsby. "That's our craft, with our men in it paddling for dear life. I can see 'em plain; can't you?"

Along the opposite bank crept the canoe—yes, it held two paddlers—now it was quartering across, making for the village; its crew certainly looked like Maria and Francisco.

Hurrah! Maria and Francisco they were; and indignant they proved to be, as their three passengers proceeded to the water's edge to meet them. They were panting and wringing wet, for they had come in a great hurry. The villagers flocked curiously down, to listen and inspect.

"Quick!" called Francisco, in Spanish, as he held the canoe to the bank, "Get in, Americans." He held up the severed rope attached to the prow. "Those rascals cut us adrift, but never mind. We'll hurry."

"We were almost down to Chagres again when we woke up," called Maria, to friends ashore. "We have been paddling ever since."

"Get aboard," bade Mr. Adams. "All right," he added, to the boatmen, as Mr. Grigsby followed him and Charley tumbled into the bows. Francisco gave a vigorous shove, out shot the canoe into the current; and instantly Maria and Francisco were digging again with their paddles.

"We've lost about six hours," remarked Charley's father. "And it's too late for even Grigsby's boa constrictor to help us out."

Maria seemed to have understood, for he grunted, encouragingly: "Go ahead! Ever'body go ahead!" And tacked on a sentence in Spanish.

"Maria says they'll paddle all night," translated Charley's father, for Charley. "That will help, but I expect a lot of other fellows will do the same."

"Well, we can do the best we're able," spoke Mr. Grigsby. "I reckon we'll get thar. The river's falling. That'll help."

By the looks of the water-line on the banks, this was so. Maria and Francisco made good progress, as they cunningly took advantage of every eddy. Speedily the village of Gatun disappeared in the heavy foliage behind, and once more the dug-out was afloat in the tropical wilderness.

The river was extremely crooked, and in spots was swift; and Maria and Francisco worked like Trojans to gain a few miles. (Of course there was no Gatun Lake here yet. The Chagres had not been dammed for any Panama Canal, but flowed in a course between high green hills bordered with lagoons.)

About noon another little hut village appeared in a clearing on the right bank. This was Dos Hermanos (Two Brothers), where people who left Gatun early in the morning usually stopped for breakfast, and their boatmen stopped for gossip. But Maria only shook his head at sight of it, and he and Francisco paused in their paddling not an instant. So Dos Hermanos faded from view, behind.

How they worked, those two boatmen—the muchos caballeros (much gentlemen) as they claimed to be! And certainly white boatmen never could have served more faithfully. Maria no longer sang his funny "Yankee Doodle Doo." He and Francisco saved their breath, while the perspiration rolled from them in streams. All day they paddled, pausing only twice for a bano, or bath. Other villages were passed, and one or two ranches; and in due time the sun set and dusk flowed down from the densely green hills.

With one accord Maria and Francisco swung the canoe in to the nearest bank, and tethered it to a leaning tree. Maria spoke in Spanish, and shrugging his shoulders, wearily stretched.

"Rest for two hours, and eat, is it?" quoth Mr. Grigsby, likewise stretching, and then standing up. "All right. These boys have earned it."

They certainly had. Still none of the gold seekers' flotilla ahead had been sighted, but assuredly some of the lead had been cut down. As for the long-nosed man's canoe, its four paddlers probably had kept it in the fore, and there was not much chance of overtaking it. Charley was rather glad. Maria and Francisco seemed to be so angry that there was no telling what they might not do to the men who had cut them adrift. And his father and Mr. Grigsby were to be reckoned with, too!

The forest on either side darkened rapidly. New birds and animals issued, for the night, and filled the jungle with strange, new cries. The river also was alive with splashes, from fish and reptile and beast unseen. But after they all had eaten supper of bananas and cold pork and cold plantains, washed down with cocoanut milk, Maria and Francisco laid themselves out in the boat, and slept. Their three passengers nodded and waited.

In two hours precisely the faithful boatmen awakened. Francisco lighted a pitchy torch and stuck it upright in the bows. Then the boat was shoved out, he and Maria resumed their paddles, and on they all went, up the river again.

This was a fascinating voyage. Great birds and beetles and bats swooped for the torch, and fled; fish leaped before the prow; and from the jungle on right and left harsh voices clamored in alarm. Charley, perched in the bows by the torch, which flared almost in his face, peered and listened. The ruddy light cut a little circle on the water, and shone on the dark, glistening forms of the two boatmen, and on the staring faces of Mr. Grigsby and Mr. Adams, sitting amidships.

The night seemed to be growing darker. Over the forest, on the right before, lightning was glimmering, and there was the low growl of thunder.

"Going to get wet," announced Mr. Grigsby. "It rains at least once every twenty-four hours, at this season."

Maria and Francisco exchanged a few sentences in Spanish and doubled their efforts. The dug-out surged along, but even when it was close to a bank the trees could scarcely be seen in the blackness.

"Well, Charley," called his father, "if we don't reach Peña Blanca (that was the next village, and the name meant White Rock) in time we are liable to get wet."

"Hark!" bade Mr. Grigsby. "Somebody's shouting."

Maria and Francisco had heard, also, for they rested on their paddles a moment, to listen. Again came the new sound—a shrill, prolonged cry wafting across the velvety river. Francisco looked back inquiringly at the two men amidships.

"Go over," said Mr. Adams, with motion of hand. "Somebody's hailing us."

Maria whooped loudly, and was answered. The dug-out turned, and slanted across the current.

Not a thing could be seen. The torch flared low, for a chill, damp breeze began to blow, in fitful fashion, heralding the storm. Maria whooped at intervals, and back came the cry in reply.

"They sound right ahead," spoke Mr. Grigsby. "Easy, boys."

"I see them! I see them!" exclaimed Charley. A lightning flash more vivid than any of the glimmers preceding had lighted the river with dazzling white; and peering intently he had seen a boat, with dark figures in it, limned not one hundred feet before. "They're straight in front—people in a boat."

"Hello!" now was wafted the shout, in English. "This way."

Maria and Francisco paddled slowly, awaiting another lightning flash. It came, disclosing the other boat only a few canoe lengths away. Maria and Francisco paddled cautiously; the lightning flashes were frequent, as if the storm was about to break, and the two boats could see one another constantly.

"What's the matter here?" demanded Mr. Adams, as Maria and Francisco held the dug-out a paddle's distance from the stranger boat. By the flare of the dying torch, and the flashes of the lightning, this was revealed as a native canoe, with two boatmen and two passengers.

"Be careful," warned a white man's voice. "We're hung up here on a snag, and need help. We've been here five hours, and not a boat would stop to lend a hand. If you've the hearts of men you'll stand by and give us a lift. Our boatmen are worn out, and one of us is sick as a dog."

"Well, sir, you can depend on us," assured Mr. Adams. "We're probably in the biggest hurry of all, but we're not brutes. Let's see what's to be done." He spoke to Maria in Spanish, and Maria and Francisco began to chatter with the other boatmen.

"We've sprung a leak, too," said the spokesman in the wrecked canoe. "It keeps two of us bailing. I won't leave my partner. He's too sick to swim. Cholera, I might as well tell you. Can you take us aboard?"

"We'll try," replied Mr. Adams. "Much baggage?"

"We've thrown the baggage over, or else we wouldn't be on top. All we ask is to get to Peña Blanca or some nearer place if there is any; and we'll pay your price."

"There's no price, sir," said Mr. Adams, firmly. "We can take them in, can't we, Grigsby?"

"You bet," responded Mr. Grigsby. "They can count on us some way or other. I'd not desert friend or stranger in distress for all the gold in California."

"Thanks later, then," spoke the other, shortly. "But our torch is out, there's a foot of water in the bottom, and if that storm breaks on us we'll be swamped. Fetch your boat alongside, will you?"

His tone was the tone of authority, as if he had been accustomed to command. Mr. Adams delivered a sentence to Maria; and the dug-out was carefully worked in to the wrecked boat. Now edge to edge they floated. The other boat was hard and fast on a sunken tree, and a sharp branch had jabbed clear through the bottom.

"My partner first," bade the man. "We'll have to lift him. He's far gone."

While the boatmen held the two crafts together by the gunwales, the helpless form, swathed in a blanket, was passed across and propped beside Maria in the stern. Then in stepped a short, stout, red-faced man, and the two boatmen nimbly followed, with their paddles.

The dug-out was weighted almost to the gunwale by the new load, and Charley caught his breath, in dismay. But she ceased sinking, and still floated.

"Cast off," bade the short man, brusquely. "Thank God," he breathed, wiping his brow. "I guess we'll make it now, storm or no storm. My boys will help paddle."

With an exclamation all together Maria and Francisco and the two new boatmen dipped their paddles, as the two boats parted; and the dug-out leaped ahead.

"My name is Captain Crosby. I'm a sailor, from Boston," the stranger introduced himself.

Mr. Adams explained who they were. Captain Crosby continued:

"I've followed the sea all my life, since I was a small boy, and this is one of the narrowest escapes I've ever had, afloat or ashore. If it hadn't been for you, my mate and I would have been drowned, or would have died in the jungle. As for those cowardly whelps who passed us by—faugh! Each one left us to the boat behind. Fiji Islanders would have had more heart than that. It was the cholera that scared 'em."

"I'm afraid your partner's very sick," commented Mr. Adams. And indeed, lying limp and unconscious, wrapped in the blanket, his features pinched and white in the glare of lightning and flare of torch, the partner certainly looked to Charley to be a very sick man.

"Yes, sir. He'll not recover. I've seen cholera before. But I'll stay with him to the last, and then I'll bury him. Seems to me you're late on the up-river trip, aren't you?"

"We are. But evidently there was a purpose in it," responded Mr. Adams. "Things work out for the best, in this world."

"You'll not lose by it, sir," asserted Captain Crosby. "Wait and see. You'll not lose by it. I've something up my sleeve. But now the main thing to be done is to land us and be rid of us."

That may have been so; in fact, it behooved them all to land, if the approaching storm's bite was as bad as its bark. The torch flickered and went out; but the lightning was light enough, illuminating river and wooded shores with blinding violet blazes. The bellow of the thunder was terrific—and while the four boatmen heaved with their paddles and encouraged each other with shrill cries, in a solid line down swept the first sheet of rain.

In an instant Charley was drenched to the skin. So were the other passengers, and the stinging drops lashed the bare bodies of the paddlers. The water swiftly gathered in the boat, so that Mr. Grigsby and the captain began to bail with gourds kept handy for the purpose. But, hurrah! There, on the near shore ahead, was another little village, Peña Blanca, its low huts showing dimly through the spume of the storm. Straight for it made the canoe—hit the sloping bank, and stuck while out stumbled the passengers, the captain shouldering his partner.

Francisco ran ahead, to show the way; and calling, dived in through the doorway of a hut larger than its neighbors. Charley followed, and in they all scurried. The other boatmen had stayed behind to spread rubber blankets over the baggage.

IX

TIT FOR TAT

Francisco spoke to the family in the hut, and rising, one of them lighted a candle. It was a two-story hut, and quarters were engaged in the up-stairs room for the three in Charley's party; while Captain Crosby and the sick man were given a place on the ground-floor.

The up-stairs was entered by a ladder. There was nothing better to be done than to sleep in wet clothes; and Charley, on his grass mat, was just beginning to be drowsy and fairly comfortable, and barely heard his father say to Mr. Grigsby: "We ought to pull out at daybreak, but that depends on what we can do for the captain," when the captain himself came poking up through the hole in the floor.

"Hello!" he said. "It's Crosby. Are you awake?"

"Yes, sir. What's wanted?"

"Nothing, thank you. I suppose you'd like to get away early."

"As early as possible, captain. But we're at your service."

"Your time is valuable now, gentlemen. Mine isn't. If you're going to catch the California, you haven't a moment to waste."

"We'll miss the California, rather than leave you in the lurch."

"You'll not miss her, if you make an early start and go right on through. I told you you wouldn't lose by your kindness to my mate and me, and you won't. I stay here; you go on whenever you choose."

"No, sir," said Mr. Adams. "If we can help you any we'll stay by you."

"I stop here," announced the captain. "As for my mate, he stops, too. He'll never travel again. Tomorrow I bury him. He's gone, making his last trip, and I expect he's landed in a better port than California. What I do next I don't know. Go back to Chagres, maybe. At any rate, here's his ticket from Panama up to San Francisco." By the flicker of the storm, now retreating,

Captain Crosby was revealed groping across the floor, and extending a folded paper.

"What's that for?" demanded Mr. Adams.

"You're to take it and use it. Sell it, is my advice. You can get six hundred or more dollars for it, at Panama."

"I'll take and sell it, if you say so; but I'll send you the money. Your friend's family ought to have that."

"My mate had no kin alive. I don't want the money, and I know him well enough to know that he'd want you to have it. Yes, I understand that you didn't help us out for pay — you or any in your party. This isn't pay; it's just a little tit for tat. Sell that ticket and divide the proceeds among you, not omitting the boy. It may tide you over a tight place, just as you tided us over a tight place. You see, the ticket's no good to me. And now there's another thing or two, before we part. You've run a big chance of getting left; and even if you reach Panama in time for the steamer, you're liable to find her full up ere that. Here's a note I've written to Captain Flowers, of the California. He's an old ship-mate of mine. I sailed with him before I got my papers, and we're as close as brothers. He's expecting me, at Panama, and he'd hold the ship for me, if possible. I've asked him to take your party on instead, and he'll do so even if he has to give up his own cabin. My two boatmen will ship with your craft and help your boys up-river from here to Cruces. There they'll find you the mules to carry you on to Panama. Without these fellows you might have difficulty to find any mules, for the crowd in advance probably has hired every tassel-tail in sight. But I'm known all along the trail from Chagres to Panama; I've been across time and again, and I have my lines laid. Now I think you're fixed for a quick passage."

"But, my dear man!" exclaimed Mr. Adams. "This is too much. We can't accept——"

"It isn't, and you can," retorted the captain, bluntly. "I'm not inconveniencing myself a particle, whereas your party took a risk. Now good-bye and good luck to you, gentlemen; and the same to you, my lad. Here are the documents. You'll find my boatmen with your boatmen in the morning. There'll not be much time to say good-bye then, if you start as early as I think you'll start. I'll leave word for you to be called at four o'clock."

So saying, the bluff captain shook hands all around, declined to listen to further thanks, and ducked back down the ladder.

"There's a good turn repaying another in short order," remarked Mr. Grigsby. "If we help somebody else off a snag we're likely to have a whole ship put at our disposal!"

"Well, don't look for that," laughed Mr. Adams. "I'd help the next man anyway."

"Certainly," agreed the Frémonter. "So would I."

And Charley sleepily determined that he would, also. But anyway, the future looked bright again.

"We ought to reach Cruces to-morrow, and Panama the day after," remarked Mr. Adams; which were the last words that Charley heard until he was shaken by the shoulder and his father's voice was saying: "All right, Charley. Time to start."

The interior of the room was not yet pink with very early morning. Charley stiffly scrambled to his feet, and followed his father down the ladder, and through the room below—treading carefully so as not to disturb the sleepers there. Mr. Grigsby already was out; and if Captain Crosby was awake he pretended to be asleep so as to avoid more thanks!

A little fire blazed on the river bank, near the boat. The boatmen had made coffee and boiled some rice in cocoa-milk for the breakfast, so that within fifteen minutes the boat was headed up-stream, on the spurt for Cruces.

Now urged by four paddlers instead of two, it fairly flew, cleaving the current while the dim shores and water grew lighter. The mountain divide ahead was gradually drawing closer, and all the country along the stream seemed steeper. One by one ranches were passed which in the midst of cleared forest and jungle looked more prosperous than the ranches of the lower river.

Well it was that the boat was equipped with four boatmen, for the current ran very swift off the high hills, and contained several rapids where two of the men—yes, and once all four of them—had to shove with poles. They constantly chewed sections of sugar-cane cut from an armful that had been tossed in at Peña Blanca. Charley tried the same stunt, and found that the sugar-cane juice was good for a lunch.

Shortly after noon the course made a long turn about the foot of a mighty, rounded hill, standing alone. Great trees clustered thickly to its top; and here, high above all, up rose a single straight palm, like a plume in the crown of a noble chief. The boatmen spoke, one to another, and Francisco pointed.

"There you are, Charley," said Mr. Adams. "That's Mount Carabali. It used to be a lookout for Indians and pirates. From that palm you can see both the Atlantic and the Pacific. We're about ten miles from Cruces."

In four miles more a large village called Gorgona was passed. During half the year this was the place where people crossing the Isthmus changed from boat to mule-back, but during the other half Cruces, six miles above, was the junction. (As for old Gorgona, to-day it has been swallowed, the most of it, by the greedy Gatun Lake of the big canal.)

Above Gorgona about two miles the Chagres River, whose course had mainly been east and west, turned sharply to the left, while a fork called the Obispo River continued on toward the Pacific. (Here, to-day, at the forks, the Gatun Lake ends, after swallowing Gorgona, and the celebrated Culebra Cut proceeds on west into the mountains, making a path for the great canal, with Panama only fifteen miles away. However, in 1849 and for many years afterward, the Panama Canal across the Isthmus was not visible to the eye. There was no Gatun Lake and no Culebra Cut; there was only the beautiful, tricky Chagres River, flowing between its high jungly banks and divided, above Gorgona, where the Obispo entered.) So the canoe carrying Charley and his party turned south up the Chagres, and toiled on, amidst rugged green walls, to Cruces, at last.

Las Cruces (The Place of Crosses) was situated on the west bank of the Chagres, and as the canoe approached appeared to be a village of much importance. As Charley had heard, it had been a famous old town, connected with Panama by a paved stone road called the Royal Road, over which treasure of gold and silver and pearls was borne by slaves and mules and horses, on the way from the Pacific to the Atlantic at Porto Bello and Nombre de Dios. Yes, and in 1670 Las Cruces was captured by the pirates of Henry Morgan (Morgan the Buccaneer, who sacked the whole Isthmus), on their way overland to attack Panama.

As the canoe grounded, old Cruces, with its regulation thatched cane huts and a few—very few—wooden buildings, looked sleepy enough in the late afternoon sunlight, as if treasure-trains and pirates and even those other gold seekers, the California Forty-niners, never had been here. One of Captain Crosby's boatmen, named Angel (and a queer black angel he was!), sprang nimbly ashore, to proceed on "up town." The other boatmen hauled the canoe higher.

"Angel's gone to find the mules," explained Mr. Adams, as all disembarked, glad to stretch their legs. "There's not an animal in sight; that's sure. The crowd ahead of us cleaned out the place."

"They didn't all get away, though. See the tents, yonder?" spoke Mr. Grigsby; for three tents had been pitched, not far back from the river, on the edge of the town.

Francisco saw, too, and shook his head vehemently, as did his comrades.

"Muy malo. Colera—mucha colera. Cuidado (Very bad. Cholera—much cholera. Be careful)," he said.

"Shouldn't wonder," muttered Mr. Adams.

"I'll go over," volunteered Mr. Grigsby, "and see if we can do anything." Shouldering his faithful rifle, the tall Frémonter strode for the tents.

When he returned he reported that Francisco had guessed truly: the tents held sick gold seekers, laid by with the dreaded cholera. But in a couple of more tents, beyond, were some engineers on a survey for the new Panama railroad. They had insisted that every horse and mule in the region had been gobbled by the gold-seeker crowd, and that the Adams party must wait for several days, at least, until the pack trains returned from Panama. However, here came Angel, grinning, and beckoning. He called shrilly; whereupon the three other boatmen promptly shouldered the baggage and started for him.

"Angel evidently has fixed us out," asserted Mr. Adams, as with Charley and Mr. Grigsby he followed.

"If he has he deserves his name," answered the Frémonter.

Angel led the way straight through the hot town, where the natives stared languidly at the little procession, to a large plantation beyond. Here, in a clearing devoted to maize and sugar-cane, amidst bananas and plantains and palms, and huge acacias laden with fragrant yellow blossoms, was nestled a white wooden house, two storied, encircled with porch and wide upper veranda. A path of white crushed shells led through luxuriant flowers to the front porch, where somebody was lying in a hammock. Charley felt rather awed, for this evidently was a wealthy ranch, belonging to cultured people.

As the party approached, crunching over the walk, the person in the hammock rolled out, to receive them. He proved to be a stout, heavy man, in loose white trousers, slippers, and white shirt. His complexion was swarthy, a magnificent black beard covered his chin and cheeks, and he plainly was a Spaniard. But he spoke good English.

"Welcome, señors," he greeted, with a wave of his hand. "I understand you are from my good friend El Capitan Crosby. If so, my house and all that is mine are at your disposal—a su disposición, señors."

That was a pleasant speech, indeed. Still, Mr. Adams, like Charley, felt a little doubtful.

"Thank you, sir," he responded. "Captain Crosby was kind enough to tell us that we would find accommodations at Las Cruces, that is true. We left him down at Peña Blanca. But we do not wish to intrude upon you. Our main thought is to get to Panama; and if you know of any mules or horses, and a guide——"

The stout man courteously interrupted.

"Enough said, with your permission, señor. Horses and guide shall be found, of course; and meantime you will honor me by spending the night. You would gain nothing by attempting the trip before morning. The trail is bad enough, by day. This is the Hacienda las Flores, and I am Don Antonio de Soto. Let your men drop your baggage, which will be properly attended to, and be pleased to enter."

Mr. Adams introduced himself and party; and with Don Antonio refusing to listen to any apologies, into the house they went. It was delightfully cool there, where the rooms were high and large and simply furnished with cane chairs and couches. Don Antonio's wife, the Señora Isabella (and a beauty), came forward also to welcome them. In white dress, with a red rose stuck into her black hair, she took Charley's fancy at once. Then there was a boy, Pascal, about Charley's age—a handsome young fellow, slim and dark, with wonderful black-brown eyes and dazzling white teeth. Servants glided hither-thither, to bring glasses of lemonade and pine-apple juice, and to distribute the bed-rooms; and when Charley found himself confronted by a real bed, with a bath at his disposal, he thought that they all were in right good hands. He wished that his mother was here, too. The Señora made him rather homesick. How his mother would enjoy this place! "We noticed the tents of some of the new railroad engineers, at the edge of town, sir," remarked Mr. Adams, at supper, where Charley, arrayed in his last clean suit of white, found the creamy beaten cocoa, served on a spotless table, was the most delicious thing that he had ever tasted. "I wonder how the work is going on."

"Excellently," responded Don Antonio. "I believe that a partial survey has been made clear across. From the Atlantic end at Limon Bay the line follows up along the right bank of the Chagres, about to Gorgona, where it crosses and uses the old treasure-trail over Culebra Pass to Panama."

"Then we'll see the survey, to-morrow?"

"No, señor, I fear not. You will follow the Camina Reale (Royal Road) from Cruces, which runs far to the northward of the other trail from Gorgona. But tell me, you being so lately from the United States, what is the report upon this Panama Railroad? The Americans are to build it, we hear."

"Yes, sir. A French company had the contract to cross this part of New Granada with a railroad, but they didn't do anything, and at the beginning of this year an American company got the right. The company is formed by William Henry Aspenwall, John Lloyd Stevens, and Henry Chauncy, of New York. The contract runs for forty-nine years from date of completion of the road, which must be finished within six years. No doubt the active construction will begin this fall or winter, at Colon; and I am glad to know that the preliminary survey is already being made. A railroad is badly needed."

"Ah, but the difficulties will be immense, señors," said the Dona Isabella. "Swamps, mountains, fevers, wild beasts, rains—!" and she exclaimed in Spanish, with despairing gesture of her white hands.

"It will be done, if the Americans go at it," asserted Don Antonio. "You Americans are a wonderful people. I shall send our Pascal north, this coming winter, to be an American. Eh, Pascal? He must learn English, too. I myself was educated at Lima, where there are many Americans and English."

"If I was going to be home you could send Pascal to St. Louis, Don Antonio," spoke Charley, impulsively. "Then I could show him 'round." "He would enjoy that, I'm sure," answered Don Antonio; and Pascal, as if understanding, smiled friendly across the table at Charley.

"Yes, sir; a year or so in the States would do him good," agreed Mr. Grigsby.

"Our friend Captain Crosby will take care of him," said Don Antonio. "The matter has been arranged. And now after the railroad," he continued, "will come the ship canal, no doubt. That will be a still greater undertaking."

Mr. Adams nodded.

"Yes, I believe you. A canal across this Isthmus of Darien, as the old navigators termed it, has been talked of ever since 1520, when Charles the Fifth of Spain ordered a survey made. I expect to live to see the railroad completed; whether I or you or any of us here will see a canal, I don't know. But there'll be one; there'll be one."

That evening, after supper, Dona Isabella played charmingly on the guitar, while amidst the shrubbery before the house the enormous fire-flies made long streaks of light or blazed like jewels on leaf and twig. With the graceful Pascal Charley chased and captured some. Pascal had a wicker cage partly full of them, and used it as a lantern. He lent it to Charley to go to bed by!

From the chase Charley returned to the porch in time to hear Don Antonio discussing the road to Panama.

"The distance is twenty miles," he said, "and must be made in daylight. The old road is not what it was in the time of golden Panama, when it was kept open by the treasure trains. I would not hurry you, gentlemen, but you should start early in the morning, for this is our rainy season and you are liable to be delayed."

"It is a paved road, you say, sir?" queried Mr. Adams.

"After a fashion," smiled Don Antonio, "but laid more than 300 years ago. From Panama to Cruces it was paved with flat stones, and was made wide enough for two carts to pass one another. That, too, señors, was a great undertaking, through the jungle and over the mountains, and hundreds of poor natives died at the work. Ah, what millions in gold and silver and precious stones, to enrich us Spaniards, have traveled that long road all the way from the Pacific to the Atlantic! The portion between Cruces and Panama has been kept open the longest, for soon after the completion of the whole vessels began to ply back and forth between Cruces and Chagres, and the lower road was not so much used."

"You spoke of animals for our use to-morrow," suggested Mr. Adams. "They shall be ready, señor. We at the Hacienda las Flores do not need to keep horses and mules for hire, but I have plenty for my friends."

"We wish to pay for their use, sir," spoke Mr. Adams, quickly. "We would not think of accepting them, otherwise. That is only fair. Isn't it so, Grigsby?"

"I say the same," agreed the Frémonter.

Don Antonio politely bowed.

"In that case," he answered, "I shall yield. The regular hire from Cruces to Panama is ten dollars each for the riding animals, and six dollars for each 100 pounds of freight. However, the animals ate at your disposal without price, if you permit me. With the packers and guide you can settle among yourselves."

Lighted to bed by his firefly lantern, that night Charley slept between sheets, under a mosquito-net canopy. He slept soundly, but he dreamed of being a pirate, and capturing a long treasure train of mules piled high with golden bars and shining pearls and rubies on the way from old Panama.

X

ALMOST LEFT BEHIND

Don Antonio proved as good as his word. After the early breakfast, at which all the family hospitably presided, back of the house were found waiting three saddle horses, and two bullocks for pack animals. The trunk was balanced on the broad back of one bullock, and firmly lashed there; considerable of a trick it was, too, to fasten it in place on the rolling hide, but Don Antonio's packers did the job in short order. On the other bullock were lashed the bedding rolls. Now there remained only to bid good-bye to host and hostess, pay off Maria and Francisco, thank everybody, mount and follow the guide to Panama.

Maria and Francisco refused to accept anything extra for their faithful services; so did Angel and Ambrosio, Captain Crosby's boatmen. They shook their heads. "No, we may be black, but we are very much gentlemen. When Americans treat us right, we treat them right," they asserted.

"It is well that you have no ladies in your party," vouchsafed Don Antonio. "The trip is hard for ladies, señors. They must either ride astride, through rain and mud, or trust themselves to chairs upon the backs of natives. Sellero do we call that kind of a contrivance."

And when Charley had seen the road, he was rather glad, after all, that his mother had not come. However, as Don Antonio remarked, "women had gone that way, and many others probably would do the same." Charley felt certain that his mother could get through, if any woman could! She was spunky.

The horses were thin, scrawny fellows, so small that Charley himself stood higher than they. On the other hand, the saddles were prodigious; they covered the little animals completely, and the large wooden stirrups nearly grazed the ground. It seemed to Charley that the saddle alone was weight enough for such horses; but when at word from his father he cautiously mounted into the seat, his horse appeared not to mind. With its high horn and cantle, the saddle fitted like a chair. To fall off would be hard — which was one good thing, at least.

So they started; the guide (who was a real Indian) walking barefoot before, Mr. Adams, Mr. Grigsby and Charley riding in single file after, the two pack bullocks plodding behind, and another Indian, to drive them, trudging at the rear of all.

The narrow trail led first through a large tract of sugar-cane growing much higher than one's head, and forming a thick, rustling green wall on either side. As the little cavalcade proceeded, the Indian guide, who wore a peaked plaited straw hat called jipijapa, a pair of white cotton pantaloons, and a heavy-bladed knife — a machete — hanging at his waist, with his machete occasionally slashed off a cane, to suck.

Suddenly the trail left the cane, and plunged into the jungle; and for most of this day the party did not see the sun again. Here the guide did a queer thing: he halted a moment, took off his pantaloons and hung them about his neck. Evidently this was the sign that the plantation and town had been left behind!

The horses' hoofs clattered and slipped; and looking down, Charley saw that he was riding over a rude pavement, made by flat stones embedded in the soft soil. This, then, was the ancient Royal Road — the Treasure Trail from Panama! The stones were tilted and sunken and covered with mud; a thicket of plants and brush crowded either edge, and gigantic trees, enveloped with flowering vines, towered over, forming an emerald archway through which a few faint sunbeams filtered to fleck the way. Monkeys swung from branch to branch, and jabbered and gathered cocoanuts and other fruit; gayly colored parrots flew screaming, or hung upside down and screamed. The whole dense forest was alive with strange animals and strange cries. Charley's eyes and ears were constantly on the alert. He was having a great experience.

Ever the old road led on. In places it disappeared, swallowed by mud and vegetation. There were numerous holes, where the stones had sunk or been displaced; and picking their way the tough little horses and the panting bullocks floundered to their knees. The trail seemed to be climbing; it also was growing rougher. It crossed dank, dark ravines; skirted their sides; and wound along the rim of precipices so deep that the sight made Charley dizzy.

Toward noon the customary daily thunderstorm descended. So they halted under a spreading plantain tree, whose leaves, broader even than banana leaves, really were very good umbrellas. Here they ate their lunch, too.

The rain made traveling worse, and worse waxed the old road.

"I vow!" exclaimed Mr. Adams, as his small horse staggered and almost fell on a steep, slippery place. "This is as bad as storming the City of Mexico. How do you like it, Grigsby?"

"I thought I'd seen bad trails, on some of my overland trips with Frémont, but this beats them all."

Several times dead mules, perhaps with their necks broken, were passed; and frequently were passed trunks and other baggage, thrown aside, all of which showed that this trail of the old fortune-hunters was now the trail of the new fortune-hunters, also, bound for California.

"We must be on top of the range," presently remarked Mr. Grigsby. "Feels like it, anyhow."

Scarcely had he spoken, when on a sudden the trail emerged from the forest, to creep along the face of another precipice. The path was only a ledge jutting out not more than three feet from the solid wall hung with vines; at the edge was a sheer drop of thousands of feet—or maybe not more than 2000, but to Charley, whose left foot hung over the drop, it looked like 20,000.

The horses trod gingerly, with ears pricked, carefully avoiding scraping the wall lest they be forced over. This was wise, but not pleasant for the riders. Behind, the bullocks snorted. Gazing off, Charley saw what might have been a whole world spread beneath him: league after league of rolling, misty green, where the jungle was dwarfed by distance so that it looked like a lawn! Above it circled and circled huge vultures; and although these were high in the air, he and his party were higher yet!

"I smell salt water!" exclaimed Mr. Grigsby. "We're at the Pacific slope!"

Charley sniffed; he heard his father sniffing; but he must admit that Mr. Grigsby's nose was better than theirs. Now the trail entered another jungly forest, and it certainly led down instead of up, as if indeed they had crossed the divide. Hurrah!

However, the journey was not done, by any means. The road grew worse still, as if the rain here had been harder. Making a misstep, down slipped Charley's horse from the trail, over the edge of a clay bank, and landed on his side twenty feet below. Charley sprawled on his face in mud and rotted branches.

Down slipped Charley's horse from the trail

"Hurt?" called his father.

"No, sir," answered Charley, grabbing the lines; and pulling his horse along, he struggled to the trail again. He was not hurt, but he was a sight to behold. The only thing to do was to laugh, and go on.

"Yes, boys; I smell salt water," insisted Mr. Grigsby. "And," he added, "I'll be mighty glad to see it."

The paving was now so bad that the horses and bullocks preferred walking at one side, following little paths that made long cuts and short cuts through the brush. These paths were so narrow that the riders had to clutch tight and bend low, or be swept from their saddles. But there was no use in trying to guide those little horses, who seemed to know what they wanted. Soon Charley and the others were wringing wet, from the rain-soaked trees and bushes. This was part of the game, but Charley was beginning to feel tired and cross. Still, he wouldn't have missed the trip for anything. He'd have a lot to tell Billy Walker, when they met in the gold fields.

It was late afternoon when the Indian guide (whose name was Pablo) stopped short, at a mud puddle, washed his feet, and put on his pantaloons!

"Hurrah!" cheered Mr. Adams. "That means Panama. Pablo's dressing. And now I do smell the ocean, and no mistake."

"I've been smelling it for hours," reminded Mr. Grigsby.

Yes, the smell of ocean was in the air! Charley recognized it. It smelled the same as the Atlantic, but of course it must be from the Pacific. And within a few minutes the road had broadened; huts began to appear, alongside. Through an opening, ahead, were disclosed buildings of stone—a crumbling old church, almost covered with vines, was passed—and beyond appeared a wide stretch of beautiful blue: the Pacific Ocean!

Amidst ranches and huts and buildings of white wood and weather-beaten stone; on a broad level road crowded with people light and dark, and horses and mules and goats, and fringed with palms and bananas and plantains, oranges, cactuses, citrons, magnolias and acacias, crossing an old moat or wide ditch, through an arched gateway in a thick stone wall the belated little party entered famous Panama. Over the broad Pacific the sun hung low, and in the harbor, about a mile and a half from the end of a street which gave the view, lay a large black steamer with smoke welling from her stacks.

"That must be the California," exclaimed Mr. Adams, quickly. "She has steam up."

"I reckon," said Mr. Grigsby, peering keenly, "we're just in time."

What a bustling city was this Panama! And what a number of Americans were here! The buildings, of stone, wood, and clay, were two and three stories high, with iron balconies bordering the upper stories. By the open doors of some of the houses Charley caught glimpses, through the halls, of charming flowery courts within, where fountains played. The air was sweet with many scents and the fresh sea breeze. The narrow-paved street down which Pablo proudly led his procession was well crowded with animals and men—the latter being of all nationalities. Spaniards in peaked hats and long velvet cloaks, Indians and other bare-footed natives, and many foreigners, speaking English, and clad in white linen, or miners' costume, or even broadcloth.

As the party threaded their way through the strange gathering, hails constantly reached them.

"Where you from?"

"Hello, Georgians!"

"Say, you're too late for the California."

"You needn't hurry, misters."

"How's the trail?"

"Oh, misters! Got a ticket to San Francisco?"

And so forth, and so forth.

The street opened into a large public square, or plaza, surrounded by stores and fruit stands, and supplied with benches under the palms and magnolias. On three sides the streets gave views of the ocean. Many people were lounging about, but it was no place to stop and rest, for this party. No, not when the favorite hail said, "You're too late," and when, as emphasis, there lay the California with smoking stacks.

"We'd better go right on down to the beach, Grigsby, hadn't we?" queried Mr. Adams; and he spoke shortly to Pablo, directing him.

So they crossed the plaza (where several tents had been erected by stranded gold seekers), and took another street which led straight through a gateway in a crumbling wall to the water.

Panama was built upon a long point, and the ocean washed it on three sides, bordered by a beautiful sandy beach unbroken by wharves or piers. Line after line of surf came rolling in, the last line shattered by the shallows before it reached the shore. Southward were high mountains, veiled in mist. Far out across the white-flecked blue rose green islands. Between the islands and the curving shore lay several ships at anchor — one of them the California. Just beyond the inner line of surf were stationed a regular flotilla of canoes; their boatmen were lounging about on the beach, alert for passengers, and at sight of the little procession of travelers filing down they made a grand rush.

"This way, señors!"

"One medio to big ship, señors."

"My canoe biggest."

"Try me, señors. Ver' hones'."

"No. I hones', señors."

Plainly enough the only way to get out to the California was by canoe. Mr. Adams tried to make himself heard. More gold seekers were loafing and waiting on the beach; and these added their shouts and advice to the clamor of the boatmen.

"Going out to the California, strangers?" demanded a red-shirted man, pushing his way through the uproar.

"Yes."

"No use. She won't take you. She's full up and all ready to sail. Don't listen to these boatmen. All they want is a fare. You might just as well unpack, and wait for the next boat, like the rest of us."

"We'll go out, anyhow," declared Mr. Adams. He picked on one of the jostling boatmen — a yellow fellow with a tiny moustache and earrings. "Two boats," he said, holding up two fingers. "The California."

"Si, si," nodded the boatman. He beckoned to a partner, who sprang to help him; and the remainder of the boatmen calmly dispersed and sat down again.

Pablo and the packer began to unlash the luggage from the bullocks, and following the example of his father and Mr. Grigsby, Charley stiffly dismounted. Immediately the yellow boatman stooped and motioned to Charley to climb aboard his back.

"We'll have to be carried out to the canoes, Charley," spoke his father. "They can't come inshore. Hurry up."

But at this instant there was another interruption. "You are Americans, aren't you, gentlemen? Then will you help another American? I hate to ask it, but I've got to."

He was a young man, of not more than twenty-one or two, exceedingly thin and sallow. Otherwise he would have been good-looking. His voice and manner were refined.

"What's the matter?" asked Mr. Adams.

"My name is Motte. I'm flat broke. I came through a month ago; was taken with cholera and robbed. I sent my wife on, by kindness of other strangers; and I've been here ever since, waiting for a chance and trying to get work. She's up in San Francisco, alone, and what's happened to her I don't know. There are 300 people here now, sir, waiting for the next vessel, and tickets are selling at from six hundred to a thousand dollars! If in any way you can take me along with your party, I'll do anything in the world." He choked with his earnestness. "I hate to beg—but I must get to my wife. I'll pay you back at my first opportunity. There's work at the gold fields, they say. I— I——" and he choked again.

"We can't stand here talking," said Mr. Adams. "We must catch that steamer. Come along out with us, and we'll talk on the way."

Charley clung pickaninny fashion to the back of the yellow boatman, who waded with him into the surf. This was great sport. Staggering and slipping, and wet almost to his shoulders by a swell, the boatman landed Charley in one of two canoes that were being held ready. Mr. Adams was landed in the same way; so was young Mr. Motte. Into the other canoe were plumped Mr. Grigsby and the baggage. The canoes—larger and heavier than those other dug-outs used on the Chagres—were swung about and pointed out for the steamer. The smoke from her stacks seemed thicker, as if she was on the very point of leaving her anchorage. Charley, anxiously gazing, imagined that he could see her move! Oh, thunder! Were they to be left behind, after all? It was a long way, yet, to the steamer, and although Mr. Adams urged the two paddlers to hurry, the canoes appeared only to creep.

But line after line of surf they skilfully surmounted—first rising high, then sliding down, down, upon the other side, to meet the next line. Gradually the shore receded; the white and gray buildings of Panama, set amidst bright green, against the background of great Ancon peak, outspread wonderfully behind the ruined battlements of the old wall that fronted the harbor. And the California, smoking as if to bid "Hurry!" still waited. Gangway stairs were still lowered, down her side; and Charley kept his eyes on these. If they were hauled in, then that would be a bad sign. Meanwhile Mr. Adams talked with the young man, who impressed Charley more and more as being honest. Mr. Adams was convinced of the fact, also, for he said:

"All right. If they'll take us on the ship you can come along with us, and welcome; can't he, Charley? If they won't, we'll see what else is to be done."

Presently the black steamer loomed over. From her high rails hundreds of faces were peering curiously down; and the captain himself, in uniform, was standing at the head of the stairs. He did not look pleased, as the two canoes reached the stairs.

"Hello!" he bawled. "You can't come aboard. What do you want?"

"We want to go to San Francisco," replied Mr. Adams.

"You can't do it, in this ship. We're full up. Stand clear; we're pulling out." And Charley, to his dismay, heard the clank of the anchor chains.

"One minute! Just one minute!" shouted up Mr. Adams, standing and waving his letter. "I have a note for Captain Flowers."

"Come aboard with it quick, then. But you can't stay," ordered the man above. And up the stairs hastened Mr. Adams.

The captain snatched the letter without ceremony (and as if he was very cross), opened it and read it. Watching anxiously, as the canoes rose and fell on the waves at the foot of the stairs, Charley could hear most of the conversation. The captain spoke loudly and decisively.

"Where'd you leave Crosby?"

"Back at Peña Blanca."

"I'd given him up. His places are taken. But I'll do the best I can for you. How many in your party? Who is your extra man?"

"A young fellow I'm trying to help along."

"Does Crosby know of him?"

"No, sir, he does not," truthfully answered Mr. Adams.

"Well, you can come aboard, you and your two, but he can't. I'll do that much for Captain Crosby. More I cannot do, and I positively won't. I'm stretching a point now. We're overloaded already. Hustle your baggage in; the anchor's afloat and you've no time to lose."

"Come on, Charley, you and Grigsby," called Mr. Adams.

"Bear a hand with that baggage," bellowed the captain; and several sailors sprang to the head of the stairs.

Mr. Adams ran rapidly down again, passing Charley, who scampering gladly up.

"You'll have to wait over, Motte," he said.

Mr. Motte's face fell.

"All right," he muttered.

"Why don't you give him that extra ticket?" proposed Mr. Grigsby, over his shoulder, as he followed Charley.

"I was thinking of that. Here," Mr. Adams extended the ticket. "That will help you out, won't it? We've no use for it. It will take you to San Francisco."

"I'll leave on the next boat, then," stammered young Mr. Motte, flushing. "I'll see you in San Francisco or the diggings, and pay you. I surely will."

"No pay expected," returned Mr. Adams, now remounting the stairs, and pressed close by the baggage. "It was given to us; we give it to you, and glad to do so. Good-bye."

"Good-bye."

Charley was about to call good-bye, also, but the words died on his lips, for almost the first face that he saw, beyond the captain, as he gained the deck, was the face of the long-nosed man. The long-nosed man had touched the captain on the shoulder.

XI

CHARLEY LOSES OUT

"Who are you?" demanded the captain, brusquely.

"I'm one of your passengers; that's enough. I've paid my money to get to San Francisco with reasonable comfort and dispatch. We are late now, and overloaded, and I protest against your delaying to take more passengers aboard."

"I'm running this ship. You get back where you belong," ordered the captain.

"This is a party of tramps," bawled the long-nosed man. "They've come off the beach with a forged letter. I know 'em. I'll report you to the company. I'll see if the United States Government won't — —"

"For shame!"

"Put him out!"

"Throw him overboard!"

Cries from the other passengers interrupted him; and so did the captain.

"Here! Chuck this fellow aft!" he called, to the sailors. "If he makes any more fuss, put him below and keep him there." And he summoned, to Mr. Adams: "Come aboard, and hurry up."

So on up the stairs clambered Charley.

"Good-bye," he called back, to young Mr. Motte.

Mr. Grigsby and Charley's father followed; and on the instant the captain hurried to the bridge. The steamer's paddle-wheels began to turn; she glided ahead.

Sailors closed the rail, and Charley and his two companions were left standing there. Below, the two canoes fell behind. Charley waved to them, and was answered.

So at last they actually were off, on the last leg of their journey to California. It had been a narrow squeak.

"That long-nosed individual seems to prefer your absence to your company," remarked Mr. Grigsby, leaning upon his rifle and glancing coolly about.

"Yes. We've some information he thinks he can use better than we can," answered Mr. Adams.

"You may have to deal with him pretty smartly, if he crosses your trail many more times," observed Mr. Grigsby.

"We will, when necessary," promised Mr. Adams. "We'll take care of ourselves; eh, Charley?"

"Yes, sir," promptly agreed Charley.

"Very good," said Mr. Grigsby. "As I size him up—and his two pards, too—he'll be afraid to do much more, aboard this ship. He's gone as far as is safe for him. But when you reach San Francisco, then look out. Meanwhile I'll help you keep an eye on him."

"Thank you, sir," responded Mr. Adams.

Out through the open Bay of Panama majestically swept the California; past several small rocky islands, with some islands ahead on the left or south which were said to be the famous Pearl Islands, where pearls as large as filberts were found plentifully. In about an hour stop was made at the equally famous Island of Taboga—the most beautiful place, as seemed to Charley, in the world. It had a white beach; from the beach rose long slopes of green, shaded by bananas, palms, figs, plantains, oranges, limes—every kind of tropical growth. And these slopes were gayly colored with tiers of peak-roofed huts and houses, in pink and yellow and brown and blue and red. Along the beach were scores of white canoes. The people of Taboga, mostly negroes and mixed breeds, appeared to have nothing to do but loaf about and fish and eat and play. It was a sort of a resort place.

At Taboga the California took on fresh water, and on she steamed, for the open sea.

Gradually the walls and houses of Panama, and even mighty Ancon Hill, faded from view.

The captain came down from the bridge, and approached the little party.

"I'll turn over my cabin to you, for sleeping quarters," he announced, rather more kindly than before. "You'll all have to bunk in together, some way, but I'll rig you up a cot. I'll pair off with the first mate."

"We can't permit that, sir," answered Mr. Adams, at once. "Not a bit. Any place on deck will do. We slept on deck, to Chagres, and we can do the same here."

"No, sir," and the captain spoke decisively. "We're overloaded, and you'll not find a spot vacant. I'll fare very well with the mate. I can use the cabin daytimes, when necessary. You must have done the handsome thing by Crosby, and I'll return the compliment as far as possible. The steward will have your luggage stowed away, and show you where you belong."

So saying, the captain left, not waiting for thanks.

The cabin, of course, was airy and convenient, and to occupy it made Charley feel like a personage of importance. Mr. Grigsby chose the cot (which was to be folded away during the day), and insisted on Charley and his father taking the berth. After arranging their baggage, they might stroll about and inspect the ship.

By this time the California was headed well out to sea. Evidently the Pacific Mail Steamship Company was wealthy and progressive. The Californiawas much larger and finer than the Georgia, her decks were scrubbed smooth and white, her brass-work highly polished, and everything looked to be in apple-pie order. Her table, too, proved to be better supplied than the table on the Georgia. In a large pen, forward of the wheel-house, surrounding a platform built for the purpose, were confined a quantity of cattle, sheep and hogs, for fresh meat. Every day or so several were slaughtered. Over the upper deck were stretched shade awnings. Officers and crew were smart and spick and span.

But, like the Georgia, the California was too crowded for real comfort. From the steerage, below, to the first cabin or upper deck, the passengers had occupied every kind of quarters; the sea was smooth, so that few were seasick, but the sun beat down from directly overhead, out of a sky almost cloudless, and even under the awnings the heat and moisture were well-nigh unendurable. The gold seekers who clung to their heavy boots and trousers and flannel shorts fairly panted.

However, it was a three weeks' voyage, now, and there was no retreat. Anyway, people said that after crossing the Tropic of Cancer, there would be more of a breeze, and the weather would cool off rapidly, the nearer the California got to San Francisco.

The majority of the passengers had come across the Isthmus from the Georgia, and Charley recognized a number of them. The long-nosed man and his two cronies carefully kept away from the Adams party; Charley saw them only occasionally. After all, they were cowards, with guilty consciences.

"Charley," said his father, that afternoon while they were together, "what do you think of telling Mr. Grigsby about the mysterious miner we took care of, back home, and his Golden West mining claim? Seems to me Grigsby's a thoroughly honest man, he's been of great help to us, and while he hasn't asked any questions he must be wondering why our friend Jacobs is hounding us so."

"Yes, sir; I think he ought to know," asserted Charley.

"All right; we'll tell him to-night. Then he'll understand the situation, and it may save us trouble. Besides, it's only fair. We don't want him to support us blindfolded."

"No, sir," agreed Charley.

So that night, while turning in, in the cabin, Mr. Adams laid the situation before the tall Frémonter. He explained the whole affair, from the beginning to the sailing of the Georgia. And he showed the scrawl by the mysterious miner, and the rough sketch and the buckskin bags.

Mr. Grigsby thoughtfully nodded.

"I see," he mused, studying the sketch map. "Map's not very clear, though. Might be a map of the American River, out of Sutter's Fort. That's the main overland emigrant trail, down from the Sierra, and where the first gold excitement led. Or it might be the Feather, or the Yuba. 'G. H.' of course means 'gold here'; it's the regular sign. Six G. H.'s—one of 'em smudged. Huh! Yep, if I were you I'd try the American River first; but you want to look mighty sharp. It's no great feat in the gold fields to jump another fellow's claim, and even if you get there ahead that other party's liable to be hot after you to oust you."

"Charley and I'll defend our rights," said Mr. Adams, stanchly.

"Well," continued Mr. Grigsby, "if I'm around you can count on me. And there'll be other men who won't be inclined to stand for skullduggery. The diggin's will be put under law and order, after a bit, or else no man's life or property will be safe for a day. But until then, look out, and keep looking out."

"We will," assured Mr. Adams, nodding confidently at Charley, who soberly nodded back.

"And if I were you," added the Frémonter, "I'd tuck those papers in a safe place. Wouldn't leave them around anywhere. See?"

"I've been carrying them on my own person," explained Mr. Adams.

"The very place where anybody wanting them by hook or crook would look first," said the Frémonter.

"Humph!" admitted Mr. Adams. "That's probably so." He looked about thoughtfully. "But I don't know of a better place—'twouldn't do to stick them anywhere in the cabin, or the baggage. Here!" he exclaimed, struck with an idea. "What's the matter with Charley! Nobody would suspect that a boy was in charge of valuables. Charley, you take these and tuck them away on you where they'll be safe."

"Put them in your shoe—or in your bootleg when you wear boots," instructed Mr. Grigsby.

"What about night?" asked Charley.

"I'll tend to the nights," grimly said the Frémonter. "You might change them to your pillow, nights, and they wouldn't be any safer and you'd be apt to forget them. But my cot will be across the doorway, nights, and I in it."

"Very good," approved Mr. Adams. And so Charley carried the papers in his shoe.

For a week the California sped on, over a smoothly rolling blue sea, accompanied by the gulls and porpoises and the steady thumps of her huge paddle-wheels. On the right, or east, the coastline was at first high and mountainous, but soon became only a bluish line, across the miles of water. The decks were hot, amidst this summer sea! Almost every night there was a gorgeous sunset; yet even after sunset the thermometer stood over eighty in the cabins.

On up the full length of Central America ploughed the California; past Costa Rica and Nicaragua and Salvador and Guatemala—all of which looked about the same, at this distance, no matter how they were colored on the maps. Next came the coast of Mexico; and swinging in, the California made for Acapulco.

Beautiful was the coast of Mexico, hereabouts: a long strip of white beach where the blue surf broke; behind, vivid green hills, their bases dotted with white towns; and further behind, tremendous mountain-ranges, piercing the clouds.

Acapulco seemed as hard to find as Chagres. The California acted as if she were going to butt right into the beach; and the passengers, crowded along the landside rails, eagerly waiting, could make out no harbor. Yet Acapulco was said to have the finest harbor between Panama and San Francisco; and there was Acapulco itself—the old fort guarding the harbor, the roofs of houses beyond it, and the tips of masts betokening where ships lay at anchor.

Between horizon and sky, far up the coast, over the sea floated a thread of black smoke. Another steamer, this, passengers said; and Mr. Grigsby, whose eyes were so keen, agreed. The smoke seemed to attract considerable attention from the ship's officers, and the captain surveyed it long through his spy-glass. However, Acapulco, where they were to be permitted to land for an hour or two, was of more importance to the passengers; and landward the majority of eyes were turned.

Only when the California had passed between a rocky island and a high bluff or headland, did the harbor of Acapulco unfold, so cleverly was it fashioned. Like a huge basin it was, scooped from the cliffy shore, as if a giant shark had taken out a big bite. So steep were the whitish cliffs, that several small vessels were lying right under them. A dazzling beach fringed the edge of the great basin; palms and other trees shaded it. On a high point was the castle, or fortress of San Diego, similar to, but not so ruined as old Fort Lorenzo at the mouth of the Chagres.

The California steamed on, when suddenly "Boom!" sounded her signal gun, to announce her arrival.

From the leafy town people came running down to the beach, and a regular flock of canoes made a mad race from the beach for the ship.

The ship's boat was lowered, and was pulled away for the shore, bearing the first mate. Word was spread that passengers might go ashore, for four hours; the gun would be fired again at sailing time.

"The hottest place on the American continent," pronounced Mr. Adams. "So I heard when I was in Mexico during the war. Those hills shut off the breeze, and the heat hangs night and day. Thermometer stands at 120 degrees in the shade, for days at a time. That gap in the hill-line yonder must be the gash cut by the Spaniards, in early times, to make a current of air. Now do you want to go ashore, Grigsby?"

"Well, I rather think I will," drawled Mr. Grigsby, good-naturedly. "It may be the last chance to stretch our legs for some days. I'm not used to cramped quarters, after having had half a continent to tramp over."

"All right, I'll go with you," said Mr. Adams. "How about you, Charley?"

Charley decided that he'd as soon stay where he was, for things around the ship began to look interesting. The foremost of the boats from shore had reached the vessel. They were heaped with cocoanuts, bananas, oranges, limes, plantains, cakes, and shells, the smaller shells being stitched together in odd patterns. As more boats arrived, a sort of a market was opened. Many of the boats were rowed by women, who smoked cigars while the men with them did the selling. A line attached to a basket or bag of matting was tossed up over the rail. Any passenger who wished to purchase drew up the basket or bag, put a piece of money in it, and then the man in the boat exchanged fruit or cakes or shell-work for the money, and the passenger drew up the basket or bag again.

But the greatest sport was to watch the little boys diving for dimes and quarters. Almost every boat had a boy or two aboard, who immediately jumped over into the water, and paddled around the ship. None of the boys wore any clothing—and how they could swim and dive! It seemed no effort at all for them to stay on top, wriggling their hands and feet a little, like fishes' fins; and when a coin was tossed near them, down went their heads, up went their heels, and through the transparent water they darted, for the money. They could be clearly seen until they grabbed it, and turned for the top. On the surface they held up the money, as proof that they had it; then they popped it into their mouth and clamored for more.

Charley rather wished that his father and Mr. Grigsby had stayed to see the sport; but they had gone ashore in a canoe, and so had a number of other passengers, including the long-nosed man.

It looked like great fun, down there in the smooth green water, so clear and cool. With resounding splashes several passengers, in undershirts and cotton trousers, dived from the rail and joined the naked black and yellow boys, who made much sport of them. As well try to catch eels, as those nimble urchins. Why, said a passenger near Charley, the natives down hereabouts could swim twenty miles, and those boys themselves could keep afloat all day!

"Here, you white boy," spoke Charley's neighbor, at the rail. "Can't you get in there and do something for your country? Can you swim?"

He was a pleasant looking man, with iron-gray hair and beard, and wore white linen. He might have been a banker. The California held all kinds of Forty-niners.

"Yes, sir; some. I can swim in the Mississippi," answered Charley. "But I can't swim like that."

"Well, jump in and show us, anyhow. You're the only boy aboard. Maybe those fellows never saw a white boy swim. Maybe they think you can't swim. Show them."

"All right," agreed Charley, not a bit afraid to do his best, although he knew very well that he was only a boy and not a fish. It would be fun, anyhow.

So he hastened to the cabin, stripped like the men had stripped, and in his undershirt and cotton trousers back he pattered to the rail. The water looked farther down than he had figured, but of course he wouldn't back out, now; and accompanied by a hearty cheer from the passengers, over he plumped. As soon as he struck the water, all the boys near there made a rush for him, yelling.

Up he rose, right in their midst — and just as he had expected, he was no match for them at swimming or diving. They cut circles around him, and under and over, and the "showing" he made did not amount to much, he feared. Still, he proved that he could swim, and was not afraid, and as he paddled about he grinned. They soon found out that they could beat him easily enough, getting the coins; but he didn't want the coins, and the water was delightfully luke-warm—just right; so they all were contented.

Really, it was much better here than up on the hot deck, and Charley was well satisfied with the change, when aloft, along the rail, a great hubbub sounded. Passengers were pointing and craning about, and most of them rushed away, to the other side.

"The Panama!" they were calling. "That's she! Down from San Francisco. She's coming in. Now for some news."

Even the natives were gazing. For the stairs swam the men who had jumped overboard, and for the stairs swam Charley also. The Panama? Sure! She was sister ship to the California, and by the talk she was coming in, bound down from California.

When Charley gained the deck he, too, looked. He saw the thread of black smoke increased to a wide plume and very near. Beneath the plume was a large steamer, already headed into the harbor entrance. Great excitement reigned aboard the California.

Majestically the Panama glided into the harbor, and dropped anchor only a long stone's throw from the California. "Boom!" spoke her signal gun, and for her raced, again, the fleet of bumboats.

Her rail was black-and-white with passengers, staring across at the passengers of the California. Men began to yell back and forth.

"Where's your gold?"

"Here! Where's yours?" and some of the Panama's passengers held up round little buckskin sacks; others slapped their shirt bosoms; and one man, amidst laughter, even held, in both hands, a large gunny sack which probably contained potatoes or yams.

"How are things at the mines?"

"Booming. Better hurry or you'll be too late, stranger."

"Plenty of gold?"

"Millions of it."

"How much can one man dig in a day?"

And so forth, and so forth. Several of the California passengers, who had been in the water before, plunged in again and daringly swam over to thePanama, so as better to get the news.

Lighters, or scows, had been unloading live-stock and other supplies into the California, and what looked to be the ship's boat was putting out from the shore. Suddenly "Boom!" spoke the ship's gun, as signal that she was about to weigh anchor. Down to the beach hurried the passengers who had gone ashore. Charley knew that his father and Mr. Grigsby would be among them. The sun had set, and a little breeze blew coolly on his wet garments, so he scampered to the cabin, to change.

Just as he reached the threshold he thought of his shoes. Shucks! He had never thought, when he had taken them off in such haste, and he had left them lying with the precious papers in one of them! In fact, he had not locked the door, had he? Anyway, the door was unlocked now—and in he hastened, his heart in his mouth. His shoes were lying there. He picked one up, but it contained no papers. He grabbed the other and explored it. It contained no papers. Maybe they had stuck to his stockings, then. He hoped so. But, alas, no papers were to be found, anywhere, on his stockings, or near his stockings, or under the bunk, or—anywhere.

He rushed out on deck again, peering, following his course to the rail. That was no use, either. The papers were gone; he had lost them, or somebody had taken them.

What a foolish boy he had been!

XII

CALIFORNIA HO!

What a foolish, foolish boy! How could he tell his father, and Mr. Grigsby? Maybe, though, he could find the papers, and then he would not have to tell. The scheme tempted him, but he decided that it was cowardliness. He had done the thing, and now he was afraid to accept the consequences. Huh! This was not playing fair with his partners. Besides, the longer he waited, the worse he made it for them and himself too.

So he soberly dressed; then he went out, this time carefully locking the door behind him, which of course was rather late in the game. The boat containing his father and Mr. Grigsby was at the ship, and they two came up the side. They were laden with stuff that they had bought ashore.

"Hello, Charley," greeted his father, cheerfully. "Had a good time? Phew, but it was hot on shore! You didn't miss much. Lend a hand, will you, and help us carry this truck into the cabin?"

"You must have been in the water," remarked Mr. Grigsby, keenly noting Charley's wet, salty hair.

Charley tried to smile, but it came hard. He picked up an armful of cocoanuts, and followed his partners to the cabin. They waited at the door for him.

"Got it locked, I see," quoth his father. "That's right. I told Grigsby we could depend on you."

They dumped the spoils in the cabin. Up to this time Charley had said scarcely a word.

"What's the matter, boy?" queried his father. "Didn't you have a good time? Aren't you feeling well?"

"I've lost the papers," blurted Charley, wanting to cry.

"I've lost the papers"

"What?" His father and Mr. Grigsby stared at him. "You don't mean it!"

"Yes. I lost them, or somebody took them." And Charley did begin to cry. "I went in swimming and left my shoes in the cabin. And when I came back the papers were gone. Boo-hoo."

"Pshaw!" muttered Mr. Grigsby.

"Well, don't cry about it," spoke his father, sharply. "Brace up, and tell us about it."

Charley did.

"You're sure they aren't around the cabin somewhere?"

"I looked. I'll look again, though."

They all poked about, to no result.

"Did you look on deck, where you were?"

"Yes, sir."

"Did you lock the cabin door when you went out?"

"I think I did," answered Charley, honestly. "I meant to."

"But you aren't certain?"

"N—no; not exactly."

"Anybody could pick the lock, I suppose," said Mr. Grigsby, from under his bushy brows. "The thing looks to me like a put-up job. Who was the man that urged you to jump over?"

"I don't know. I'd never seen him before."

"Well, describe him," bade Mr. Adams.

Charley described him as best he could—a medium sized man in white linen suit, with iron-gray hair and short beard iron-gray to match.

"What color eyes?"

"I don't know," confessed Charley, truthfully. "B-black, I think."

"Don't know!" grunted Mr. Grigsby. "After this, notice those things. A man can change his hair, but he can't change his eyes. When you've followed the trail a while, like I have, you'll learn to size a man up at a glance, and never forget him. Kit Carson was a great fellow for that. So was Frémont. Well, the first thing to do is to look for Charley's man. What do you say, Adams?"

Charley's father gravely nodded.

"I agree. Did you see any of that gang go ashore, Charley? Either of the Jacobs cronies, I mean. Jacobs we saw ourselves, in the town."

"No, sir," said Charley. "But they might have gone."

"Didn't see them aboard ship, then?" asked Mr. Grigsby.

"No, sir; I didn't."

"Wait a minute," spoke Mr. Grigsby. "We did glimpse that fellow who tried to use the knife, going into a grog shop. Remember?"

"I do," affirmed Mr. Adams. "That accounts for two, then. Well, Charley," and he laid his hand on Charley's shoulder, "it's up to you to find your man for us, and then we'll investigate him. Take a brace, now, and don't feel bad. There's no use crying over spilled milk; you're only wasting time. You simply made a mistake, and everybody makes mistakes once in a while. The thing to do now is to go ahead and correct that mistake, the best you can. We'll help you."

What a brick his father was! And so was Mr. Grigsby. Instead of scolding him and confining him on bread and water, or sending him back home, they were standing shoulder to shoulder with him.

"The papers don't amount to so tearing much," mused Mr. Grigsby. "You know what the sketch looks like. That assignment of the claim may be important and may not. But of course nobody likes to be robbed."

Charley was now all eagerness to retrieve himself and find that man with the iron-gray hair and beard. Out he went, with his eyes open; but though he trudged everywhere, while the ship got under way and steamed, with a cheer, out past the Panama and to sea again, he found no passenger who looked anything like the one wanted. And he didn't see him at the table. Neither, so his father and Mr. Grigsby reported, on coming up after dining, separately, did they.

However, while most of the first-cabin and second-cabin passengers were loafing about, that evening, enjoying the long twilight, who should saunter to the Adams party but the long-nosed man himself. He certainly had nerve!

"How are you?" he accosted, very pleasantly. "I saw you gentlemen ashore. How'd you make out? Hot place, wasn't it!"

"We made out very well, sir," answered Mr. Adams, shortly. "But while we were gone our cabin was robbed. How do you account for that?"

"Meaning, I suppose, that you think I can account for it."

"Anybody who would tamper with boats would tamper with a cabin, we reckon," growled Mr. Grigsby.

"You seem bound to be personal," retorted the long-nosed man. "That little controversy on the Georgia came out in your favor, but you can't rile me. I want to let by-gones be by-gones. I'm a peaceable man. You've beat me, and I'm willing to say so. Who robbed your cabin? What'd you lose? Speak up."

"We lost some small papers, entrusted to this boy, here. I have witnesses to prove that they were in my possession, so they won't be of use to anybody else," informed Charley's father, "and the safest thing for the present holder to do is to return them."

"That's the captain's cabin. Tell the captain," urged the long-nosed man.

"No," growled Mr. Grigsby; "we thought we'd tell you."

"Meaning, I suppose, that I did it," returned the long-nosed man. "You're overshooting. You saw me ashore."

"Yes, we saw you," replied Mr. Grigsby.

"Meaning, I suppose," resumed the long-nosed man, "that if I didn't do it some of my friends did. You saw them ashore, too, didn't you?"

"Saw one of them, perhaps," admitted Mr. Adams.

"Well, you prove that the other was on this ship—you find anybody who can swear he saw the other on this ship, and then you've the right to question him," challenged the long-nosed man. "But he couldn't enter your cabin when he wasn't here, could he? Or I, or anyone else, either! Now, listen. I've come to you, wanting to be friendly. I don't deny it was to my interests to keep you back, so I could get to Californy first, and I tried my levelest. But you've beat me, and here you are. I'm a fair man; I know when I'm licked, and I don't bear you ill-will. Understand? The passengers on this steamer," and the long-nosed man raised his voice so that the people around would hear, "are witness to my coming to you and saying, 'You've licked me; but I'm friendly. Let by-gones be by-gones.' And what do I get? Why, you call me a thief, when you know very well I didn't do it. That hurts my feelings, gentlemen," and with this appeal, the long-nosed man walked off, apparently indignant.

"That's the most remarkable speech I ever heard in all my life!" exclaimed Mr. Adams, struggling between laughter and wrath. "He threatens Charley and me, and tries to cut our boat down and drown us, and assaults you (to Mr. Grigsby) and gets you almost knifed, and sets our canoe adrift, on the Chagres, and when we finally, by luck, reach the steamer just as she's weighing anchor, he orders the captain not to take us aboard—and now after our cabin is robbed very suspiciously and we've lost what he wanted, he says, 'I forgive you. I'm friendly. Shake hands.'"

Charley felt the same way. Evidently so did Mr. Grigsby, whose eyes were glinting shrewdly. He beckoned Charley and his father and led them out of earshot of the other passengers.

"That talk doesn't go, of course," he said. "It's regular Injun talk, after they've stolen your hosses. Humph! We can't find Charley's man, can we? At least, we haven't found him. Why? Because there isn't any such man. I'll wager my rifle against a cocoanut that the hair and beard were false. If they'd been stripped off, the third rascal in the gang would have shown up. As soon as Jacobs blustered about our 'proving' that the third fellow was on ship and not on shore, I made up my mind. He and Charley's man are one and the same. See?"

"I believe you're right," declared Mr. Adams. "What do you think, Charley? You said his eyes were black, as you remembered."

"He might be the same," admitted Charley. "At any rate," continued Mr. Grigsby, "the best we can do is to keep quiet and lie low. It hasn't worked any harm to tell those fellows that we know what's happened and we're not afraid of 'em. We've given them something to think about. But we'll not burn more powder until we're pretty certain of fetching a scalp. That's my opinion."

"No, it won't do any good to run circles," said Mr. Adams. "We can be thinking while they're guessing. We know what we'll do better than they know what they'll do—and they'll never, never keep possession of that mine," and he set his jaw hard. "That is," he added, "if any of us finds it."

The news spread that the "Adams party" had been robbed, and presently queries came from the curious, even from the captain himself. But people soon found that the "Adams party" weren't much of a hand to talk at random about this or any other of their affairs, and the little excitement soon died away. The captain said he was sorry, he'd take up any line of inquiry that Mr. Adams would suggest, etc., etc.; and Mr. Adams replied that there was nothing to be done, yet—they'd decided to let the matter rest.

The long-nosed man and his two partners appeared, now and then, swaggering with great air of being unconcerned—the long-nosed man especially assuming to be a hail-fellow-well-met who could not possibly be guilty of any meanness. But nevertheless, none of the three was especially popular, except among the gamblers and drinkers.

As for Charley, he did not enjoy the rest of the voyage. He had lost the papers, and he had failed to identify the man who had challenged him to jump overboard, and he was simply crazy, now, to have the voyage at an end. What he wanted, was to get ashore at San Francisco, and race that long-nosed man for the Golden West mine. He was determined to "make good," was Charley.

Up the beautiful coast of Mexico steamed the California, with a stop at San Blas, and another at the fine port of Mazatlan, almost on the Tropic of Cancer. The scenery was wonderful; the white surf of the shore, and misty blue mountains rising high above the green background, being ever in sight from the deck. The water was alive with flying-fish, porpoises, sharks, whales, dolphins, and now and then an immense turtle; while over the ship's foamy wake the gulls and terns and pelicans sailed and dived.

From Mazatlan the California veered westward, right on the Tropic of Cancer, to clear (said people) the Gulf of Lower California. When she pointed in again, in the morning, she crossed the path of the steamer Oregon, southward bound out of the gold fields. The Oregon was too far to be hailed. However, no matter—for aboard the California, now arose a cry, while people pointed.

"There's California, at last! Hooray!"

On the starboard quarter appeared, hazy across the sparkling whitecaps, a long line of low land ending in a lofty cape—San Lucas, which meant, in English, Saint Luke. Even through a spy-glass, which Mr. Adams borrowed from another passenger, the land looked to be uninhabited, and was brown and bare, with mountains rising back from the surf-dashed coast. People said that amidst the brownness were wonderful green valleys, occupied by ranches and villages; but if this was really the Land of Gold, Charley was disappointed. It did not look very inviting to tramp over. However, this was only Lower California, still owned by Mexico; and San Francisco and the true Land of Gold, Upper California, was a week ahead.

As the steamer skirted the brownish, rugged, mysterious coast of this Lower California, the weather grew more bracing, for the tropics had been left behind. Flannel shirts and heavy trousers were comfortable. The great albatrosses became few, but the gulls and Mother Carey's chickens, the nimble gray petrels that flew all day with their feet grazing the waves, were thick. The bright Southern Cross dropped low into the horizon behind, while the Great Dipper, circling the North Star, rose higher before. Yes, the California surely was making northward rapidly.

"We don't cross into Upper California until we reach San Diego," said Mr. Grigsby. "That will be to-morrow, I reckon. I remember San Diego very well. I was there in Forty-six, with Carson and Frémont; and we raised the Flag in the plaza. It's still there, too, I bet you. Commodore Stockton of the Navy took the place and held it. It used to be a great station for hides, and has one of the finest harbors on the coast."

The next morning, sure enough, the good steamer swept in for the port of San Diego, of the California of the United States. The entrance was very narrow. On the left jutted out a high, brown, brushy point named Point Loma, with a solid white lighthouse, built long ago by the Spaniards, standing forth as a landmark on the very nose. On the right was what looked to be a long, low, sandy island, fringed by the dazzling surf, and shimmering in the sun.

Through the narrow channel steamed the California, at half speed, everybody gazing hard to "size up" this first town of American California, and the first place under the American flag since New Orleans was left, over a month ago.

At the end of the channel appeared several low white-washed buildings, along the foot of the ridge which made the point.

"The hide-houses," said Mr. Grigsby, with satisfied nod, "where the cow-hides used to be stored, waiting for the ships. Smelled bad, too; shouldn't wonder if there were some waiting now. We'll see the town in a minute."

A bay began to open on the right; and sure enough, beyond where the channel broadened, ahead, at this end of the bay, on flat land came into view a group of houses, both brown and white, and a flag, on a tall pole, floating over their midst. It was—it was the Stars and Stripes! Hooray! And again hooray!

"We raised that flag—Frémont and Carson and we others in the battalion—or one like it, in July, Forty-six," declared Mr. Grigsby. "Sailed down from Monterey on the fine sloop-of-war Cyane, to help Stockton. Yonder, just back of town, on the first hill, is where the commodore located his fort, Fort Stockton, to hold the town. He anchored in the bay and sent his men ashore to do it. On the rear edge of town, on the first little rise below Fort Stockton, was the Spanish presidio, or fort—but Fort Stockton had the bulge on it. About thirty miles northeast (can't see it from here, of course) among the hills is where General Kearny and his First Dragoons were corralled by the Californians after they had marched overland from Santa Fé, New Mexico, a thousand miles across the desert. The dragoons were surrounded and in bad shape; but Carson and Lieutenant Beale of the Navy and an Indian crawled and sneaked through the California lines, the whole distance to San Diego, and brought word to Stockton to hurry up and send reinforcements. Carson nearly lost his feet, by cactus, and Beale was laid up for a year. During the war San Diego was no easy place to get into, or out of, either."

"Where's the mission?" asked Mr. Adams. "The first of the California missions was here, wasn't it?"

"It used to be in town, before there was any town, they say," answered Mr. Grigsby. "That was 1769. But when the town had started, the priests moved the mission about six miles up yonder valley, so as to get their Injuns away from the fandangoes."

Meanwhile, the California had swung to, opposite the hide-houses. Out rattled her anchor chain; "Boom!" announced her signal gun. A number of people had collected in front of the town, which was separated from the water by a wide strip of tide-land; but on a road which bordered the point and connected the hide-houses with the town, other people came at a gallop, horseback. The captain went ashore, in the ship's boat; but stay here was to be short, so no passengers were allowed to go.

"Is there gold in those hills yon, mister?" asked a lean, lank Arkansan, of Mr. Grigsby, who was accepted as an authority on the country.

"There might be; I dunno," responded the Frémonter. "But it's powerful dry, according to Kit Carson. You can't mine without water. Of course, those flat-tops to the south of us are in Mexican territory. To my notion, it isn't gold that will make this southern country; it's climate and commerce. The climate down here is the finest in the world. Warm like this all the year 'round, and cool enough nights for sleeping. No bad storms, either. This bay runs about three miles southward, yet every inch of it is landlocked. When that railroad across the Isthmus is finished, to help emigration, I look to see a big city here, and a harbor full of ships."

"A ship canal across the Isthmus would help this country a lot," mused Mr. Adams. "The west part of the United States is too far from the east part; a canal would bring them together."

"Yes, and so would a railroad clean from the Missouri to the Pacific," agreed the Frémonter. "That will come, too, in time; and to go to California will be as easy as to go to Washington or New York."

"Looks as though a toler'ble lot more passengers were comin' aboard, don't it?" remarked the Arkansan, staring fixedly at the beach.

"Yes, sir; and overlanders, too!" exclaimed Mr. Grigsby, his gaze narrowing. "I reckon they must have got in by the southern route along the Gila River. And if so, I pity 'em. It's a terrible trail."

XIII

INTO THE GOLDEN GATE

The captain's boat was returning from the landing at the hide-houses, accompanied by a large whale-boat filled with strangers. Gun barrels out-thrust from the mass, baggage was visible, and as the whale-boat drew nearer to the steamer the persons in it were seen to be tattered and gaunt, as if they had been through great hardships. The captain's boat contained a guest in United States Army uniform—an officer, evidently.

The captain and his guest climbed into the steamer; then the whale-boat unloaded. Goodness gracious, there were not only the travel-worn men, but two women also! Up the side they all toiled, the men lean and brown and whiskered, the two women fully as distressful looking, with their hair faded, and their skin tight over their cheek-bones. The majority of the men were clad in old deer-skins and moccasins, and carried only hand-baggage of bundles.

The passengers of the California, crowding curiously, respectfully gave way.

"Well, holy smoke!" exclaimed Mr. Grigsby, at sight of one of the men. "Is that you, Bentley?"

"Hello, Sam," wearily responded the man. "It's what's left of me."

"Where'd you come from?"

"From the States, by way of the Gila trail across the desert. Nigh starved to death, too."

"You look it," commented Mr. Grigsby. "Is this all your party?"

"No. Part of us branched off for Los Angeles, on this side of the Colorado Desert; part of us never got through, and some are buried and some aren't. The rest of us struck for the sea, by the San Diego fork, as fast as we could. And I tell you, this steamer looks mighty good!"

"Pshaw!" murmured Mr. Grigsby, while Charley felt a great wave of sympathy for Mr. Bentley and all. And the Frémonter added: "I suppose you're bound for the gold fields, like everybody else."

"Yes," answered the tattered emigrant. "But all the gold in Californy can't pay me for what I've gone through. Hunger and thirst and heat and cold and Injuns—we met 'em. It's a terrible trail, Sam, as I reckon you know. And queer enough, those two women—those two wives in the party—stood it without a whimper. Gentlemen," he spoke to the crowd, "those are the heroes."

"You bet," responded several voices. "And there are more women like 'em."

The emigrant Bentley passed on, following his fellows. Mr. Grigsby had known him in trapper days. They had hunted beaver together.

No one made any objection to taking these additional passengers aboard. Anyway, now it was only a few days to San Francisco. The new gold seekers all had harrowing stories to tell. As Mr. Bentley had said, the most of them had traveled from the Missouri River, in Arkansas and Missouri, by a southern route across New Mexico which included what is to-day Arizona, from Santa Fé striking west for the Gila River. It was a parched and barren country, rife with the Apaches and Navajos and Yumas and other fierce tribes, who stole their horses and cattle and harassed their camps. Skeletons of men and animals, from other parties, lined the trail; and there was one march of fifty miles without water.

Two in the company had even crossed Mexico, and had been lost, until they emerged from the mountains and sighted the desert of southern California. All in all, thought Charley (and his father agreed) people were taking astounding risks to get to California.

There was the trip clear around Cape Horn, by boat; and the trip across the Isthmus; and trips across Mexico, from Vera Cruz and other points; and the Gila River trail, through the dry desert; and several trails, further north, more crowded and almost as perilous. Why, the whole West and

Southwest must be divided off every few hundred miles by regular processions of gold seekers! He hoped, did Charley, that Billy Walker would get through all right.

The army officer proved to be a young lieutenant—Lieutenant William T. Sherman, Third Artillery, now Adjutant General of the Division of the Pacific, with headquarters at San Francisco, whither he was returning. Mr. Adams managed to strike up a conversation with him, for the lieutenant was affable, especially with anyone like Mr. Adams, who had been a soldier under General Scott.

"Have you any news for us gold seekers, Lieutenant?" invited Mr. Adams.

"From where, sir?"

"From San Francisco and the gold fields."

"News!" exclaimed the lieutenant, smiling with his steady gray eyes. He had a long, rather stern face, of russet complexion, but he was pleasant. "There's news every hour. This crowd you've taken aboard is only a sample of the people who are pouring in by thousands."

"Gold is plentiful?"

"It exceeds any reports, sir."

"How about other business? What is the chance in San Francisco?"

"San Francisco is growing at the rate of thirty houses and a hundred people a day. All kinds of supplies are in demand, and all kinds of labor and professions. The chief trouble is to get them. The harbor is full of vessels without crews, stores are without clerks and houses without servants, and the army almost without soldiers. You are aware, I suppose, that this very steamer, the first steamship into the harbor, last February, was immediately deserted by every sailor, who all put out to the mines. She was held at anchor for a week or two, trying to ship a crew so as to make the return trip to Panama. Whole companies of soldiers have followed the example of the sailors. Colonel Mason, when he was military governor of

California, found himself obliged to cook his own meals; and General Persifor Smith, the present commander of the division, has been abandoned by every servant. We officers all are doing our own housework. As it is, ordinary laborers are getting ten and twenty dollars a day, and house servants ask and are getting $200 a month! Everybody figures on making twenty dollars a day at the mines, with chance of making much more; so ordinary wages don't tempt. The whole country is simply crazy." And Lieutenant Sherman turned on his heel and marched off, as if indignant—and well he might be, for it was soon found out that the army officers in California were having hard work to live within their small pay.

The California steamed northward, with the hilly California coast much in sight on the right, although distant. Some of the table-lands and hills shone yellow as if gold-plated, and raised high hopes among many of the passengers. Wasn't this the Land of Gold, at last? But Lieutenant Sherman and Mr. Grigsby, and a few others familiar with the country, explained that the yellow was immense fields of wild oats, already ripening.

At sunset was passed an island called Santa Catalina Island, inhabited by thousands of wild goats. It was owned by a Spanish family who annually killed the goats for their meat and hides. Out of sight inland, was said to be the town of Los Angeles, the largest inland town of California, and older than San Francisco.

The next stop would be Monterey. During the night the wind blew hard, kicking up the roughest sea of the whole voyage, and once throwing Charley out of his bunk, almost on top of Mr. Grigsby's cot.

"Hello," grunted the Frémonter, "hold fast, there. We must be rounding Cape Conception, above Santa Barbara. That's a sort of a Cape Horn of this coast, dividing it off. But we'll have fair sailing again, on the other side."

In the morning the storm had waned, but the seas still ran high, in immense white-crested waves that tossed and foamed, and leaping at the steamer tried to climb aboard. The sky was gloriously blue, without a cloud, and the air tasted salty crisp. Now the Coast Range of California loomed large; its hither bases spotted with the yellow of oats and the green of trees. Ramparts of high cliffs, separated by strips of green and brown lowlands, bordered the ocean.

After breakfast a long point, jutting out from the shore ahead, was hailed by the knowing ones aboard as Point Pinos (Pines Point), guardian of the harbor of Monterey. Gradually the steamer turned in; another harbor opened, with a cluster of white, red-roofed houses behind it, at the foot of the hills. Sweeping in past the pine-ridged point the California, with boom of gun, dropped anchor in the historic bay of Monterey.

The captain and Lieutenant Sherman, and any passengers who wished, went ashore here, for the California was to take on wood for fuel to San Francisco.

Monterey had long been the capital of Upper California, and was the first place captured by the United States, in July, 1846, after war with Mexico was begun. Mr. Grigsby knew it well, for hither he had marched from the north with Frémont's battalion of Volunteer Riflemen. It was a pleasant old town, of white-washed, tile-roofed clay buildings, a custom-house at the wharf, a large, yellow town hall, and an army post on the bluff overlooking town and bay. The town sloped to the low surf of the wave-flecked bay encircled by cliffs and bluffs. Beyond the town rose higher hills, well timbered with oaks and pines.

"The flag was raised July 7, Forty-six, over this custom-house," stated Mr. Grigsby. "Commodore Sloat sent ashore 250 men from the flag-shipSavannah, and the ships Cyane, Warren and Levant, which he had in the bay; and Lieutenant Edward Higgins did the raising, at ten in the morning. Purser Rodney Price made the proclamation to the people."

"Where were you, then?" asked Charley.

"Oh, I was up north at Sutter's Fort, with Frémont and the rest, waiting to get supplies—this shirt, among other things." For Mr. Grigsby had donned his star-collar shirt, as if in honor of the occasion. "We marched in later."

Monterey seemed to be a very quiet, sleepy old place. The majority of the citizens were the native Californians, wearing their picturesque costumes of slashed velvet trousers loose at the bottom and tight at the knee, red sashes about their waists, silk shirts and short velvet jackets, and peaked, wide-brimmed, tasseled felt hats. The morning air was chilly, although the sun shone brightly. In front of many of the stores and in the plaza or square little fires had been built, around which the people were huddling, to get warm. Mr. Grigsby explained that there wasn't a stove in town, probably, that everybody cooked in small fireplaces, and that until the Americans came and introduced the bonfire the natives were "too blamed lazy" to do more than shiver themselves warm!

"Why, these natives wouldn't walk across a street," he said. "They all rode—that is, the men. And why not, when horses were to be had for nothing. Ten dollars would buy the best horse in the territory."

Considerable of a crowd had gathered in front of the town hall, clustered and craning and gazing at some object in their midst. Mr. Grigsby, stalwart and proud in his Frémont shirt, sauntered to see. Presently he called and beckoned.

"Here you are. Here's what you're looking for."

So Mr. Adams and Charley crossed, also. The crowd gave way courteously, exposing a smiling, good-looking Californian, leaning against the heavy saddle of his horse.

"Here you are," repeated Mr. Grigsby, who was fingering the contents of a small canvas sack, evidently the property of the horseman. "You want to see gold? Take a look at it."

Following his father, Charley peeped within. The canvas sack was half full of dull yellow—a yellow like the yellow which the buckskin sack had contained, in St. Louis. However, this yellow was coarser.

"Flake gold," announced Mr. Grigsby. "Straight from the mines. Is that not so, amigo?"

"Si, señors," smilingly answered the native. And continued, in good English: "From the American River."

"Did you get—find it?" queried Charley, eagerly.

"Yes, and more. Everybody finds it who looks."

"How long were you gone?" asked Mr. Adams.

"Who knows, señor? Coming and going, perhaps two weeks, but I stopped with friends along the way."

"How long were you in finding this, then?"

"Four, maybe five, days. It is easy."

"What will you do with it, señor?" inquired Mr. Grigsby.

The man shrugged his shoulders.

"Who knows? When one has money he has friends. For a few days I can be rich. When I am poor again, there is plenty more gold to be had."

"Were there many other people searching?" asked Mr. Adams.

"An army, señor. They are working like ants."

They thanked the man for his courtesy, and returning him his treasure started on, for the town hall doorway.

"He'll spend that before another morning," declared Mr. Grigsby. "That's the curse of easy money—especially out here, where the natives can get along on a little. Wait a minute. I'll go in and find the alcalde—he's the mayor. Colton's his name. He was chaplain on the frigate Congress, and was appointed alcalde after Monterey was captured. I knew him in Forty-six. Fine man. Maybe we can call on the governor, General Bennet Riley, and pay our respects."

Mayor Colton sent word that he'd be pleased to see them, but that the governor was in San Francisco. However, the mayor (who, as Mr. Grigsby had said, was a minister, a navy chaplain, and indeed a fine man) showed them through the town hall, which he had caused to be built out of the fines and fees in the town treasury. It had been finished only this March, and contained a large public hall on the second floor, and a school and jail and other departments on the ground floor. It certainly was a credit to Monterey, away out here in California.

"Gold?" exclaimed Alcalde Colton, waving his hands in despair at the mention of it. "Yes, I've been up to the mines myself, on several occasions. I was there as early as last September, and dug some for myself. But it's the ruination of Monterey and the rest of the coast. Nobody'll work, except we Government and other public officers who have to; everybody's crazy, talking and dreaming only of easy riches; and even an old woman cook of mine, too feeble to go away, won't clean a fowl until she's examined its crop for a nugget."

"By the way, where's Colonel Frémont?" queried Mr. Grigsby. "Is he still out here?"

"Certainly. You're a Frémont man, I see. He's here, and so are his wife and daughter. They came out just ahead of you, on the Panama. They make their home in Monterey, but they're up north now, with the colonel. He's mining on his big Mariposa ranch, in the interior back of San José. They have the only four-wheeled vehicle in the territory—a surrey brought around the Horn for them."

However, interesting as Monterey was, nobody aboard the California wanted to stay long here. San Francisco was only about twelve hours ahead; and then, the gold!

On again steamed the California, threshing the waves with her huge paddles, and all the passengers scrutinizing the shore line, many of them rather expecting to see gold out-cropping on the cliffs and ridges.

"We'll probably get in at evening, and spend the night aboard," remarked Charley's father.

During the day the coast grew more bare and sandy, with sandy, rolling hills behind it. In the afternoon it appeared to bulge out, before, and in the bulge appeared a gap.

"There you are," directed Mr. Grigsby, to Charley, and pointing. "See that gap? Yes? It's the Golden Gate channel into the Bay of San Francisco."

"The gate to the Land of Gold, eh?" mused another passenger, near.

"That's what it's reckoned at, now," assented the Frémonter. "But it was named before gold was discovered. Frémont named it; you'll see it on his map of Forty-seven. It's the Golden Gate, whichever way you look at it— from the outside, toward the land, or from the inside, toward the sunset."

True enough. Even now the sun had set, and all the wide west fronting the gateway was a deep golden sheen, and the water and the shore was dyed with the richness. Turning her stern on the sunset, the steamer headed in, for the golden shore.

The gap opened, wider and wider, to form a broad strait. In it an island gleamed white.

"That's Alcatraz Island, at the inside end of the channel," explained Mr. Grigsby, who served as a very good guide. "You'll see Yerba Buena Island—some call it Goat Island—in a minute, on the right of it, and Angel Island on the left. That big round peak straight ahead, on the mainland, is Mount Diablo. Now we're getting opposite Fort Point; see the flag. The town is around on our right, other side of this first line of hills separating the bay from the ocean."

Through the Golden Gate was slowly and majestically steaming the California. The gate was really a pair of jaws, set half-open—great promontories of rock and sand, the one on the left or the north being almost a mountain chain. Within the jaws was the bay, like the mouth. Everything was tinged with the wondrous golden glow.

Several sailing boats were beating in and out of the strait, which was narrowest at Fort Point. Beyond Fort Point the tips of masts began to appear, over the tops of the lower hills on the right; and as the California gradually rounded the further side of this peninsula, ships at anchor came into sight. The bay itself opened, extending on right and left of the entrance, against a background of rolling, yellowish hills.

"Around the corner, now—and there you'll see San Francisco," announced Mr. Grigsby, he peering as intently as anybody.

Between Alcatraz Island and Goat Island passed the California, swinging to the right more and more, describing a half circle; the ships at anchor increased to a dense mass floating many flags; and then, hurrah, on the near shore, against the hills of this the west side of the bay appeared a straggling jumble of low buildings, already enshadowed by dusk and dotted with lights, some stationary, others moving. The murmur of many voices, punctuated by shouts and hammering, floated across the smooth water, and from the shipping sounded frequent hails. Through the shipping weaved the California, with all her passengers peering excitedly; then "Boom!" spoke her signal gun, and not far from the water-front, where a clear place had been left, she dropped anchor. From her decks arose a mighty cheer; and listen—the people running down to the water-front replied! So everybody cheered again, Charley swinging his hat and "hooraying" as hard as anybody.

XIV

ALL ASHORE

So interested had most of the passengers been, that they had omitted to collect their baggage and make the grand rush as at Chagres. But now at the dropping of the anchor the charm was broken. Helter-skelter they all ran, to be ready for the first landing, but suddenly were halted by the word that nobody could go ashore until morning. The ship must first be examined by the health officer. So a howl of dismay and wrath arose.

"The captain thinks he'll keep us aboard all night, does he? Well, he can't and nobody else can, either. Ain't that right?"

Charley had been carried along by the rush to gather the baggage; and now this voice spoke at his elbow. He looked quickly, and saw the profile of the long-nosed man, who was talking to one of his partners.

"There'll be plenty of boats sneaking around, and plenty of sailors taking French leave for the mines," continued the long-nosed man. "We'll just join 'em. We've got too big a stake ahead of us, to waste a night here."

"Sure. We'll let the other party do the wasting," answered the partner. "We're ahead, so far, and we'll stay ahead."

"All right. Keep your eyes and ears open, and a little money in your hand, and at the first chance, we leave. Tell Jack, if you see him before I do."

Charley slipped away. So the long-nosed man's party were planning to go ashore anyhow, were they? Well, he'd see about that. He'd tell his father, who'd tell the captain, and the captain would make them play fair.

But his father shook his head, after Charley had excitedly appealed.

"No, we won't do a thing. Grigsby and I had decided anyway that we'd better stay on board till morning. We'll all gain nothing by going ashore in the dark, Charley. Lieutenant Sherman says it's a miserable place to find your way around in, and it's full of the riff-raff of all nations, besides the better people. As for the Jacobs party, what they do is none of our business.

They'll deny that they have any notion of going—and then they'll go, just the same. The captain has other things to tend to, than watching the passengers."

"But they'll beat us," complained Charley.

"Nonsense," laughed his father. "The crooked trail is the longest way 'round. When they get ashore in the dark they'll not be much nearer the end than we are. We'll mind our own business and play fair, and then you'll see who comes out ahead at last."

"Is that San Francisco?" quavered somebody near them, at the rail. She was one of the worn, plucky women who had traveled the Gila trail. "It looks like a big camp-meetin'."

And so San Francisco did! Many more lights had been struck; a few flickered here and there, as if they were being carried about, but the majority appeared to be behind canvas, through which they shone with pale yellow glow. Evidently even some of the business buildings were only canvas; and these, and the multitude of tents, gleamed dully like a great encampment. Voices sounded constantly, echoing across the water; hammering never ceased; music floated—strains of violin and trumpet and piano! From the water-front clear back up the sides of the hills San Francisco was alive by night as by day. And on the hour all the vessels in the harbor struck their bells, in a great, melodious chime.

Charley and his father and Mr. Grigsby stood long at the rail, as did the other passengers, gazing at the dim shore and its multitude of spectral lights, and talking. The whole ship seemed to be athrill with great expectations; row-boats approached, circled and mysteriously lingered, as if awaiting; and the little waves murmured low and invitingly, as they slapped against the steamer's sides.

Yes, after the trip of forty days and nights from New Orleans (fifty from New York!), and of six thousand miles, by water, and twenty miles by land, here they all were, at anchor off the Land of Gold.

Charley rather hated to turn in. However, the three of them went to bed, at ten o'clock, and San Francisco was still as lively as ever. Once, in the night, Charley woke up, thinking that he heard a soft hail and the splash of oars. He wondered if the long-nosed man's party were taking their "French leave." He sat up and peered out of the open door; and there, across the water, were the lights of San Francisco, and the uproar of voices and hammers and music. Apparently, San Francisco didn't sleep.

All in all, it wasn't a very good night for sleeping, anywhere. Some of the passengers on the decks talked the whole night through, it seemed to Charley, discussing plans. At daylight began a general stir, to prepare to go ashore, the Adams party were ready about as soon as anybody, waiting for the boats to start their trips. Luggage was piled high, everywhere aboard; and by sunrise people were impatient.

It happened to be a beautiful morning, with wisps of fog drifting out to sea. How large the bay was, extending north and south and three miles wide! Porpoises were numerous, rolling their backs through the tumbling gray surface; gulls sailed and circled and screamed; and there was a hoarse, grunty barking which Mr. Grigsby said was from sea-lions, on the rocks of the shore.

Now San Francisco lay revealed, sprawled from the wharves of the water's edge, on back up the sides of the bare rounded hills behind.

"Who would have thought, when I came out here with Frémont," murmured Mr. Grigsby, as they three gazed again at the town, "that the old hide landing of Yerba Buena would have jumped to this. My idea for a city would be the other side of the bay, on the mainland. But here was the starter, boats were used to it, and nothing can stop the place now."

"It's not very pretty, that's sure," commented Mr. Adams.

And indeed, evidently built of anything that came to hand, with its houses squatted in haphazard, hasty fashion, and the country around bare and brown and bleak, San Francisco did not look attractive. But the bay was grand; and the hundreds of ships flying the flags of the United States, and England, and France and Spain and Mexico and Germany and Denmark and Sweden, were interesting beyond words. There were several United States men-of-war. One, the line-of-battle-ship Ohio, lay not far away from the California. How tremendous she looked, with her yards all aslant, and the round, black muzzles of her cannon staring out through her open ports! Nothing could lick her, decided Charley, proudly.

A bustling fleet of rowboats put out to the California, yelping for the business of taking passengers and baggage ashore. The ship's boats also began work early; and now, at last, Charley found himself embarked in a skiff and making for the shore. He did not see any of the Jacobs party, on the decks or in the other boats. As like as not, then, they had sneaked away during the night.

The one wharf toward which the boat seemed to be making was crowded with people and piled high with baggage. Every inch appeared occupied — and now another difficulty presented. The tide was out, for the water ended a quarter of a mile from the shore! The boat sluggishly stopped.

"Here you are," said one of the boatmen. "Tumble out."

"What do you mean?" demanded Mr. Adams. "We've paid you two dollars each to take us ashore. You don't expect us to walk through this mud, do you?"

"Walk or fly. This is shore, as you can see for yourself. Boats don't travel on stilts, in this country."

Other boats also were being stuck, and many of the passengers were already wading knee-deep in ooze, for the dry land.

"An outrage!" exclaimed Mr. Adams.

"We can't control the tides, stranger, even in California," spoke the other boatman. "We can leave you here and come again in about four hours and take you the rest of the way for two dollars more. Tide'll be turned by that time."

"What'll you charge to carry us in from here, now?" asked Mr. Grigsby.

"Five dollars apiece for self and baggage."

"Come on, Charley," bade Mr. Adams. "Off with your boots and stockings. We can do as the rest do."

"That's the talk," approved Mr. Grigsby.

Barefooted, trousers rolled high, out they stepped, and lugging their bed rolls and other hand baggage, stumped for the shore.

"Five dollars apiece!" muttered Mr. Grigsby. "Money must be mighty cheap out here."

"If that's a sample of prices, the quicker Charley and I get out of town, the better," answered Mr. Adams. "Eh, Charley?"

All along the stretch of tide-flats passengers from the California were wading ashore. The women were being carried pickaback—and screamed when their helpers stumbled. It was a comical sight, for several men already had tripped and fallen, and were a mass of mud.

A number of men and boys were digging in the mud for clams. One man they passed had such an odd appearance that Charley turned and stared back at him. He was of a strange yellow complexion, his eyes were set slantwise, he wore a short, loose, bluish frock with wide sleeves, and a round little hat, and down his back hung a long pig-tail.

"There's a queer sort of Injun," remarked Mr. Grigsby. "Some sort of a Sandwich Islander, I reckon."

"No; that's a Chinese—a Chinaman they call him in New Orleans," said Mr. Adams. "I've seen some down there, and in Mexico, too."

"Well, he's an odd one, all right," insisted the Frémonter. And Charley agreed.

The crowd on the wharf and shore were cheering and laughing at the antics in the mud. From the wharf a long, steep flight of steps led down, and up this, in the procession, toiled the Adams party.

It was a very good-natured crowd, almost all men, in rough costumes of miner's red or blue or gray shirts, and trousers tucked into boots, slouch hats, faces well whiskered and pistols and knives thrust through belts. Some of the men were uproariously greeting newly-arrived relatives and friends; but there was no one here to greet the Adams party. So the first thing to do was to find the trunk, and then a lodging-place.

"What's the proper hotel, Grigsby?" inquired Mr. Adams.

"I'll find out." And Mr. Grigsby addressed the nearest citizen—a small, gray-shirted man with a beard almost as gray. "Pardner, what are the lodging-houses here now? City Hotel still running?"

"City Hotel, Parker House, Portsmouth Hotel, United States Hotel; they're all running, and full to the roofs, too, stranger. If you want a bed you've got to make tracks—and I reckon by the looks of your feet you'll make 'em."

"We'll go up to the plaza, I reckon, then," said Mr. Grigsby, to his partners. "Better put on our boots first."

They wiped their feet on a piece of old canvas lying near, and donned their stockings and boots.

"How'll we get our trunk up to the hotel, I wonder?" spoke Charley's father. "Here——" and he called to a couple of Mexicans standing near. "Want to earn fifty cents?"

The Mexicans laughed, and shrugged their shoulders; and one of them, in a very impudent fashion, made a derisive answer in Spanish. Charley's father colored, and took an angry step forward; but a miner stopped him.

"Go easy, stranger," he said. "This is a free land." He thrust his hand into his pocket, and actually extended to Mr. Adams two dollars. "Carry your trunk yourself," he said. "Fifty cents wouldn't take it to the end of this wharf." And the onlookers shouted at the joke.

So Mr. Adams laughed.

"All right," he uttered. "I offered what I thought was a fair wage. If somebody'll kindly help us up with that trunk we'll tend to the other baggage and pay the regular tariff."

"Now you're talkin'," approved the miner. "Why, most of us out here wouldn't stoop over to pick up four bits. What's four bits, in these diggin's? 'Twouldn't buy a cup of coffee. But say, if you really want to make easy money, instead o' spendin' it, I've got a little investment worth your attention."

"What is it?"

"Best water lot in the city."

A score of voices interrupted, and the Adams party found themselves almost mobbed.

"Don't listen to him. Hear me!"

"If you want a water lot——"

"No, no; I've got 'em all skinned."

"Wait a minute, now."

"The most valuable proposition in California."

"A water lot is what you ought to have. As soon as the city builds out——"

And so forth, and so forth. It was most bewildering.

"Where is your lot, sir?" demanded Mr. Adams.

"Right under the red skiff yonder," directed the first miner. "Level and sightly, as you can see as soon as the tide's full out. Straight in line for the extension of Clay Street. Can't be beat."

"What's your price?" asked Mr. Grigsby, with a wink at Charley.

"You can have that fine lot for only $10,000 cash. It's worth $15,000."

Mr. Adams threw back his head and laughed, and laughed. Even Mr. Grigsby guffawed. And Charley was indignant. These San Franciscans must think them awful green, to offer them "lots" away out in the bay — and at $10,000!

"Come on, boys!" bade his father. "I'm afraid, gentlemen, that your real estate doesn't appeal. It might make a good navy yard, but not the kind of a yard that I could use for my family."

"You'll see the day when you'll wish you'd taken some of those lots, strangers," warned the man, after them.

And so they did—although that seemed ridiculous. The "water lots" are now almost in the centre of the business district of great San Francisco, and worth ten times ten thousand dollars.

It was an amazing town that they traversed, carrying their hand baggage and followed by a couple of Mexicans who for the promise of two dollars had deigned to pick up the trunk. Few of the buildings seemed finished, and all looked as if they had just been put up, in a great hurry. They were made from canvas rudely tacked on warped boards, of rusty sheet-iron and tin, of brown clay or "adobe," of newly-sawed rough lumber, of pieces of boxes and flattened cans, and one was even built of empty boxes piled up for walls, with a canvas roof. But all these stores were full of goods, many not yet unpacked, and of buyers, and every third or fourth store was a saloon and gambling house, fuller still. As for the streets, they were full, too,—and with what a queer mixture of people!

The Americans were evidently as widely varied as on board ship. The best dressed were smooth-shaven, quiet men in white shirts, black ties, and well-fitting broadcloth and polished boots—the cool, professional gamblers, as Charley somehow guessed. He had seen their like in St. Louis, and on the ship. The others wore mainly the regulation Californian costume of flannel shirt, etc.,—and with them it seemed to be the fashion not to shave at all. Such whiskers! But every nation under the sun appeared to be represented. Why, it was better than any geography book.

Everybody seemed to be in a great hurry, acting as if should they linger anywhere more than a minute they would be missing something. There was something in the cool, windy air, fresh from the lively bay, that made Charley himself throw out his chest and step lively. The talk, right and left, was of the jerky, impatient type, and in terms of dollars—dollars, dollars, thousands of dollars. Nobody acted poor, all walked and talked gold; one would have thought that the very dirt was gold—and as he trudged briskly, following the lead of Mr. Grigsby, Charley saw people grubbing on hands and knees, with knives, in the very street. Yes, he saw some boys, no older than he, doing this, and one with a grin showed him half a handful of golden specks and dirt mixed, that he evidently had scraped up!

The streets had no sidewalks, and in spots were thick with dust, blown by gusts of wind. Mr. Grigsby plainly enough knew where he was going, for at last he led into a vacant square, which was the plaza. A sign on a long, two-and-a-half story wooden building, unpainted, said: "Parker-house. Board and lodging." Under the sign Mr. Grigsby stopped, and eased his arms.

"We'll try this," he said. "It's been built since I was here last year. Great Jimmy, but how the town has grown! I'm mighty near lost in it. I remember this old plaza, though. There's the City Hotel, across. There's the old custom-house, too; that adobe building, with the flagpole in front of it, where the flag was raised in Forty-six, by the Navy. Well, let's go in."

They entered. The place was crowded.

"Yes, sir; I can give you one room, with two beds in it, upstairs," informed the clerk at the counter. "It's positively all we have, and you're lucky to get that."

"What's the tariff?" queried Mr. Adams.

"Rates are twenty-five dollars a week, each, for bed; twenty dollars a week for board."

Mr. Adams shook his head, and looked at Charley.

"I'm afraid we'll have to try elsewhere," he said. "Let's go across the street."

"City Hotel is full; you can't get even blanket room," declared the clerk. "The Frémont Hotel, down on the water-front, charges the same as we do, and supplies fleas for nothing. If you don't want the room, stand aside. Next!"

"But aren't your rates pretty high?" queried Mr. Adams, puzzled.

"High, my friend?" retorted the clerk. "Do you know where you are? You're in San Francisco, where people dig gold in the streets. And do you know what rent we pay, for this building? One hundred and ten thousand dollars a year, my friend. The Eldorado tent-building next to us rents at $40,000 the year; it measures exactly fifteen by twenty-five feet. Out here, gentlemen, a hole in the ground rents for at least $250 a month. Last April there were but thirty houses in the whole town, and now there are 500."

"We don't want the room for a week. We'll take it for a night, though. We're on our way to the mines," said Mr. Adams.

"So is everybody else," sharply answered the clerk. "For one night the room is five dollars apiece, and I'll be losing money at that."

"All right. We've got a trunk out in front. Have it sent up, please."

"Can't do it, sir. Every man is his own porter, in this town. The stairs are fairly wide. I'll show you up."

The Mexicans had dropped the trunk on the long porch, and refused to carry it another inch. And when they were to be paid off, they insisted that the two dollars meant two dollars apiece! Bystanders gravely agreed that this was the correct price.

"Whew!" sighed Mr. Adams, with a quizzical smile, after he had paid. "No wonder that twenty dollars a day is small wages, out here. What an enormous amount of money there must be in circulation! Grab an end, Charley. Come along, Grigsby. Let's inspect our quarters."

XV

THE SIGHTS OF SAN FRANCISCO

Charley took one end of the trunk, his father the other, and piloted by the hotel man, with Mr. Grigsby, lugging the hand baggage, in their wake, they climbed two flimsy flights of stairs to the third floor! The hotel man led the way down a narrow hall of rough boards, and flung open a door.

"Here's your room," he announced, shortly. "Don't ask for what you don't see. We haven't got it. You're lucky, gentlemen, not to be obliged to sleep in a tent—and San Francisco nights are cold. Five dollars each, please."

"Certainly," said Mr. Adams; and he and Mr. Grigsby settled for the party.

"Well," remarked Mr. Grigsby, when the hotel man alertly left, "I've been in worse quarters."

"Don't bump your head," warned Mr. Adams.

It was a dormer room. The ceiling, of bare rafters, sloped sharply. The walls also were bare, made of unsurfaced boards, warped and cracked. There were two "beds": one a low bunk, home-made and solid but not pretty, the other a wobbly canvas cot. Each had a pair of gray blankets as bedclothes. There were a couple of rickety chairs, a home-made table bearing a wash pitcher and a tin basin, with a towel hanging from a nail over it, beside a cracked looking-glass, and in the end of the room a small window dulled by dust. Charley tried to look out through the window, but could dimly see only the tops of the roofs, across. From below, and from the city around, floated in through the thin floors and walls a medley of voices and bustle.

"Guess we'd better unpack some of our stuff, and sort what washing we want done," quoth his father, cheerily. "When we take it out we can look about and get what other supplies we need; eh, Grigsby? What are your plans?"

"Same as yours, if you say so," answered the Frémonter.

"You mean to say you'll go along with Charley and me?"

"Why, yes. This town's too crowded for me, already. Doesn't strike me as a very healthy place to loaf in. Money, money; that's all I've heard. So I'm off for the diggin's, like the rest."

"Good. Shake," approved Mr. Adams, and Charley felt delighted. The Frémonter was such a fine man; a loyal friend in need. "We'll stick together as long as you can stand our company."

"Agreed," quoth Mr. Grigsby, shaking. "There'll be room enough in the hills for us to spread out, if we want to."

They overhauled their baggage and wrapped their wash in some old newspapers that had been stuffed into the trunk. Then they sallied forth.

"Pshaw! There's no lock on the door," exclaimed Charley's father. "I hate to leave all our stuff scattered around, in that fashion."

"It'll be all right, I reckon," said Mr. Grigsby. "Ask the clerk about it."

"The door to our room has no lock," spoke Mr. Adams, to the hotel man, when they had tramped below. "We've got quite a bunch of goods lying open."

"That's all right, sir," answered the clerk. "They'll not be touched. Not a door in this hotel has a lock. Thieves are given short shift in San Francisco, and they know it. You can leave a bucket of gold out in the street and it'll all be there when you want it again."

"Beg your pardon, gentlemen," spoke a voice near at hand, "but I see you're carrying a newspaper or two. Would you sell them?"

He was a brusque, bearded man, in miner costume, but he spoke like a person of education.

"I'll give you a dollar apiece," cried another man, hurrying forward; and almost immediately the three in the Adams party were surrounded by a crowd.

"Wait a minute," bade the first man. "I was here first. I'll give you a dollar apiece."

Charley gasped. Were they crazy?

"But, gentlemen, these are only some old papers we happened to have as fillers," protested Mr. Adams, as much astonished as Charley.

"How many have you got?" demanded the second speaker.

"Probably a dozen."

"Where from?"

"St. Louis; two or three from New York, maybe."

"I'll give you eight dollars for the lot."

"Give you nine," bid somebody else.

"But they're six weeks old, gentlemen," informed Mr. Adams.

"Only six weeks old?" queried the first man. "I'll give you ten dollars for a dozen! And here's your money." He held out a ten-dollar gold piece.

"Go up and get the other papers, Charley," directed Mr. Adams. "If these men are crazy it isn't our fault. When you see the papers, if you don't want them you needn't take them, sir," he said to the man.

"I'll take them," laughed the man, grimly. "Papers only six weeks old? Why, stranger, that's fresh news out here. You can sell a thousand at a dollar apiece."

"Wish I had them, then," remarked Mr. Adams. And Charley scuttled away. He brought back all the crumpled papers that he could find. They sold every one—the first lot at ten dollars for a dozen, and the three more, in which the washing was wrapped, at dollar apiece on delivery later!

"This will pay for our washing, at least," commented Mr. Adams. "Is there a laundry near here?" he asked, of the clerk.

"Right around the corner."

"Thank you."

They went out—Charley sighing as he thought of the big stack of old newspapers, back home. Why, they might have brought out a hundred more! What a queer town this was, where people would pay a dollar apiece for old papers! He resolved to write to his mother the first thing, and tell her when she came out to bring every old paper she could find.

The air was much chillier than when they had arrived. A strong, gusty wind was blowing, carrying clouds of dust, and because of this, and a raw fog, the sunshine had waned from gold to gray. Nevertheless, something in the atmosphere made them all step out briskly.

Around the corner of the plaza a torn canvas sign before a dingy tent-house said: "Washing Done." And in through the open door they filed. A short, stout Frenchman, apparently, stood behind the board counter, and bowed at their approach. He wore a little black spike or goatee, and his face fairly shone above a collarless shirt. From a room behind sounded vigorous scrubbing and rinsing.

"You do washing?" demanded Mr. Adams.

"Oui, m'sieur."

"Here's some. When can we get it?"

"To-morrow morning, at the ten o'clock. And does m'sieur wish ze repassage—what you call ir-ron?"

"What's the charge?" asked Mr. Grigsby.

"Seex dollair the dozen, m'sieur, for ze wash; the same for ze ir-ron."

"There goes your newspaper money, Adams," laughed the Frémonter. "I think I'll do my own washing, after this."

"We have to live, my wife and I, messieurs," explained the Frenchman, spreading his hands. "In France we live on ze very little. In New York we have one très bon café, and we charge ze very little. But out here——" and he shrugged his shoulders. "We wash, and for zis meesairable caban—what you call it? hut—we pay ze price of 500 dollair ze month."

"Wash what we've brought, but don't you dare to iron them; eh, Grigsby?" said Mr. Adams.

"Ze rough wash it shall be, messieurs," bowed the stout Frenchman.

"On the trap trail we washed twice a year—spring and fall," commented Mr. Grigsby, as they trudged out. "That's plenty often enough here, too, the way prices run."

"Look at the crowd!" exclaimed Mr. Adams, as they emerged at the corner; for part way up a hilly street a great throng had gathered in front of a low building, and a constant stream of other people were hastening that way. "What's the matter up there?" he inquired, of a passerby.

The man scarcely paused. He only turned his head, to drawl:

"Post-office, mister, and the mail's come in."

"That must be the mail we brought," cried Charley.

"If you came on the California, you brought it, sonny," informed another stranger.

"When's the office open, sir?" inquired Mr. Adams.

"Whenever the mail's distributed, of course," replied the man. "I hear the California fetched about 25,000 pieces, in all languages from American to Chinese. The postmaster and two assistants have been working all night and they'll probably work all day and another night."

"Well, we don't expect anything this time; do you, Grigsby?"

The Frémonter shook his head.

"Nor do I," volunteered the strange man. "But I've a partner up there who's been expecting a letter for six months. See those lines of hopefuls? By noon they'll be extended two blocks. The first in line must have got there as soon as the ship was sighted, last evening. I've known men to wait in line for a week, and have their meals brought to them. And then as like as not they didn't get their letter."

"I was thinking that we'd get what few supplies we need," said Mr. Adams, as they resumed their way, "and start out for the diggin's in the morning. There'll be some way of getting up there, I suppose."

"Yes, by boat, horse or foot," answered the Frémonter. "I don't reckon we want to buy any horses, and it's a long trail afoot. I'll see about a boat if you'll lay in what supplies you think we'll need."

"All right. Sugar, salt, flour, bacon and potatoes will be enough, won't it?"

"Plenty. I'll meet you at the hotel at noon. Adios."

"Adios," replied Mr. Adams and Charley; and the tall Frémonter strode away.

The throng at the post-office seemed to have no effect on the rest of the down-town, for the streets were as crowded as before with hurrying people, mostly men. New Yorkers, Arkansans, Illinoisans, Britishers, Germans, Frenchmen, Swedes, Mexicans, Malays with long curved knives, the queer Chinamen, and some swarthy persons, in brown ponchos (or cloaks with a hole in the middle for the head), who his father said were Peruvians and Chilians—all these passed hither-thither, only pausing to bargain with each other or at the shops, until Charley's brain whirled at the many odd sights. There were a few women, but none who looked to him anything like his mother.

Across the plaza his father espied a new sign, in front of a shop built of boxes. It said: "Potatoes for Sale. Just Received."

"That's what we want, Charley," he spoke; and for the place they made. The potatoes were in open sacks, just inside the door—and that was the shop's whole stock of goods.

"How much are your potatoes, my man?" asked Mr. Adams. "They look pretty good."

"One dollar and a half. Yes, sir; they are good ones; came in only this morning."

"Let me have a bushel, then, at a dollar and a half," bade Mr. Adams, with satisfaction. "That's not an unreasonable price, is it, Charley!"

"We don't sell by the bushel; I quoted you the price by the pound," explained the potato merchant.

"What!" gasped Charley's father, again astounded. "You don't mean a dollar and a half a pound?"

"You bet," smiled the merchant. "And going like hot cakes at that. I'll not have a potato left, by night."

"Come on, Charley," laughed Mr. Adams. "We'll wait and grow our own potatoes."

"I'll take all you can grow at your own price," challenged the merchant, after them, as if growing potatoes out here in California was impossible.

Suddenly a score of voices yelled: "Look out! Look out!" The crowd jostling and bartering in the plaza parted and rushed to one side and another, and people plunged headlong into the store doors. Mr. Adams grabbed Charley by the arm and dragged him in the nearest doorway, too. Amidst wild shouts and a cloud of dust, into the plaza charged a lean red bull, with curving sharp horns and frothing mouth; close at his heels pursued, on dead run, a horseman in Mexican costume, swinging his riata, or noosed rawhide. The bull dodged—bolted right over a stand where cakes were on sale—and over the stand sped the horseman, too. His noose shot forward — it fell exactly over the bull's wide horns, and to one side veered the quick horse. He braced as the rawhide tautened; it snapped tight, and head down, heels up, the bull capsized in a twinkling. The fiery horse held hard, bracing with his legs, while the Californian sat straight and easy. As the bull struggled, with a shrill whoop another rider like the first raced in, threw at full speed, and noosed the bull by the two hind legs. With wave of hand and flash of teeth the vaqueros, or cowboys, rode away, dragging the bull through the plaza and out. The plaza filled up again, the shops resumed business, and nobody appeared to be annoyed. Even the cake seller gathered his cakes and joined in the laughter while several persons helped him set up his booth again. Truly, this San Francisco was a light-hearted, generous place.

"I should think that a man would make surer money farming than digging for gold," declared Mr. Adams, after he and Charley had noted eggs priced at twelve dollars a dozen, squashes at a dollar a pound, and some cabbages at two dollars apiece! "Hello; there's Lieutenant Sherman." For a spruce military figure was briskly crossing this plaza of Portsmouth Square.

Lieutenant Sherman saw them, as he approached and smiled.

"Not off to the mines yet?" he greeted.

"Not yet. I was just saying to Charley that farming looked better to me than mining, in this country, judging by prices of common produce."

"It's all shipped in," stated the lieutenant, in his quick voice. "Nobody now has any time for farming; and before this excitement everybody had too much time. The Californians lived on beef, tortillas and beans, all of which was easy. They wouldn't take the trouble even to milk a cow. The missions tried to teach agriculture to the Indians, and now since some Americans have taken up ranches a few patches have been ploughed, for the home table. But the wheat, barley and live stock, which grow without attention, are about all you'll find on tens of thousands of acres. California is dry and barren. I've ridden over a great deal of it, and I once wrote East that I wouldn't give two counties in Ohio, Kentucky or Tennessee for the whole territory. It never will amount to anything except for gold production. When do you start?"

"To-morrow morning."

"All right. Good luck to you. Our headquarters offices are in the old custom-house; drop in if you need any information I can give you. General Persifor Smith and family are lodged in the lower room of the old

Hudson's Bay Company house on Montgomery Street. Every servant but one, and he is a negro, has deserted us; and the general does the marketing and sometimes the cooking. The rest of us occupy the second floor, and hustle for our meals the best we can. You're well out of this hurly-burly where the commander of all the United States forces on the Pacific coast must do his own housework! When we move over to the new post at Benicia perhaps things will be better."

So saying, the busy lieutenant strode on.

By the time that Charley and his father had succeeded in purchasing what few supplies they could afford, they had pretty nearly seen San Francisco. It certainly was a queer jumble. Buildings and population alike were of the hasty, rough-and-ready style; but already a brick store, for the merchant firm of Howard & Mellus, had gone up and had cost a dollar a brick! In the stores, no matter how constructed, every kind of goods was being sold, signs bore high-sounding names such as the Alhambra, Delmonico's, United States Hotel, and other signs were being added hourly; from the wharf on Montgomery Street to the top of the Clay Street hill beyond the post-office busy hammers beat a great chorus, in the bay flew hundreds of flags, and in the streets school-teachers, bankers, lawyers and farmers rubbed elbows with Mexicans, Peruvians, Chinamen and Kanakas, while all talked in terms of thousands of dollars. Why, here was New York, New Orleans and St. Louis thrown together and boiled down.

Up at the post-office the post-master and his clerks evidently were still sorting out the 25,000 letters, for the lines of waiters were unbroken.

Mr. Grigsby was promptly on hand, at noon, in the hotel. He reported that he had engaged passage on a sail-boat, the Mary Ann, for the town of Sacramento, 120 miles north up the Sacramento River.

"That is," he added, "if you want to try the American River country, where the first diggin's are. Sacramento is the old embarcadero [which, as Charley found out, was the Spanish for boat-landing] for Sutter's Fort, up the

American. The fare is thirty dollars, and I paid ten dollars apiece down, to hold our places till two o'clock."

"All right," approved Mr. Adams. "We'll go. Now let's eat. Hear the dinner bells! It must be a hungry town."

And that would seem so, indeed. From every hotel and restaurant issued a clamor of hand-bells and of gongs, each apparently vying with the other to make noise. It sounded like a Fourth of July! People began to rush into the Parker-house, and in a jiffy the long tables were filled. The Adams party got seats just in time.

The price of the meal was two dollars, for beef (splendid beef, too), bread, potatoes, and coffee or chocolate. There wasn't any milk or butter. However, as Mr. Grigsby remarked, one could easily eat a dollar's worth of potatoes at a helping! The food was very good and well cooked. Charley heard somebody say that the cook was a famous chef from New York, and drew a salary of $2000 a month. Even the waiters (who were men in shirt-sleeves) were paid $300 a month, and board.

"I believe I'll go up to the room and rest a bit," announced Mr. Adams, after dinner. "The rest of you can do as you please."

"You aren't sick, are you, dad?" asked Charley, anxiously.

"Not a bit. I feel a hundred per cent. stronger than when we left home. But I mustn't overdo. I'll take a nap and write a letter to your mother. There'll be a mail out next week, and not another for maybe thirty or forty days. Shall I leave the letter open for you?"

"Yes, please," bade Charley, a lump in his throat at the mere thought of his mother. "I'll add a lot to it after I come back."

"I'll tell her we've not found our gold mine yet, but we've sold our newspapers for a dollar apiece and spent that for washing," laughed his father.

"Tell her to send us out all the old papers she has," begged Charley, excitedly. "And potatoes and cabbages, from the garden!"

"I saw a man buy a whole cargo of eggs, down at the water-front," put in Mr. Grigsby, "at thirty-seven and a half cents a dozen, and he turned right around and resold 100 dozen of them at six dollars the dozen! You can't afford to be sick here, Adams. The doctors charge $50 for a visit, and the same for every hour after the first look-in. Come along, Charley, and we'll see the sights while I do a few errands on my own account. I hear Colonel Frémont's in town. Maybe we can catch him."

XVI

CHARLEY HEARS A CONVERSATION

"If you're looking for Colonel Frémont, you'll likely find him at the United States Hotel," hailed the hotel clerk, as Charley and Mr. Grigsby passed the counter. "He's there with General Vallejo, I understand."

"Good!" exclaimed Mr. Grigsby. "You know who Frémont is," he said, to Charley; and Charley nodded. Of course he knew. Frémont was the great explorer—Frémont the Pathfinder, they called him. He it was who, arrived in California on his third exploring expedition for the Government, early in 1846, had been on hand to lead in the taking of California from Mexico. His stories of his travels made fine reading. "Well, this General Vallejo is Don Mariano Guadalupe Vallejo. He was the military governor of Upper California before the war, but he's been a great friend of the Americans, although he was the first man they captured in the uprising of Forty-six. Nobody has a word to say against General Vallejo. He wanted California to belong to the United States, and said so, when other Californians were favoring England and France instead of Mexico, after it was seen that Mexico couldn't hold it. Fact is, General Vallejo it was who started San Francisco. Not this San Francisco, but Benicia, at the other end of the bay. He donated the land, and only asked that the city be named Francisca, after his wife, Francisca Benicia. He gave a tract an mile wide by five miles long. It's a better site for a big city than this is, they say, because it's not so steep and is only across a narrow strait from the mainland, and has deep-water anchorage. Most of the steamers go there now, to anchor, and it has the naval and military headquarters, at Mare Island and at the new post going up. This place was only Yerba Buena—Good Herb Cove—a landing-place for the San Francisco mission. But the settlers already here got ahead of the Vallejo plan, and renamed their town San Francisco, because of San Francisco Bay; and the name has made it grow. The general and Thomas O. Larkin (who was the Government consul and agent) and Doc Robert Semple, who's an old-time trapper from Kentucky and is about seven feet high, went ahead and started the other town, and having lost out on Francisca called it by Mrs. Vallejo's other name, Benicia. But it never has amounted to much as a town. I thought I'd tell you about General Vallejo. He and Frémont are a good pair—Americans both, though one is French, born in Georgia, the other is Mexican, born in California."

The same boys whom Charley had seen in the morning were scratching for gold in front of the United States Hotel, and quarreling over their finds, which stuck to the moistened heads of the pins they were using.

"There he is, now—and the General with him," spoke Mr. Grigsby, quickening pace as he and Charley approached across the street.

Two men were just leaving the hotel porch. One was of medium height, erect and slender, in a broad silvered Californian hat and a short velvet jacket embroidered with gilt. The other was taller and heavier and darker, in ordinary citizen's clothes. Charley guessed that the first was Colonel Frémont.

That was so, for going directly to him, Mr. Grigsby extended his brown, sinewy hand, saying:

"Colonel, do you remember me?"

Colonel Frémont gave him one flashing glance out of a pair of deep-set, very keen, dark blue eyes. A handsome man was the Pathfinder, with such eyes, a clean-cut, imperious nose, and a crisp full brown beard.

"Hello, Grigsby," he said, grasping the hand heartily. "Do you think I could forget one of my own men? The General remembers you, too, I'll wager."

"With pleasure," said General Vallejo; and he, also, shook hands. He was older than Colonel Frémont, was General Mariano Guadalupe Vallejo, and even more commanding in his appearance. His face was large and dignified, in its black beard, his forehead was high and broad, and his dark eyes piercing.

Mr. Grigsby introduced Charley, and they both shook hands with him.

"We're off to the mines in the morning, and I wanted to pay my respects and introduce this boy, here, before we left," explained Mr. Grigsby. "Are your family here, Colonel? And yours, General?"

"The General's are north at Sonoma, I believe," answered the Pathfinder. "Mine are on their way back to Monterey. What trail do you take, Grigsby? The northern mines, or the southern?"

"We'll try the northern, up the American; by boat as far as Sacramento."

"Our old stamping-ground of the American fork, eh?" remarked the Colonel. "I well recall our first trip in, across the mountains, in that winter of early Forty-four, when Sutter's Fort was the only habitation. Who'd have thought that in five years there'd be towns all along the old trail, and thousands of white men pushing in from mountains and ocean both, to scratch and burrow like gophers! You won't know the place, Grigsby! When were you there last?"

"A year ago."

"You won't know it, just the same."

"No," agreed General Vallejo, earnestly.

"There's still plenty of gold, is there?" queried Mr. Grigsby. This was an important question, to Charley.

The Colonel shrugged his shoulders and laughed. The General gravely smiled. Answered the Colonel:

"Gold? Lots of it, and people finding it. The diggings along the American and the Yuba and the Feather are in full blast; and then there are the southern mines, up the San Joaquin Valley, in the Mokelumne and Calaveras districts. I'm going over there myself to-morrow or next day. If you see Captain Sutter up north, tell him that any help he can give you will be appreciated by me."

"Your rancho is prosperous, Colonel?"

"Fairly so. You know we've named it Mariposa, or Lily Ranch. I had intended to stock it to cattle, but the mining excitement has changed my plans and all my ranch machinery is stored here in town. The land has so much mineral on it, we've discovered, that I'll work that first if the Government doesn't object. Unfortunately mineral claims are not supposed to go with Mexican land grants. While my family are here we make our quarters in the Happy Valley section. I have a saw-mill started back of San José, too. Should you come that way, be sure and stop off with me."

"And should you come to Sonoma, do me the honor of making my house your home," said the General. "And pray do not forget that in September we of California hold a statehood convention at Monterey, to frame a State constitution. All good citizens are requested to be present."

"The State of California, already! Think of that!" exclaimed Mr. Grigsby.

"And a free State, too, if we can make it so," added Colonel Frémont, his blue eyes aglow. "California's free now, to everybody. One man is as good as another. I was born in the South, but I'm against slavery. California has started gloriously free, and she ought to remain so."

"I'm with you, there, gentlemen," quoth Mr. Grigsby. "Certainly this is the one population, away out here like a big family, where slavery has no place or reason. Anybody who will work ought to be allowed to make a living. This gold and land weren't put here for the benefit of a few."

They all shook hands again. The Colonel and the General paced away, on their business. Mr. Grigsby and Charley went ahead on theirs. And Charley never forgot his first meeting with the celebrated Pathfinder and the stately ex-governor.

He was tired enough when he and Mr. Grigsby had completed their errands. But he found his father rested and up, and waiting with the home letter just finished. Charley added four pages; but he had so much to tell that he didn't say half of it. 'Twas a wonderful country, let alone the marvelous journey behind it. He only regretted that he didn't pick up a little gold, in the streets, so as to enclose that in the letter, too.

His father had made arrangements to store their trunk, and what clothes they would not need while at the mines.

"Now all that remains is to get our washing early—and, by the way, the Frenchman promises to have it ready by six o'clock—and a pack animal at Sacramento," he pronounced. "That is, if we can find one."

"If Captain Sutter is there, we'll find our pack animal," asserted Mr. Grigsby.

"And if we don't, we can carry our own packs," declared Mr. Adams. "That's the way the majority of the people are going in. By the way, several persons have told me we ought to try the southern mines, up the San Joaquin, beyond the new town called Stockton. But of course we have our reasons."

"It's all luck, to the greenhorn," replied the Fremonter. "But I think the American or the Feather country fits that map better."

After supper they took a stroll, before they turned in early to get a good night's sleep. Surely there never was a gayer, busier place than San Francisco at night. The wind, which had been blowing most of the day, dropped, at evening, and a dense fog floated in. In the fog the lights of lamps, lanterns and candles shone weirdly from doors and windows and through canvas walls. Now about every other store appeared to be a saloon or gambling room, all crowded. There were other places of amusement, also, even to a sort of a theatre, where miners were dancing with one another, on the floor, to the sound of a fiddle and cracked accordion, while on a stage a thin woman with painted red cheeks was singing and prancing. An auctioneer was selling real estate, from a dry-goods box in the plaza. Stores were open, the streets were thronged, hammering and music and shouting were mingled just as in the night before; and after the Adams party had gone to bed they found it hard work to sleep.

The hotel itself was noisy, for voices carried right through the floors and the thin partitions. Charley tried not to listen, and was just dozing off at last, when a new conversation, somewhere along the hall, made him prick up his ears. There evidently were two men.

"You've never heard of Tom, have you?" asked one voice.

"Not a word, since he started back to the States to find his relatives," answered a gruffer voice.

"Hadn't many, had he?"

"Nephew by marriage, is all he ever mentioned."

"He did well while he was here, and it's a pity he threw up and left. Somebody's jumped his claims by this time, sure. Fact is, you can't leave a claim over night, without having somebody jump into it and squat. People are getting crazy, running 'round wild-like and grabbing any land they fancy. The Government will have to step in and make laws."

"That's right; but Tom had one claim that he banked on and said nobody could find."

"You mean the Golden West?"

"Yes. Somewhere up north."

"In the American or the Feather country, I always imagined. He was saving it till he could get that nephew, I reckon, to work it with him. A quartz claim. I saw specimens from it. Well, let's go to sleep. So long."

"So long."

Charley's heart beat rapidly. "The Golden West!" That was the very name of the mine they were seeking—the mine that had been given to them by the mysterious Californian back in St. Louis! In the American River or Feather River country, the two men had said; and "Tom"; but beyond that they didn't seem to know much more than did anybody else. They had spoken of a nephew, though. He wasn't entitled to it, was he—even if the man in St. Louis had been looking for him? The man had given it to him,

Charley, and to his, Charley's, father, because they had helped him. Shucks! Now the nephew might be hunting for it, and the long-nosed man and partners were hunting for it, and it didn't belong to any of them.

Charley had half a mind to get out of bed and find those two men. He wanted to see them, at least. But to snoop through the hall, asking people in the rooms if they had been talking about "Tom," would be a crazy proceeding. No; all he could do was to wait till morning and tell his father and Mr. Grigsby what he had heard. He wished that they weren't sleeping so soundly, and snoring without a pause. He could scarcely wait—until he fell asleep himself.

It appeared to be the fashion in San Francisco to sleep late. Perhaps everybody was tired out. The early morning hours were the only quiet hours, and when Charley was wakened by the movements of his father and Mr. Grigsby, the rest of the hotel seemed to be still in bed.

"All aboard, Charley," bade his father, leaning over the bunk. He was dressed, and so was Mr. Grigsby. The air in the room was chill and gray.

"All right," answered Charley. "But wait a minute. I want to tell you and Mr. Grigsby what I heard, while you were asleep. Got to speak low, though." And with them listening, close to him as he sat up, he repeated every word of the conversation. "That nephew doesn't get any of it, just the same; does he?" he added. "It's ours."

"Now, Charley," laughed his father, "you're going too fast. Nobody can have it till after somebody finds it. We've come 6000 miles, and what do we know? There was a man named Tom, who is supposed to have had a mine in Northern California named the Golden West, and a nephew back in the States. That's too indefinite to argue about."

"A quartz claim," reminded Mr. Grigsby. "That's one clue of value. There aren't many quartz claims in the country. Nearly all the mining is placer. People prefer to dig in the dirt rather than blast in the rock. It's quicker."

"Quartz let it be, then," agreed Mr. Adams. "That does help out a bit; but we won't discuss ownership yet, except with that man Jacobs. Him I'll resist to the full extent of law and strength."

"What is a quartz claim?" queried Charley.

"Well," said Mr. Grigsby, "gold may be loose in the dirt, or held in rock. The first is a placer, the other is a vein or lode. Nearly all the mining out here is placer mining, where the dirt is dug out and washed away, leaving the gold. But of course the gold in the placer beds must have come out of a vein somewhere above. It doesn't grow like grass. 'Cording to the scientific idee it was melted into the rock, first, like into quartz, and then was worn away by the weather and carried into the dirt. I don't fancy breaking up rock, to get gold, when in a placer it's already been broken for you. But they say quartz mining can be made to pay well, if you have the proper machinery. As like as not this man 'Tom' was waiting for machinery."

"Tom." Tom who? And what was his nephew's name? And did his nephew know about the mine? And was he out here looking for it? These and other questions Charley kept putting to himself, because nobody could answer them for him. The main thing now, anyway, was to get off, to the "diggin's."

They paid their bill, shouldered their baggage, and wearing their complete miner's costumes (Charley sporting his knife and his belt) they proceeded down to Long Wharf and the Mary Ann. On their way they collected their washing from the bowing Frenchman.

Long Wharf was the principal wharf, where they had climbed the stairs when landing from the California, and was at the foot of Clay Street, just beyond Montgomery, only a few blocks from the plaza of Portsmouth Square. The tide was half in, partially covering the ugly mud-flats, and extending all around the wharf.

Considerable of a crowd had collected, on the wharf. They were in flannel shirts and boots and coarse trousers belted about with pistol and knife, and were laden with baggage rolls. Evidently they, too, were off to the mines; perhaps by the Mary Ann.

"That must be the schooner, out yonder—I can see Mary Ann on her stern," spoke Mr. Grigsby. "And I reckon that's her boat coming in."

"I'll get you out quicker'n that, stranger, if you're for the Mary Ann," cut in an alert by-stander. "Five dollars for the trip; safety guaranteed."

"Not to-day," smiled Mr. Grigsby.

A skiff was being pulled in, from a schooner anchored out a short distance. At a nod from Mr. Grigsby, Charley and his father pressed forward with him, to meet the boat at the foot of the long stairs. Yes, it was from the Mary Ann; and they and a dozen others (or as many as the boat would hold) tumbled in.

The Mary Ann was a small schooner, about fifty feet long and twenty feet wide. She had one little cabin with four rooms, so that the passengers were expected to sleep on deck or in the hold, where bunks had been built along the sides, with the dining table (of boards) in the middle! However, who cared, when they were off to the mines and this was one way to get there?

"How long'll it take us, to Sacramento, captain?" hailed one of his passengers.

"Five days with luck; two weeks without," snapped the captain, a very short, red-faced little man, giving orders right and left and sending mate and sailors running, as the Mary Ann swung free from her anchorage. Up went the foresail and out shook the jib. Leaning, the Mary Ann slowly gathered way, gliding through the ripples.

The great Bay of San Francisco was beautiful. The morning sun had broken through the fog, to gild the hundreds of ships, and the dancing water. Heeling to a smart breeze, the Mary Ann soon passed vessel after vessel lying at anchor—among them the California herself. The jumble of low buildings and tents forming the city of San Francisco dwindled, behind; the uproar of voices and hammers died; and heading for the north the Mary

Ann clipped merrily along, the Golden Gate entrance on her left, the rolling hills of the California mainland distant on her right.

Her passengers numbered thirty-seven—about seven more than she ought to hold, decided Charley. Everybody was in high feather at the prospects of being on the way to the "diggin's." They pressed against the weather rail, mounted atop the cook's galley and the cabin roof, and several of the boldest even climbed aloft to the cross-trees of fore-mast and mainmast, where they cheered and whooped. Yes, it seemed to be a sort of pleasure excursion. Voices were constantly shouting.

"That's Goat Island, isn't it? The first one we passed."

"There's Alcatraz."

"Hurrah for Angel Island! Anybody want to land?"

"Is this still San Francisco Bay?"

"Of course it is."

"Where's San Pablo Bay, then?"

"At the end, before we turn into the Sacramento River."

The Mary Ann was making good time. The red-faced little captain stood near the wheel, with folded arms and vigilant eye, as if he was very proud of her. All the shipping at anchor had been left behind long ago, and now the schooner seemed to have joined with a regular procession of small boats, hastening in the same direction as she. Some were sail-boats, many were skiffs and launches; all were crowded, and in a great hurry.

The bay narrowed, and between two points called San Pablo (or Saint Paul) and San Pedro (or Saint Peter), guarded by islands called the Brothers and the Sisters, the Mary Ann entered San Pablo Bay, which really was a round basin forming the north end of San Francisco Bay.

The bell below was ringing for dinner, but the Mary Ann had turned more toward the east, and against the land, in front, could be seen the masts of more shipping.

"That must be at Mare Island, and at Benicia beyond," said Mr. Grigsby. "You know how Mare Island gets its name? Because there used to be a big herd of elk on it, led by an old mare. The Government's going to make a naval station of it. Benicia is the town General Vallejo donated the site of. There's where the army headquarters are being built. Well, guess we'll have time to eat, before we get there."

"Come ahead, Charley," bade his father.

The dinner really was very good; and if anybody still was hungry, a sign on the cook's galley announced, invitingly: "Pies One Dollar." Charley saw several of the miners buying pies and eating them.

When the Adams party came up on deck again, the Mary Ann had passed Mare Island, where some vessels, among them two ships of war, were anchored, and was entering a narrow opening named the Straits of Carquinez. On the right the mountains approached very close. On the left appeared more shipping, and the houses and tents of a town. This was Benicia, and a prettily located place it was, too, with the ground sloping upward, behind it, and the massy brown crest of Mount Diablo, landmark seen from the Golden Gate, rising across the strait, before.

Beyond Benicia the straits opened into Suisun Bay—a pocket into which emptied the Sacramento River and the San Joachin River. The San Joaquin River came in on the south. Anybody going to the southern gold mines would sail up the San Joachin to Stockton; but the Mary Ann was bound for the Sacramento and the northern mines; so she kept on, through Suisun Bay, past a town of one house, on the south side, and named (people said, laughing) the New-York-of-the-Pacific, for the mouth of the Sacramento.

XVII

ON TO THE DIGGIN'S

Suisun Bay was bordered with reedy marshes where the rushes grew higher than a man's head. It seemed to be a great hunting ground, for ducks, geese and swans flew in armies—a beautiful sight in the sunset. These quite excited the Mary Ann's passengers, until suddenly somebody noted, distant in the east, ahead, a long broken line of bluish white.

"Mountains!"

"Look at the mountains, boys!"

"No! Those are clouds."

"No, siree! Mountains, with snow on 'em!"

"Hooray for the Sierras, boys! There's where the gold lies."

"See them?" bade Mr. Grigsby, to Charley and his father. "That's the main range of the Sierra Nevada—the Snowy Range, as the Spanish goes. It divides California from the Great Desert. Over it Carson led Frémont and us other fellows, in winter, through ten and twenty feet of snow, to the headwaters of the American River and down the American River to Sutter's Fort and the Sacramento. How far away is that range, do you think?"

"Near a hundred miles, I should judge," calculated Mr. Adams.

Various passengers were guessing twenty, fifty, one hundred and two hundred miles—making all kinds of wild assertions. But Charley's father had struck pretty accurately, for he had seen mountains before, in Mexico.

"Just about," approved Mr. Grigsby. "The nearest perhaps seventy-five. But Sacramento's more than sixty miles yet, by the river, and the high Sierras are one hundred miles up the American from there."

As evening fell, the Mary Ann was entering a wide channel through the marshes where the San Joaquin River from the south and the Sacramento, further on the east, emptied into Suisun Bay. The mouth of the San Joaquin, said several people, was narrow and shallow, and boats ascending for Stockton and the southern mines frequently went aground if the tide was out; but the Sacramento was wide and deep. A mist or fog began to veil the shores and water, and passengers prepared to go to bed. The Adams party decided to sleep rolled in their blankets on deck—which suited Charley exactly. He had grown fond of this open-air sleeping, and planks did not seem hard any more.

The breeze died, and in the dusk the anchor rattled out, holding the schooner short, near the mouth of the Sacramento. All night the wild fowl screamed—and all night the mosquitoes hummed. Charley stuck his head under his blanket and slept fairly well.

The sun rose red, and so did many of the passengers, for the mosquitoes had been fierce indeed. But everybody was good-natured; a few hardships must be expected, in making a fortune. With the morning breeze the Mary Ann hoisted in her anchor. All sails set again, she glided through the slough, and struck the current of the Sacramento.

The Sacramento proved to be a fine, noble stream, flowing 200 and 300 yards wide, with gentle current and plenty of "sea room" around and under. The banks were heavily timbered clear to the water's edge, flowers blossomed gaily, and through grassy openings in the timber on the right were given glimpses of the distant foothills, over-topped by the blue-misted snow-crests behind them. It certainly looked like a wonderful country, not only for mining but for farming, also.

The banks appeared mainly deserted, save where squatters, as they were called, had taken land, cleared it, and had piled up wood to sell. There was one spot which Mr. Grigsby said was an Indian village, and he pointed out reed huts. But the most interesting feature was the boats, most of them going up, a few coming down.

There were two schooners, larger than the Mary Ann, but crowded as full, which, just ahead, tacking back and forth, sometimes were near, sometimes far. There were also smaller boats, skiffs and scows, full to the gunwales, their passengers rowing and paddling hard, as if in a race. In one funny hand-made skiff the men were using boards and even pans. They scarcely paused to cheer the Mary Ann as she triumphantly glided past, and her passengers yelled:

"Bye-bye!" "See you later!" "We're bound for the mines. Where are you going?" "Want a tow?" And so forth, and so forth. Another boat was a suspiciously built yawl, which looked much like the boat in which Charley had slept, over the stern of the California. It held nine men, three of them in sailor costumes; and on the bows a name evidently had been scratched out. Rowing desperately, the men in it barely glanced up as the Mary Ann passed. They appeared to be anxious to sheer off.

"Here's a runaway, I'll bet my hat," exclaimed the captain of the Mary Ann, who happened to be standing near the Adams party. "It's a ship's boat, and those men row like sailors—let alone their clothes. They've taken French leave, for the mines. It's impossible to hold a crew, in San Francisco Bay. If they can't steal a boat they'll swim ashore and make their way on foot."

Now down the river came a broad scow, made of rough planks, and steered by sweeps. As it passed, the men in it (who wore miners' costumes) waved their hands—and see; they held up gunny sacks and salt bags, stuffed full and heavy.

"Just from the mines," they shouted. "Back from the land of gold. You're too late. We got it all."

The sight of those fat, heavy sacks created intense excitement aboard the Mary Ann. The passengers rushed to the near rail; eyes bulged and voices volleyed in a chorus of questions—and several persons almost jumped overboard.

"Where'd you get it?"

"How much?"

"There's more, isn't there?"

"Wait a minute!"

"Stop the ship, captain!"

"Hey! Show us a handful!"

Charley was as excited as anybody. Big sacks of gold! Think of that! Look at them! But the captain laughed, winking at Mr. Grigsby.

"Sand, boys; sand," he drawled. "That's a trick of those up-river fellows. They load with bags of sand for ballast, and show them to the other crowd. Bah!"

At this Charley felt better, although he did not begrudge anybody a sack of gold, if only there was enough left.

The Mary Ann made rather slow progress. The river, always broad and smooth, curved in mighty sweeping bends, so that sometimes the breeze was dead ahead. Then the Mary Ann must tack and tack, gaining only a few yards in several hundred. At night she tied up, to a tree; and several of her passengers caught some fish from the rail. Charley tended a line, for a few minutes, and caught a cat-fish that weighed twenty pounds; he couldn't pull it in until his neighbor helped.

The Sacramento evidently flowed through a wide valley, for mountains were visible beyond the timber on either hand. Each evening the schooner stopped for the night, tying or anchoring. Not until noon of the fifth day on the river was any sign of settlement along the banks encountered, although boats continued frequent. But that noon a large ranch was passed, where a settler by the name of Schwartz had been wise enough to start in raising vegetables. He had made over $15,000 already, claimed people aboard the schooner—yet for all that nobody on the Mary Ann seemed ready to farm instead of mine.

Next, ahead on the right bank, above the Schwartz ranch, appeared a collection of houses and tents. The Mary Ann waxed excited again.

"There's Sacramento!"

"Get your things together, boys."

"Is that Sacramento, cap'n?"

"No, sir," answered the captain, shortly. "That's only Sutterville."

"Do we stop?"

"No, sir; we do not."

"Where's Sacramento?"

"Three miles above."

"This must be the town old Captain Sutter's started," remarked Mr. Grigsby, surveying it narrowly. "Well, he's taken plenty of land to spread out in." And that was so, for about twenty houses were scattered along the high bank for half a mile. "Hope the old captain's up at Sacramento. I'd like to see him."

"How large is Sacramento, stranger?" asked a neighbor at the rail.

"Large, you say?" answered another. "Make yore guess. Last April when I came out with my pile it had four houses. Now I'm told it's boomin' wuss'n San Francisco—and you know what that means."

"So you've been to the mines, have you?" invited Mr. Adams.

"Yes, sir; I have, sir. You bet I have, sir."

"How'd you make it?"

"To the tune of $20,000 in two weeks, sir. Then I was fool enough to quit, and spend it all in San Francisco. But here I'm back again, for $50,000."

Instantly everybody within sound of his voice deluged him with questions, as to "How much could be dug in a day," and other foolish remarks. Charley stared at him. This certainly was a wonderful land. If a man could make and spend $20,000 and then expect $50,000 more, why should anyone remain poor?

"Look at the ships!" cried voices, as the Mary Ann rounded a curve.

Against the timber to the right, before, rose a score and more of mast-heads. Above the timber floated a cloud of brown dust, as if stirred by many feet. And beyond the masts, in the midst of the trees, could be descried tents and houses—a great number, laid out in streets, with a levee of earth and sod piled high with freight and baggage, fronting the river. This was Sacramento, at last!

The Mary Ann glided in on a long tack. Down fluttered her main-sail, presently down fluttered her fore-sail; and as she swung to, spilling the breeze from her jibs, close to the bank at the end of the levee, a sailor sprang into the water and swimming until he could wade carried a hawser ashore. This he made fast to the great root of a tree, washed bare by the waters. All up and down the banks other vessels were moored likewise, to trees and trunks and roots, so that some of the branches brushed the yards and spars. A number of cook's galleys had been set up on shore, as cabins, and several ship's figure-heads were established like sign-posts! It was a queer water-front—and what a swarm of people it exhibited!

From the Mary Ann Sacramento looked even busier than San Francisco. It was better laid out, too, for the streets were regular and straight.

"Four houses and fifty people three months ago; 5,000 people now and houses going up so fast you can't count 'em," said the red-faced captain, as in obedience to his orders the mate dropped the schooner's boats. "Wish I'd bought some lots here when they were offered to me—three for a thousand apiece."

"What are they worth now?" asked Charley, breathless.

"Well, sonny, a lot twenty feet wide is selling for $2,300." And the captain turned away.

The passengers were piling ashore; some would not wait for a boat; the Mary Ann had swung close to the bank, and they made running jumps from the rail, to land sprawling in the shallows or to plump out of sight and swim. When the Adams party finally stepped from the skiff to the levee (which was calledembarcadero, of course) they were fairly deafened by a multitude of cries from citizens who insisted upon their buying lots. But Mr. Grigsby sighted a stout, ruddy-faced man; and exclaiming: "There's Captain Sutter!" made for him.

He and the captain shook hands heartily, and Mr. Grigsby brought his friend over to the rest of the party.

"Captain Sutter, gentlemen," introduced the Frémonter (and Charley felt quite like a man, to be included in "gentlemen"). "The first American settler in California, and the friend of all the other Americans who came after. You've heard of Sutter's Fort. He was the boss."

Captain Sutter was a short, stoutly built man, with crisp mustache and goatee, and a military way. His complexion was florid, his eyes very blue, and his forehead so high that probably he was bald. He looked to be German (though really he was Swiss), and he spoke with a German accent. His manner was very courtly, as he bowed and shook hands.

"Yes, of Sutter's Fort—but where is that now?" he said. "These gold seekers, they run over it; they leave me nothing. They have no rights of land to respect. Ach, what is the country coming to? All here was mine, once. See, now! Somebody put up a city, on this embarcadero where I landed my supplies for my fort. My saw-mill is a hotel—the City Hotel—and for it and the land it is on somebody gets $30,000 per year, they tell me. Nobody work for me any more; even my Indians go to mining gold, and my wheat fields are stepped all over. My new city which I start only three miles below, and call by my name—my gute name which when I was useful was so popular—is neglected, and everybody flock here. I once was rich; now soon I am bankrupt; all because my men discovered this gold. This gold, I hate it. It will be the ruin of this country."

"Well, captain, I'm sorry to hear this from you," said Mr. Grigsby. "But I'm powerful glad to see you, anyway. You've been too generous. You gave away your land, so as to help build up the country."

"Yes," answered the captain. "I did not want the gold, but I did not think the people would go crazy and flock over everything and obey me not at all. Well, what can I do for you, my friends?"

"We're going in to the mines, captain," informed Mr. Grigsby. "How's the horse and mule market? We want a pack animal of some kind. Colonel Frémont said you might be able to help us. I saw him in San Francisco."

"The grand Colonel!" exclaimed Captain Sutter. "For my real American friends I would do anything yet." He spread his hands. "But horses and mules? One time I remember I had many for you—that time you came out of the mountains so nearly famished to my fort. Now times are different. Horse and mule sell for $100, where they used to be ten. Maybe when the emigrants begin to come in, over the mountains, with their beasts, things will be different. I hear 30,000 are on the way, for the American River and the Sacramento. But I guess I know of one mule. I will try. Come this way, gentlemen. Leave your baggage. It will be safe—safer than the land it is on."

Captain Sutter led the way from the levee, crowded with people and baggage and freight. What a beautiful city this Sacramento was growing to be! The buildings were mainly of rough-sawn timber, with some of clay, and of course many tents; but the streets were wide, and straight, and everywhere great trees had been left standing, many of them six feet through at the ground. Business of buying and selling real estate and goods was at full blast. As he trotted along, the captain proved talkative.

"You saw my own city of Sutter's Ville, below?" he asked. "That is a much better site; not? It is high and dry, while this place—bah! Gentlemen, in the spring I have moored my boats to the tops of trees on that very embarcadero! But we shall see. I have hired Lieutenant Sherman of the Army to survey between my town and this, and connect the two; and maybe soon they will be one. Lieutenant Davidson, of the Army—he is surveying my town now, for fine streets and big lots."

"Davidson? Lieutenant J. W. Davidson, I suppose," remarked Charley's father; and Captain Sutter nodded. "He was with General Kearny in that overland march with the First Dragoons, from Santa Fé to San Diego, in the summer of Forty-six, when the Army was sent to capture California."

"Yes, sir," answered the captain. "But my friend Frémont and Kit Carson and Mr. Grigsby, here, and the American settlers, they got in ahead of the United States Army. Still, we needed the Army, like we needed the Navy; and we need them still. It is another of General Kearny's officers, Lieutenant John Warner, who surveyed this Sacramento City. A brave man, a very brave man. Three lance wounds he got, in the battle of San Pasqual, when the Californians would have prevented the Army from entering to San Diego. He is now already far up in the Sierra Nevada, at the head of the Feather River, surveying for a railroad route, I hear. Think, gentlemen! Soon a railroad, maybe!"

Captain Sutter had led the way to a rude hut of woven grass walls and thatch roof, on the outskirts of the town. Here he halted, and called:

"Ho, Pedro! Amigo (friend)!"

An Indian came out. Yes, an Indian — but different from the Indians whom Charley had seen in Missouri. He was squatty, dark and wrinkled, his hair cut short, and cotton shirt and trousers as his clothes. The captain spoke to him in Spanish. Pedro listened, and with a nod, turning, made off at a trot. In a moment he came back, leading from a shed among a clump of trees a small donkey.

"A burro, 'pon my word!" exclaimed Mr. Adams. "I haven't seen a donkey like that out of Mexico!"

"It is the best Pedro has," explained the captain. "These gold seekers so crazy they have robbed him, because they think he is nothing but an Indian. There will be troubles with my Indians, if the whites do not treat them better. Anyway, gentlemen, this animal is not so small as his size. He will carry all you put aboard him, and Pedro will sell him for twenty-five dollar, since you are friends of mine. Otherwise, he would not sell him at all."

"Good," said Mr. Adams. "Bueno," he added, so that Pedro might understand. "We'll take him, and glad of it."

So they bought the burro (a funny little creature with shaggy head, enormously long ears, and small hoofs) and led him away, Charley proudly holding the rope.

"You are lucky, my friends," spoke Captain Sutter; "one other animal there was, which I found for those friends of yours who came through the day before yesterday."

"What!" exclaimed Mr. Adams, sharply. "Who were they?"

"A rather small, dark man with a very long nose, sir, and two companions. They came by trail, from San Francisco, they said, and wanted a pack animal. They told me of my friend Grigsby, who had recommended them to me if they saw me, and of course I was happy to oblige them."

"Great thunder!" muttered Mr. Grigsby, as he and Mr. Adams stared at one another. But he quickly added, as if not to hurt the honest captain's feelings: "Very good, captain. When did they leave? Going up the American?"

"They left immediately, and I think they spoke of the American," answered the captain. "Yes," he continued, placidly, "it was a large bay mule, with one ear under-bitten—a notch taken out of it. I was of course happy to oblige them; but this burro I saved for you."

No, there was no use in telling the captain of his mistake, and making him feel bad; and Mr. Adams shook his head warningly at Charley. But what nerve, on the part of the long-nosed man! However, Mr. Adams only said:

"We'd better set right out, then, Grigsby."

"Can I do anything more for you, gentlemen?" inquired Captain Sutter.

"No, thank you, captain. We're fixed nicely. Now we'll pack up and leave at once. Time is precious, you know, to us gold seekers. Where is Jim Marshall? Up at the saw-mill?"

"Yes, at Coloma, but the saw-mill is not running. We have nobody to run it. Ah," mused the captain, "everyone is in a great hurry, like you. They see nothing but gold, much gold. It was not so in the old days. Well," he added, extending his hand, "good-bye, gentlemen, and good luck. Maybe we shall meet again."

They shook hands with him, thanked him once more for his kindness, and he trotted off — evidently as "hurried" as other people.

XVIII

THE TRAIL OF THE ENEMY

"Evidently we have to do with a very cunning gang of rascals," remarked Mr. Adams, as with the burro they hastened back for the levee and their baggage. "How did they know enough to trade on your name, Grigsby?"

Mr. Grigsby smiled grimly.

"They probably saw I was a Frémont man—may have heard us talking; and they took the chance. Naturally enough they'd guess that I knew the captain. All we early Americans in California knew him, and he stood ready to help us out. Well, sir, they left a clue, at any rate. We'll follow as fast as we can."

"Do you think we'll catch them?" asked Charley, eagerly.

"We'll do our best, whether we catch 'em or not," answered the Frémonter. "It's a big country, up yonder in the mountains, as they'll find out. Now, I'm thinking that we can't do better than to take the trail up the south branch of the American, to the saw-mill, and see Jim Marshall. He's been living right in the middle of things and may know something we'll want to hear."

"You mean the Marshall who discovered this California gold, for Americans?" queried Charley's father. "Well, I'd certainly like to see him, and have Charley see him; and the place, too."

"All right. Maybe we can kill two birds with one stone," answered the Frémonter. "And from the mill we can work north, to the other branch of the American."

The baggage was undisturbed, on the levee. Charley held the burro, and his father and Mr. Grigsby proceeded to pack her. Mr. Grigsby had stopped at a store, on their way, and bought two crowbars, a new rope and a pack-saddle, and some dried-beef. The crowbars cost $1.50 each, the rope cost $5, and the pack-saddle, of oak and rawhide and shaped like two letter

X's fastened together by the middle, cost $8. The meat was the cheapest. It came in long strips, and sold by the yard—six yards for fifty cents!

The Frémonter was of course an expert at packing a horse or mule, and Mr. Adams knew considerable about it, from his army experience. Charley wondered at the neatness with which his comrades hoisted aboard all the variously shaped articles, and tied them fast so that they balanced.

"They call this the diamond hitch," grunted Mr. Grigsby, as he hauled tight, while the little burro stood with ears meekly drooped. "Rope makes the shape of a diamond—see? But it's only the regular trappers' pack throw. I've used it a thousand times and more. Well, we're all ready; hurrah for the gold mines. Charley, you can lead the critter. I'll go ahead, to show the road."

"Hurrah for the gold mines!" echoed Charley; and away they trudged.

As they left the hurly-burly of the embarcadero, and threaded their way through the bustling town, which was like another San Francisco, nobody appeared to notice their march. It probably was an old story, and besides, the people were too busy running about, bargaining in real estate, making money quick.

The dust was floating high, from the many feet; and as the street became a road out of the town, the dust was thicker than ever, from parties on before. It lay brown and powdery, ankle-deep and hot to the boots. The sun blazed down fiercely. Leading the little burro, in his heavy clothing Charley soon was streaming with perspiration; before, tramped with long stride the Frémonter, a rifle on shoulder; at the rear stanchly limped Mr. Adams, well laden with gun and pistol and the few articles that he and Mr. Grigsby had divided.

The burro's pack displayed crowbars and shovels and picks and gold pans and camp equipage; and to Charley's mind the little procession looked very business-like.

After following the dusty road through a flat brown plain, in about a mile and a half they passed what Mr. Grigsby said was the famous Sutter's Fort. With its thick clay walls and square towers at the corners, pierced with loopholes, it did indeed look like a fort. Inside the walls were several clay buildings where the captain had lived and stored his goods and taught his Indians to do white man's work. He had erected his fort here in 1839, and had been given all the land about, by the Mexican government of California. But now the fort was deserted; the doors and windows had been broken in, most of the wood had been torn out and carried off, and the fields about had been used as pasturage by the gold seekers. No wonder that the captain felt aggrieved; and it was pretty hard on him, when really because of his saw-mill had gold been discovered. This was poor reward for having settled the country and built a saw-mill—and a flour mill besides.

"There's the Rio Americano," spoke Mr. Grigsby, pointing ahead, after they had passed old Fort Sutter.

About a quarter of a mile before on the left, a line of trees indicated the course of a river—the American. And a fine stream it proved to be, flowing clear and sparkling between wooded grassy banks. The road, still dusty, turned slightly, and ascended along the river, making toward the rolling brown foothills which shimmered in the blue distance, with the mighty snow-crests of the Sierra Nevada range glinting beyond them.

In the shallows and on the bars of the American parties of miners were at work digging away with spades and picks, and squatting to wash out the gold in their pans. They all were so busy that they seemed to note nothing on either side of them or overhead. Their eyes were glued to the sand and the holes and the pans. Other parties had halted by the way, for rest in the shade of trees; and these hailed the Adams party with the usual calls: "How far to the diggin's, strangers?" "This is the American, ain't it?" "Say! How much do you s'pose a man can dig in a day, up there?" "Where you folks from, and where you bound?" "Is it always this hot in Californy?" And so forth, and so forth.

Several parties on their way back to Sacramento also were met; they were brown and hairy and rough and ragged, and some of them limped weakly as if they could scarcely carry their weapons, picks, spades, crowbars and blanket-rolls. They all were received with a perfect volley of excited queries from the resting parties—to which they replied with wave of hand and sometimes with a triumphant flourish of a fat little sack.

But Mr. Grigsby paused not for the gold seekers in the river, or under the trees, or on the way down. He tramped stoutly, with his long stride; Charley just as stoutly followed behind, leading the packed burro, and at the tail of the burro strode, a little unevenly, the tall and soldierly Mr. Adams.

The dusty road continued through the wide rolling plain which formed the east half of the great Valley of the Sacramento. The herbage was short and brown, except at the margin of the streams, and the hot landscape was broken by occasional large spreading trees, singly and in clumps. As the foothills gradually drew nearer, the number of miners became greater. Finally, at sunset, Mr. Grigsby halted at a grassy hollow, near the American, where there was a considerable camp of men, and even two women. A rude sign announced the title "Woodchuck's Delight."

"We'll camp, too, I reckon," he quoth, dropping his pack; and Charley was glad to hear the words. "How are you?" greeted Mr. Grigsby to the nearest miners, as he turned to unpack the burro.

"Howdy, strangers? Where you from and where you going?"

"Just coming in, or have you made one pile?"

"That's a burro, ain't it? Will you sell him?"

"What might your names be, strangers?"

To these and other queries Mr. Grigsby answered good-naturedly, as he and Mr. Adams stripped the little burro. The camp consisted of a few tents and of men who merely had thrown their blankets down here and there, as if to cook their suppers and rest till morning. The great majority had come afoot, many without even pack animals; a sprinkling of horses and mules were staked out, at pasture; and speedily Mr. Grigsby led the burro aside, to stake him out, too. He laid back his ears, stretched out his shaggy head, and made short runs at the other animals near him, until he had cleared a grazing spot all his own. Then he hee-hawed triumphantly, and lay down for a luxurious roll.

Mr. Adams and Charley tossed the bedding to a place which appeared as good as any other, for sleeping, and got out the "grub" and cooking utensils.

"Charley, you're expected to supply the wood and water, and help me with the camp chores generally," directed his father. "We'll let Grigsby do the hunting and camp locating and burro tending, and I'll cook and wash dishes. That will be our regular system. How about it, Grigsby?"

"Sounds like a pretty good arrangement," agreed the Frémonter, tersely. "But I'm perfectly willing to chip in wherever necessary."

"Get some wood, Charley," bade Mr. Adams. "That's first. There's the axe." And he proceeded to sort out the food, while Mr. Grigsby busied himself with the bedding.

Charley seized the axe from amidst other tools, and lustily chopped wood from a tree which already had been half demolished by other campers. In fact, it looked as though very soon no trees would be left, along this trail; which was a great pity.

Having brought enough wood, he took an iron kettle and trudged to the river. Several miners were at work, along the banks, and on a bar in the middle; one was working right where Charley arrived — a low place, like a miniature gully, where the soil was bare and sandy clay. He had dug a small trench, and was shoveling some of the loose dirt into his gold pan.

Charley could not help but watch, for a moment.

"Are you getting anything?" he ventured.

The man appeared to be a rough fellow, unshaven and tanned red, in faded blue flannel shirt, old trousers belted with a leather strap, and bare feet. But when he smiled, and pausing a second, answered, he spoke in a pleasant voice, with as good language as from Charley's father or any other cultured person.

"Oh, a few pinches. See — —?" and he swirled his pan level full of water, until the water and much of the dirt had flowed out over the edges. He did this again — picked out a number of pebbles and large particles of dirt — swirled once more, and tilted the pan, almost empty, for Charley to see.

Hurrah! Sure enough, there was a thin seam of yellow, lying in the angle of sides and bottom! And breaking it, was a small irregular particle, of blackish hue tinted with the yellow in spots. Charley's eyes bulged. Gold! Was this the way they did it?

The man picked out the small lump, and turned it in his fingers.

"One little nugget. Worth probably twenty dollars," he remarked. "The rest of the pans — these are two pans washed out — average about twelve cents." Then, at sight of Charley's excited face, he laughed heartily. "You look as though you had the gold fever, boy, and had it bad," he said. "But these pans are nothing. They wouldn't sum up more than four dollars a day — and nobody in California would work long for four dollars a day. It's too low down on the river to pan out real wages. I'm just amusing myself. Got a pan? Come in and try your luck. The ground's free."

"I can't, now," stammered Charley. "I'm getting water for supper. Maybe I can later, though. Will you be here after a while?"

"Oh, as like as not," answered the man, calmly scraping out the yellow stuff with the point of his knife, and dropping it into the usual brown buckskin sack—which, Charley noted, bulged a little at the bottom. "I used to be a preacher; now I seem to be a miner. What's your name and where'd you come from and where are you going, as the fashion of asking questions is."

Charley briefly told him (for he liked this ex-preacher immensely), but of course he didn't mention that they were on the trail of the Golden West claim. He simply said that they were bound up the American. Then he dipped his water and hastened back to the camp, where he found his father waiting.

"I saw a man panning gold," he announced.

"Getting anything?" asked Mr. Grigsby, not at all excited.

"Yes. A nugget and a lot of dust besides. He said he'd help me pan, if I'd come back after supper. Can I, dad?"

"Oh, I guess you can, if you have no chores," consented his father, with a smile at Mr. Grigsby.

Charley had no idea that his father was such a cook. Mr. Adams went at the matter in great shape—and even Mr. Grigsby, lying near, rewrapping a place on the pack saddle, apparently found nothing to criticise.

Mr. Adams (and it looked odd to see him, a man, busy cooking!) had bread batter already started. He took one of the gold pans, dumped into it some flour, a pinch or two of saleratus, and a quart or two of the water. He mixed away with his hands, adding flour and water until the batter was correct, formed it into a loaf, laid it in another pan, well greased with bacon rind, covered it with the first pan, and set the "oven" well down among coals that he had raked out to one side. He poured a little water into the fry pan, or spider, laid in a lot of chunks and strips of dried-beef or jerky, and salted it and put it on the fire. He took out a handful of coffee beans that had been roasting in the fry pan before he used the pan for the stew (and how good they smelled!), crushed them in a piece of cloth between two stones, and turned them into the coffee-pot.

"You must have been there before," commented Mr. Grigsby.

"Well, I've been a soldier, you know," explained Mr. Adams. "This is soldiers' fare; that's all."

"Strangers, you're new to the diggin's, I reckon," asserted a caller, who strolled in and coolly sat down. He was an exceedingly powerful man—as tall as the Frémonter, broad and heavy, a veritable giant. His shaggy whiskers were bright red. He wore a broad-brimmed black hat, below which hung his red hair to mingle with his whiskers; his red shirt was open at the hairy throat, his stained coarse trousers were belted with a piece of rawhide, through which was thrust a knife and pistol, and he was barefooted. He certainly was the biggest and most ferocious-looking man that Charley had ever seen. Yet he acted very harmless.

"Why so?" queried Mr. Adams, examining his bread.

"'Cause you're bread eaters, 'stead o' bein' flap-jackers. By that I take it you've not been up into the flapjack country yon," and he jerked his head in the direction of the foothills and mountains. "When a man makes his squar' meals out o' flapjacks an' sow-belly, then he can call himself a miner."

"You've been there, in the flapjack country, I suppose," invited Mr. Adams.

"Have I, stranger? Wall, I should shout! I was one of the fust into the diggin's after Jim Marshall discivvered color. Fact is, I'm jest down from thar now, only stoppin' hyar at Woodchuck's Delight to rest my feet. They've got rheumatiz powerful bad, wadin' in the water so much."

Charley had noted that many of the men in the camp were barefooted, as if their feet were sore; evidently Woodchuck's Delight was a sort of a resting place.

"How are things at the saw-mill diggin's?" queried Mr. Grigsby.

"Peterin' out, stranger," replied the red-whiskered man. "Quiet as a Quaker Sunday. I was thar about a month ago."

"Is Marshall mining?"

"Not much. He's grumblin', mostly. Thar's a man, who when he struck a big thing jest natter'ly didn't know what to do with it. It made him pore instead o' rich. The rush o' people tromped an' dug all over him, an' he doesn't appear to have enough spunk to stand up for himself. He seems to think he owns the hull country, 'cause he was thar fust, an' 'cordin' to his notion nobody can mine without his leave. But as matter o' fact, he was too blamed slow to locate any claims; an' when the miners agreed to let him have 100 feet, he didn't get to work on it. He seems to expec' the Government to pay him for his discivvery, while he sits 'round waitin' an' grouchin'. But that sort o' thing doesn't go, out hyar, whar every man must look out for himself an' do his part."

"Never heard of a claim called the Golden West, in those parts, did you? A quartz claim?"

"Nary Golden West, stranger; or any other quartz claim; 'cept that thar was a party through on the trail a day or two ago, inquirin' for that same name—the Golden West. But they didn't say whether it was lode or placer."

"Three men, with a bay mule—one man small and dark, long nose?" pursued Mr. Grigsby.

"You've got 'em, stranger."

"Which way were they bound?" asked Mr. Adams.

"I reckon they went on up the American."

Mr. Grigsby and Charley's father exchanged glances; then Mr. Adams spoke quickly, as if to drop the subject.

"Will you have supper with us, sir?" For the bread was done.

"No, thank 'ee; I'm well lined with flapjacks and sowbelly, to last me till mornin'," replied the red-whiskered man. However, he stayed while the party cleaned up everything that Mr. Adams had cooked.

Now it was near the close of twilight; and Charley, fidgeting anxiously, wondered whether he might not try for gold, just once. His father must have read his thoughts, for he said suddenly:

"Get out your pan, Charley, if you want to, and try your luck. We'll tend to the chores."

Charley needed no second bidding. He grabbed the one clean pan, and down to the river he ran. He fancied that he heard the red-whiskered man call after him, with joking advice, and he knew that other campers, whom he passed, laughed at his eagerness; but who could tell — perhaps he would find gold as well as anybody.

The ex-preacher was still there, in his "diggin's," working away.

"Hello!" he welcomed, cheerily. "Come in and spell me. I'm tired. There's your dirt, all ready for you."

Into the shallow ditch jumped Charley, as bold as an old-timer, and scooped some dirt into his pan. The ex-preacher sat down on the side of the ditch and watched him.

"Don't put in too much dirt at once, boy," he cautioned. "Half full is enough. That's right. Now sink it to the rim in the water, and swirl it around and back again, so the current will carry the dirt off. Don't be afraid to keep it moving. That's it. The gold is heavy, you know; the dirt goes and the gold stays behind. Whoa'p! Let's see. No, it's all gone, this time. You've washed the pan clean. Try again. Take things easy."

That proved to be no easy job, though. The pan was large, the dirt and water weighted it down, and as Charley squatted and tried to swirl it around, at just the right level, presently his back and his arms were aching together.

"Slow, now," bade his instructor, becoming interested. "Raise the pan a bit and swash the water — flip it out along with the dirt, a little at a time. Be careful of that black sand — it's heavy and carries the gold. Here; I'll get rid of the sand for you," and taking the pan he cleverly swirled it, occasionally dipping up more water, until the sand had flowed off.

"There you are!" he laughed, gaily thrusting the pan back into Charley's hands. "And there's your color, sure enough. See it? A ten-cent pan, the first time. Good!"

Charley anxiously peered. In the rounded angle of bottom and side, a narrow gleam of yellow! Could it be possible? Yes; there it was, the gold; actually, real gold, and he had washed it — or at least, he had washed most of it.

"Shall I try some more?" he asked, excitedly.

"Sure. Go ahead. We always wash several pans, before we clean up. Now do it all yourself. You know how."

This time Charley succeeded in getting rid of everything but a very little of the sand; and behold, the yellow seam was deeper. After the third pan he could wait no longer; he out with his buckskin sack, and with the point of his knife scooped his gold in. A little sand went along with it, but who cared?

"We'd better quit for the night, I guess," remarked his new friend, who appeared as delighted as he. "I expect you've made as much as half a dollar. Now it's time for tenderfeet to go to bed."

Through the dusk Charley trudged back to the fire, with his pan and his gold, feeling much indeed like a regular Forty-niner.

His father and Mr. Grigsby were sitting by the fire, talking, when in he burst upon them.

"I got some! I got some!" panted Charley.

"Did you? All right. Show up."

"It's in my sack. See?" And Charley "showed." "I didn't stay to pan much. But I learned how."

"A trace of gold, and considerable sand," pronounced Mr. Grigsby. "But that's enough, for a starter—only you want to dry that stuff out, lad, and blow the sand away. Understand?"

"We've decided to push right along, Charley," said his father, just as if he and Mr. Grigsby considered Charley as much of a partner as they were, "up the trail to Marshall's place; then we can turn north for the north branch of the American, or for the Yuba and the Feather beyond. They're all mining districts. Do you agree?"

"I agree," assented Charley. "And whenever we camp we can wash out gold, can't we?"

His father laughed.

"Certainly. By the time the mine is reached, may you'll have filled your sack."

Charley yawned mightily. The future seemed golden bright—yet he felt as though he couldn't keep awake long enough to discuss it. His father yawned; so did Mr. Grigsby; already the majority of the campers were stretched out in their blankets, some of them snoring; and to bed went the Adams party, also.

Charley removed his boots and trousers and flannel shirt; and rolling himself in his army blanket used them as a pillow—the fashionable scheme, he noticed. He was asleep so soon, and slept so "fast," that he was perfectly astonished to wake into daylight and breakfast time.

The camp of Woodchuck's Delight was breaking apart, for a number of its tender-footed inhabitants had started on, up or down the trail. As his father and Mr. Grigsby were packing the burro, the red-whiskered giant of the evening before passed by, and waved an "Adios."

"It's almost time that we met some of the overland crowd, isn't it?" remarked Mr. Adams, as they took up the march, in the same order as before.

"Not quite," answered Mr. Grigsby. "That's a four months' trip, and I don't reckon any of 'em got away much before the middle of April. It'll be two or three weeks or more, yet, when the first of them cross the range."

"Will they all come this way?" appealed Charley. Thirty thousand there were, so people said; and what a procession they would make!

"No. There's that southern trail, around by the Gila, and to San Diego or up through Los Angeles. And the northern trail, to Oregon and then down. But the Eastern papers advised taking the Oregon trail up the Platte and across South Pass beyond Fort Laramie, to Fort Hall; then south to the Mary's River that Frémont named the Humboldt, down the Humboldt to the Sinks, over to the Truckee and across the Sierra to the head of the north fork of the American—the way we came in with Frémont in Forty-five. And there's that other way, about our trail of Forty-four: by the Carson River, which is south of the Truckee, over Carson's Pass of the Sierra, to the South Fork of the American—which would strike down this trail, like as not, to Sacramento. But in my opinion the trail up the Truckee to the North Fork is the best, and the bulk of the people will come that way."

So saying, Mr. Grigsby shouldered his long rifle, and strode out, to lead. Charley occupied the middle, with the burro. His father limped in the rear.

XIX

A GREAT DISCOVERY

Coloma, near to the celebrated Sutter's saw-mill, was about thirty miles on east, up the trail. The trail did not always keep to the American, but diverged from it. However, streams flowing into the American were crossed, and ever the trail waxed more interesting. Several new towns were passed — one, called the Mormon Diggings, was inhabited largely by Mormons from Salt Lake. Here mining was in full blast, with many improved methods, as by "cradles," which were boxes set upon rockers and rocked like a cradle so that the water and sand were flowed out as from a pan; and by long boxes called "Long Toms," set on an incline so that when the water and dirt were flowed down them, their cleats, nailed across the bottom on the inside, caught and held the heavy sand and gold. Then the cleats were cleaned and the gold separated. As further into the foothills the trail led, the more numerous were the miners; and when the first of the mountains were entered, every gulch and ravine held its busy population.

Now the mountains, high and thickly timbered, clustered before and on either side, when, on the afternoon of the second day (for Mr. Adams traveled slowly on account of his lame leg), Mr. Grigsby, ahead, pointed and said:

"There's the saw-mill."

So it was — a large frame building, apparently not all completed, amidst a clearing of stumps, on the edge of a ravine near the foot of a slope. Several log cabins and a number of tents stood near it; and shacks and tents dotted the gullies around. But, as Captain Sutter had said, the mill was not running; and as the red-whiskered man had alleged, the locality was not bustling.

"I expect the place has been all worked out, by the first rush," commented Mr. Grigsby, as he led on, up the well-marked trail.

"This is where the gold was discovered in Forty-eight, is it?" queried Charley's father, as on the edge of the clearing they paused, to take breath, and gaze about them.

"Yes, sir; and unless I'm much mistaken, there's Jim Marshall himself, in front of that cabin."

So saying, followed by his party the Frémonter crossed the clearing, as if making for one of the cabins before whose open door a man was sitting, on a stool. The man appeared scarcely to notice their approach, and barely turned his head when, halting, Mr. Grigsby addressed him.

"How are you, Jim? I met you down at Sutter's, after the war. My name's Grigsby."

"Yes, I remember your being 'round there," responded Mr. Marshall, in a soft, slow drawl, rising to shake hands. "The country wasn't so full, then."

He was a rather tall, well-built man, with long brown beard and slouch hat. He had wide brown eyes, with a sombre gaze in them. In fact, his whole countenance was sober and a bit sullen.

"So you're still at the mill."

"I have been, but I'm going out. There's no place for me here. The man who discovered this gold ain't given an ounce of it," and Mr. Marshall's voice was bitter. "What did I get for all I did when I opened that mill-race? Nothing; not even gratitude. It's Government land, they say, and so the people flock in and take it, and my only chance is to rustle like everybody else. Do you think that's fair? No, sir! If I had my percentage of all the gold being mined around here I'd be a rich man. Instead, they give me a hundred feet, and expect me to dig like the rest. Bah! I'll starve, first."

Although Mr. Marshall was trying to make this a tale of woe, Charley, for one, could not quite see the reasonableness in it.

"Well, Jim," hastily soothed Mr. Grigsby, "this is a country of hustle, and most of us have to look out for ourselves. You were here first, and I suppose people figured on your making the most of opportunity. Anyway, I wish you'd take us over to the mill-race and show these two partners of mine just where you discovered the gold. We aren't going to stay, but we'd like to see that much."

"Yes, I can do that," assented Mr. Marshall. "Leave your animal here, if you want to. There aren't many white people about" (and he spoke bitterly, again) "to steal it."

Charley tied the burro to the cabin. Mr. Marshall led the way over to the mill, which was abandoned and idle, and paused on the brink of a wide ravine that extended back to the mill wheel.

The ravine was ragged and torn, its bottom bare to the rocks and its sides gashed by countless holes. A number of Chinamen and Indians were working in it, scraping about and filling pans and wicker baskets with loose dirt, which they washed in the stream trickling through. But there were no white men.

"That was the tail-race," explained Mr. Marshall, "which led off the water after it had passed under the wheel. After we got the mill to going, about the middle of January, last year, we found the tail-race wasn't big enough to carry off the water fast and make a current that would turn the wheel. So I threw the wheel out of gear, one night, and lifted the head-gate of the race full open, to flow a hard stream through and wash the tail-race deeper. Next morning early, which was January 24, I went down with Weimer (you know Weimer, Mr. Grigsby; he served in the Frémont battalion during the conquest), who was helping me, to see what the water had done. We shut it off first, of course, above. Well, the tail-race certainly had been scoured a good bit, and we were looking in, as we walked, congratulating ourselves on the job, when I saw a sparkle of yellow on a flat bed-rock. I went down in and picked it up, and I was sure it was gold. I sent an Indian back to the men's cabin for a tin plate. I didn't want to say much about the find till I'd made certain that it wasn't copper, but during the day Weimer and I searched about and found a little more. We tried it out with potash in Mrs.

Weimer's soap kettle, and it didn't tarnish. The other men got excited, and the next day started to poking about on their own account, in the rain. I took what I had down to the fort, and the captain and I locked ourselves in and tested it with nitric acid, weighed it, pounded it, did everything we could think of, and made dead certain that gold it was. Next day the captain himself came up to the mill, and we all found gold. It was everywhere. Of course that set us up in great shape, but the captain made us promise to keep the matter a secret for six weeks until he had finished a flour-mill that he was building at the fort, or else he wouldn't be able to get anybody to work for him at wages. But some of the men showed their dust down at the store at the fort, buying goods, and the cat was out of the bag. Everybody deserted the old captain, his grist-mill hasn't been finished to this day, his crops weren't reaped, his saw-mill property was overrun with a regular army, some of the people tried to save a bed of gravel for him, but that's gone now, neither his rights or mine are respected, I don't own an ounce of gold and am busted, and he'll be busted soon. There's no gratitude in this country," and Mr. Marshall turned gloomily away.

"There doesn't seem to be much show here for mining; the whole country's been turned over," commented Mr. Adams, as they gazed about. "But I'm glad to have seen the spot where the first gold was found in California."

"By the way, Jim," spoke the Frémonter, "are there any quartz workings around here? Never heard of a claim called the Golden West, did you?"

Mr. Marshall shook his head, in his gloomy fashion.

"Not on the South Branch of the American, either fork. It's all placer work yet. That's the quickest. Lodes don't pay; they need machinery, and nobody wants to wait for machinery. But I've heard they're beginning to find lodes over in the Nevada country, beyond the upper North Branch. Several parties on their way to the dry diggin's of Rough and Ready spoke about quartz outcrops over yonder somewhere on the North Branch."

"Yes, we thought we'd go over that way ourselves," answered Mr. Grigsby.

"Whereabouts is Rough and Ready, Mr. Marshall?" asked Charley's father—much to Charley's relief, who wanted to know, himself.

"It's a dry diggin's camp, near to the Nevada dry diggin's, in Grass Valley between the Bear and the Yuba. That's all I know," responded Mr. Marshall, as if to imply that it was all he cared, too!

The directions seemed very indefinite, in such a big country, but Mr. Grigsby appeared to be impressed by something or other in Mr. Marshall's words, for he was plunged into a brown study until the party had left Mr. Marshall sitting gloomily as before and were resuming the march. Then, out of earshot of the cabins and mill, he suddenly slapped his buckskin thigh and uttered an exclamation.

"By jings!" he said. "I have it—and those three fellows had it, too. We've overrun 'em. They've turned off, below, and I'll wager they're making for that smudge! Remember that smudge on the map—what looked to be another 'G. H.,' in capital letters? Well, sir, if that sign isn't 'G. W.' instead of 'G. H.' I'll miss my guess. 'G. W.'—'Golden West'! How does that strike you? It's yonder in the new quartz country, you see."

Charley stared, agape. The idea was stupendous. Oh, if only they had that map, again, so as to re-examine it.

"Why—I shouldn't wonder if you were right, Grigsby," agreed his father, weighing the matter. "Then we ought to get over there as quick as we can."

"I know I'm right," asserted the Frémonter. "Feel it in my bones. And away we go, as straight as we can travel."

A long, long tramp across a wild country it was, now, upon which the tall Frémonter piloted the way. He seemed to know where he was going and what he was doing; and Charley and his father could only trust in his guidance. Up hill and down, through timber and brush, sometimes on a trail and sometimes not, ever making northward, on they went, with the burro the nimblest of all, and Mr. Adams having hard work, occasionally, with his lame leg. But wherever they passed, no matter how rough and high the country, they encountered miners like themselves, digging and washing and searching, in camp or on the march.

But not a word more, of the Jacobs party, or of the Golden West mine.

Mr. Grigsby appeared to be looking for certain landmarks, ahead. It was at the end of two weeks of travel and camp when they three, following a pack trail across a timbered ridge, suddenly emerged into a beautiful vista of valley and snowy range, to the north and east; the course of a rushing river, and the tents of another mining camp.

"There she is!" cheered the Frémonter, swinging his hat. "There's the trail where Frémont and we fellows came in, the second time, winter of Forty-five. Yon river's the North Branch of the American. I remember that gap, there. What that camp is I don't know; but we'll find out."

"This is an emigrant trail, then, too, isn't it?" queried Charley's father.

"It'll be the main emigrant trail, or I'm much mistaken."

"I don't see any emigrants, though," puffed Charley, as down they hastened, for the camp. He was wondering about Billy Walker.

"No; there haven't many passed yet, that's certain," answered the Frémonter. "But the rush must be about due."

"What camp's this?" he hailed, as they passed a party of miners delving and washing in a little ravine.

"This is the Shirt-tail Diggin's, stranger, where everybody's happy and the goose hangs high."

Shirt-tail Diggin's consisted of a collection of tents and of lean-to shacks made of boughs and canvas, three or four log cabins, and a store, scattered along the side of the valley, amidst great trees. To the east showed the bluish gap, of which Mr. Grigsby had spoken, in the hills, and beyond the hills was the snowy range. Through the valley coursed the river—the North Branch of the American, according to Mr. Grigsby; and in the river shallows and along the banks and in ravines and ditches on both sides, up the slopes themselves, with pick and spade and pan and cradle were working the miners.

As with his father and Mr. Grigsby and the burro he drew near, Charley was surprised to hear a cheer—and another, and another, as if in greeting. Why was that? Was it a joke? But see! Arms were pointing, hats were waving, and shout joined with shout:

"Emigrants in sight! Here they come—the overlanders! Tumble out, boys!"

XX

ANOTHER GREAT DISCOVERY

Sure enough! Following a trail out from among the timbered slopes to the east, there emerged from the gap a white-topped wagon—and another, and a succession of dots of other vehicles and of people horseback, until a long line was winding down through the green and brown. Yes, emigrants! Charley had seen such wagons, and even such a procession, before, in Missouri; but this was different, because these wagons and people had come clear across the 2,000 miles of plain and mountain and desert, from the Missouri River! Think of that!

From their ditches and ravines out clambered the miners all, to wipe their brows and gaze and cheer. And on weaved the line, until the people afoot, also—even women, and some children—could be seen trudging beside the wagons.

Riding at a walk, the horsemen who led the procession as if picking out the trail approached slowly, while the camp waited. The nearer the procession came, the worse for wear it looked: the white-topped wagons (there were only a few) were torn and battered, the other vehicles were only make-shifts, cut down from the originals, the horses, mules and oxen were very thin, and the people themselves were gaunt and ragged and pitiable. As brown as any Arabs and as bearded as the miners were the leading horsemen.

"Howdy?" greeted one, with a nod. "How far to Sutter's?"

"Seventy miles," responded a score of voices. "Where you from?"

"The Missouri River."

"When did you leave?"

"Last week in April."

The first of the wagons came lumberingly creaking in. It was drawn by two yoke of lean spotted oxen. The wheels had been wrapped with rawhide, for repairs, and the canvas top was torn and discolored and askew. From the puckered front peered a woman and two children; the man of the family was walking wearily beside, swinging an ox-goad.

"Howdy, strangers?" he hailed, as he halted. "Are these the Californy diggin's?"

"Is this Californy?" put in the woman, quaveringly.

"You bet your bottom dollar, friends," was the hearty answer. "This is Californy, and these are the Shirt-tail Diggin's, the best on 'arth."

"Haven't got any flour for trade, have you?" queried the man.

"Nary flour, nary anything for trade, stranger, but I'll give you a sack o' the best flapjack flour that ever came out a store."

"Hooray for the first woman in Shirt-tail Diggin's!" rose the cheer, and the crowd surged forward excitedly.

"No, strangers, I don't want your flour for nothin'," said the man, as if a little alarmed. "I'm busted for money, but I'll trade ye, and trade ye fair."

"Where's the gold? I'd like to see some gold," ventured the woman—a little alarmed at the uproar.

"Pass the hat, boys," ordered the spokesman of the camp; he fished out his buckskin sack, shook a generous portion into the top of his old hat, and started the hat through the crowd. Somebody hustled back with flour, somebody else with bacon; Shirt-tail camp fairly fought for the privilege of handing these and other supplies in, to the wagon, and there was added a buckskin sack half full of dust.

"Oh, we can't take these," appealed the woman, shrinking. She wasn't handsome, just now; she was thin, haggard and tanned, and wore a calico gown; but to the miners she was a woman, just the same, and Charley found himself wishing she were his mother.

"Take 'em! Throw 'em in, boys, anyway. They're for the first woman in Shirt-tail. Hooray! Hooray!"

"Charley Adams! Oh, Charley!" cried a voice, piercing the crazy clamor. Charley whirled and looked. It was—why, Billy Walker! Of course! Billy Walker! He had forgotten about Billy, for the moment—in fact, he hadn't recognized him.

But the remainder of the emigrant train had drawn near, bunching as it halted, and on foot Billy was hurrying through the crowd, followed by his father. Charley gave a shrill whoop of joy, and with a run he and Billy grabbed one another and hugged and danced. Then they drew off to shake hands; then Charley shook hands with Mr. Walker—and Mr. Adams shook hands with Billy and his father; then Charley and Billy grinningly sized one another up.

"You look like a sure-'nough miner," said Billy.

"And you look like a sure-'nough overlander," said Charley.

"What have you got? Have you found much gold? Are these the regular diggin's? How long've you been here? Have you made your pile? Were you seasick any? Did it storm at sea? What's the name of this place? Where's the Sacramento? Did you stay in San Francisco? How much gold can I dig in a day?" propounded Billy, all at once.

"I've found some gold—I've panned out half a sackful. We haven't been here long. Wasn't seasick a bit—scarcely. These are the Shirt-tail diggin's," replied Charley. "What kind of time did you have? Did you kill any Injuns? Do you have to go on? Why don't you stop now and mine? Is this all your crowd? Did you have a lot of fun? Do you want me to show you how to pan?"

"Gee, we had some fun, but we had an awful time, mostly," declared Billy, soberly. And he looked it. His flannel shirt was torn and faded, his trousers were patched with buckskin, his boots were scuffed through and resoled with rawhide, the knife in his belt had been ground down to half a blade, and his rifle was scarred and the stock spliced with rawhide at the grasp. Besides that, his face and hands were brown as brown, and scratched, he was thin as a rail, but his eyes were bright and steady and he evidently was as hard as nails. "We broke our wagon and lost our horses—they just fell down and died in their tracks—and had to leave half our outfit out in the desert. But our company's first in; there are about 200 of us—and there are about 30,000 following, strung out all the way from here to the Rocky Mountains, I guess. That's a tough trail, across the desert from Fort Hall; but we made it, though the Digger Injuns 'most got our scalps, once. Part of the crowd's coming in by way of Oregon; and that's a harder trail still, we hear. Some of our own company, branched off, other side of the Sierra, for the Carson River, but we struck up the Truckee and over to the American River this way. Don't know what dad and I'll do now. We ought to get some grub and other stuff. I'd give ten dollars for a loaf of bread."

"Huh, I guess you would," retorted Charley. "Do you know what flour's selling at, in California? Sixty dollars a barrel. Besides, we don't eat bread, up here. We eat flapjacks."

"Jiminy!" sighed Billy, his mouth watering as he smacked his dry lips. "That sounds mighty good, just the same. Honest, I've been living on old ox so long I've nearly forgotten what flapjack tastes like. I used to have 'em back home, though. Remember those old Liz, our cook, made? Yum! Just the same," he added, defiantly, "I'm glad I came. I wouldn't have missed that trip for anything."

"You bunk in along with us, and we'll give you all the flapjacks you can eat," urged Charley. "Dad can make the best you ever tasted. And I'll show you how to pan out the gold, too. Shucks! It's easy. Some days you'll just simply scoop it up, and think you're going to be rich right away—and next day you won't find color, even. But it's fun. Wish you and your father would throw in with us. There's no use in going on down to Sacramento; prices of everything are awful, there, and at San Francisco, too. Ask him, won't you?"

But Billy didn't need to ask, for Mr. Grigsby had been introduced to Mr. Walker by Charley's father, and they three were talking together earnestly.

The upshot was (to Charley's and Billy's delight) that the two parties joined.

"I've told Mr. Walker that we're on the search for a certain quartz proposition," announced Charley's father, to his partner Charley, "and if we find it we'll probably need good help to develop it. And there's nobody we'd rather have in with us than him and Billy. Now if we five can't make our way, I'll miss my guess. What do you think about it?"

Think about it? Charley and Billy uttered another war-whoop, together, and in a mutual hug gave a kick-up Indian dance—but Shirt-tail Diggin's was used to this sort of thing.

"I'd better hustle out and see what I can add to the outfit," said Mr. Walker; and accompanied by Mr. Grigsby, away he went.

He succeeded in buying a horse from one of the emigrants, and in picking up here and there a few supplies. By the time that the horse and burro were packed, and the start onward might be made, the emigrant train also was again in motion, and the miners were descending again into their ravines and ditches. The great majority of the emigrants continued eastward, bound for "the Sacramenty," there to renew their strength. A few stayed in camp at Shirt-tail. But a weary lot they all were—they and their animals; weary and seemingly bewildered now that they actually had arrived in the famed gold fields of California.

Mr. Grigsby set the pace, as usual, for his party. Straightaway he led, down the first ravine out of Shirt-tail, up the other side, and into a draw or pass which wound among the hills. The miners whom they passed, at work, gazed curiously; and one or two hailed with—"Where you bound, strangers? What've you heard? Another strike?" But the party only smiled and shook their heads.

Charley and Billy trudged together, leading burro and horse.

"Did you shoot anything on the way across?" asked Charley.

"You bet. Shot an antelope. Killed him first crack. He was mighty good eating, too. But there wasn't much game. Too many people on the trail."

"Did you kill any bear?"

"No. Didn't even see one. We were in too big a hurry to stop to hunt much, anyway, and when we needed meat the worst, we couldn't find it. That was on the desert between Salt Lake and these mountains. Where are we going now? Do you know?"

"Over to a camp called Rough and Ready, in Grass Valley, I guess."

"What's there?"

"It's dry diggin's, mostly, but it's more of a quartz country than this. We're on the track of a big quartz claim. You remember that sick man I found in St. Louis?" Billy nodded. "Well, he told us about a claim of his; he sort of gave it to dad and me. We aren't telling anybody else, but now you're a partner, I can tell you that much."

"Jiminy!" exclaimed Billy. "Hope we find it."

"Well, if we don't we can wash out a lot of gold, anyhow."

"What are dry diggings, Charley?"

"They're diggin's in dry ground, where you have to bring in the water some way. Wet diggin's are placers in the beds of streams where you're in the water already. Shirt-tail was wet diggin's. They're the hardest because your feet are soaked and get sore, and you catch rheumatism and fever and everything.

"What's quartz diggin's, then?"

"Aw, those aren't diggin's, exactly," informed the wise Charley. "Quartz is a rock that helps form a lode where the gold is carried, first, before it's crumbled out by the weather and is washed down with gravel and sand to make the placer beds. You dig the placer bed, but you have to use a crow-bar and powder on lodes, and break them to pieces. Then you have to crush the pieces and wash the gold out or unite it with mercury and get it that way. Lode mining takes machinery, if it's done right, and it's expensive; but it lasts longer, if it's any good, because you can follow the lode for miles. Placer mining is sort of luck."

"If we find a lode, what'll we do with it, I wonder," pursued Billy. "We haven't any machinery, or much powder, either."

"We'll get the machinery, all right, if we find the spot," asserted Charley. "My father and Mr. Grigsby are going into this thing scientifically; that's the only way to make a success; your father's no slouch, either.

"I should say not," agreed Billy, loyally. "I guess we all together can make a mine pay, if anybody can."

"This is awful rough traveling, isn't it!" remarked Charley, suddenly. And Billy answered: "Kind of; but we were over worse. Had to haul the oxen and horses up and down by ropes." Nevertheless, the going was, as Charley had said, "awful." Steep slope after steep slope blocked the way; the brush and timber grew thick; sometimes large rocks interposed; and when the party weren't sliding they were climbing, dragging the puffing pack animals. But the trail that had been taken always led on.

Camp was made beside a spring, in a little flat or cup surrounded by timber over which peeked the snow-caps of the main range. For supper Billy had his flapjacks, as Charley had promised; and how he did eat! Nobody's appetite was especially poor, however.

"Now you're a Forty-niner, sure," informed Charley, to his fellow partner. "You've got a fresh lining in your stomach. When we get settled I'm going to practice till I can toss a flapjack up the cabin chimney and catch it coming down on the outside. See?"

Up hill and down was it the next day, again. Shortly after noon they came to a high ridge, covered with brush in spots, and in spots bare. The three men climbed on, for a view ahead, but Charley and Billy branched off, to a place that looked lower. Then, suddenly, Charley caught sight of it—a great grayish-brown beast, lumbering along a slope just ahead, and making for the top not far before. Sometimes he was in the brush, sometimes in the open; but Charley knew him at once.

"Billy!" he cried, excited. "There's a bear! Shoot! Quick!"

"Where?"

"Right in front of us! See? Hurry, or he'll be over the top."

"That's not a bear. That's a cow."

"Cow your grandmother! 'Tis, too! A grizzly! They grow as big as cows in this country. Aren't you going to shoot? Give me that gun."

The burro and the horse had seen or smelled, for they were pulling back and snorting, ears pricked, eyes Staring. Billy stepped on his lead rope, and leveled his gun like lightning.

Billy stepped on his lead rope and

leveled his gun like lightning

"Bang!" The big bear gave a jump aside and turning sharp lumbered faster, straight for the top. "Bang!" spoke Billy's patent repeater, again. And just as the bear disappeared over the top, "Bang!" shot Billy, a third time. But the bear was gone.

"Did I hit him? Did I hit him?" panted Billy. "Whoa, there, you horse. Did I hit him?"

"Don't think so," panted Charley, just as excited. "Maybe you did, though. I heard the bullets sing, anyway. One must have struck rock. Come on; let's go over. Tie your horse. How many shots you got left?

"Four."

In a jiffy they tied the horse and burro to the brush, and away they pelted, lunging and staggering up the slope, to the place where they had seen the bear.

He wasn't there now, and he wasn't anywhere in sight, either; and though they searched closely, they could not find even a drop of blood.

"I guess I missed him clean," confessed Billy, ruefully. "I was in too big a hurry."

"It's hard shooting up hill; and he was running, too," sympathized Charley, "Let's see where the bullets hit."

That would be some satisfaction; so they searched more. Presently Billy yelped:

"Here's where one hit. It knocked a big chunk out of the rock. Funny looking rock." And then he exclaimed: "Come over, Charley. Quick! The rock's got a lot of yellow in it!"

"What color rock?" demanded Charley.

"Whitish."

"Let's see."

Billy pointed, and he also handed up the piece that the bullet had knocked loose. Yes, the fresh side of the piece was white and glistening—and the whiteness was mottled with dull yellow. The scar in the rocky ridge also was white and yellow mottled.

"Is it gold, Charley?" gasped Billy, anxiously.

"I don't know, for sure," said Charley, trying not to be foolish. "But I think this is quartz, all right enough; and if that yellow's soft enough to be scraped with a knife blade it's liable to be gold." He drew out his knife from his belt and scraped at the yellow. Where the yellow was thickest it could— yes, it could be scraped in tiny shavings. Billy was peering close; and he was breathing so fast that, Charley afterward declared, he could be heard half a mile. But no matter now.

"It's gold!" Charley's voice came tense and stammery. "Anyway, it's soft."

"Do you suppose the whole rock's full of gold?"

"Maybe. Let's knock off some more. Maybe the whole hill's full of gold—all the rock! Hurrah!"

"Hurrah! Maybe it'll get solider, deeper we go," cheered Billy, hopefully.

Charley hammered with his boot heel and pried with his knife; Billy hammered with his rifle-butt; and when they knocked off even a chip, it showed traces of gold. Why, wherever the rock stuck up, making little humps and furrows, it seemed to be the one kind: quartz-blotched and yellow-spotted.

"Hurrah!" again cheered Charley. "We ought to stake off claims. Who found it? I saw the bear."

"And I shot the bullet," returned Billy.

"Well, there's enough for all, anyway. It'll belong to the whole party. What'll we call it? Grizzly? Lucky Bullet?"

They were so busy searching and gloating that they had forgotten the pack animals below and even the whereabouts of the men of the party. On a sudden, as if replying to Charley's queries, Billy cried out excitedly:

"Somebody else has been up here! Here's a little pile of loose rock, and a stake with a board sign on it, that says——shucks. Can't quite make it out. Come on and help me."

Over scrambled Charley, to where Billy was crouching and peering at a weathered board set up in a shallow hollow. Billy's voice rang triumphantly.

"'Golden West,' it says. 'Golden West Mine.' And——'I lay claim to as much of this lode running east and west as is allowed by miners' law. Tom Jones. August 22, 1848.'"

"Golden West!" exclaimed Charley, crashing and sliding to Billy's side. "Hurrah! That's the mine we've been looking for, Billy! It's our mine. It's the one——"

"That's where you're mistaken, bub," interrupted a new voice, speaking cold and distinctly. "Now you pile out of there, and git! Don't come back again, either."

Looking up, startled (as did Billy likewise), Charley faced the long-nosed man and his two companions gazing in upon them, over the brushy rim of the hollow and the muzzles of three guns.

XXI

MINERS' JUSTICE

"No talk, now," continued the long-nosed man, with a hard smile slightly curving his thin black moustache. "Drop that rifle, you other kid. Back up the side of that hollow, both of you, and scoot. You're in the wrong pew. This happens to be our claim. See?"

Billy was so surprised and bewildered at the sudden attack that he simply couldn't say a word. He only looked, with mouth open, at Charley; and then at the men. He and Charley slowly backed away, up the other slope of the hollow. Charley saw that the three men were breathing hard, as if they had just arrived, in a hurry. He was so mad that he, too, scarcely could speak.

"'T isn't either your mine," he retorted hotly. "That's a lie, and you know it. You're only trying to steal it. It was given to me, and we've found it again, and we can prove it. You wait till we get our crowd."

The three behind the gun-muzzles laughed.

"The best thing for your crowd to do is to stay out of shooting distance," answered the long-nosed man. "We've got the mine, and the documents to prove it's ourn. Those are two p'ints hard to beat, bub."

"You haven't any right, just the same," retorted Charley, furious. "You stole those papers, but you needn't think you can steal the mine. You wait."

"We'll wait," said the long-nosed man, grimly.

"Come on," bade Charley, choking with wrath and almost with tears, to the astonished Billy. "Let's get our animals and find our partners. Those fellows needn't think they can bluff us."

"Who are they, anyhow?" gasped Billy, as he and Charley went plunging down the ridge. "Is that their mine? Did they put that sign up? I thought we found it. We were there first, weren't we?"

"It's a long story, Billy; I'll tell you later," panted Charley, hurrying. "But it's our mine, all right—same one that was given to dad and me last spring. Remember I spoke about it? And we're going to have it, too. Come on."

"And I'm going to have my rifle. They needn't think they can keep that, either," uttered Billy, waxing pugnacious.

"I see the rest of 'em," announced Charley.

"They're making for the pack animals." And there, threading their way through the brush near the foot of the ridge, beyond the burro and the horse, were the figures of Mr. Adams and Mr. Walker and the tall Frémonter. A fourth figure was with them—he looked like a miner.

Charley and Billy waved and shouted, and hurried.

"Hello! Were you doing that shooting?" demanded Charley's father, as they approached. "What did you see?"

"A big bear," wheezed Charley. "But we found the mine—the Golden West. And the long-nosed man took it away from us."

"There are three of 'em," joined in Billy. "They pointed guns at us and made us get out."

"Where?"

"Up there on top of the ridge. Billy's bullet knocked out a piece of gold quartz—see?" and Charley extended the fragment that he had been clutching tightly. "Then Billy found a sign that said 'Golden West' and is signed by Tom Jones, for a claim; and when we were looking at it that Jacobs gang surprised us and told us to 'git.' Let's go back up there. They made Billy leave his gun, too."

The four men uttered exclamations, while looking at each other; Mr. Grigsby thoughtfully stroked his beard, and gazed at the crest of the ridge. Charley was certain that the heads of the Jacobs party were peeking over the brush, there.

The piece of quartz passed around, and was examined. Most excited of all seemed to be the miner—for he certainly was a miner—who had been added to the party: a short, heavy-set man, very shaggy and weather-worn. He carried knife and pistol, and appeared to be good reinforcement.

"Did you get that up on that hill?" he demanded. "How much more is there of it? It's gold quartz, sure as shootin'—an' plaguey rich. Say—I want some o' that, myself. Hooray! Come on, all o' ye, 'fore the news gets out. You're fust, I'm second."

"You say you found the Golden West mine, and the Jacobs party ran you out, Charley?" asked Mr. Adams.

"Yes, sir. Didn't we, Billy?" And Billy nodded.

"Are they up there now?"

"Yes, sir. See 'em. They've got guns, too, besides Billy's."

"Looks as though we were in for a fight, then; eh, Grigsby?" remarked Mr. Adams, flushing. "We'll not stand to be robbed in any such fashion. Let's go and see what they have to say."

"The way I size those gentry up," said Mr. Grigsby, "they're there and we're here, and they won't let us get much closer. Maybe we can starve 'em out, though," and he surveyed the ridge.

"I'm with you, in anything you want to do," spoke Mr. Walker. "How many are there? Three?"

"Jumped yore claim, have they?" asked the miner.

"They certainly have."

"You're shore it's yourn?"

"We can prove it."

"Then best thing you can do is to prove it to the boys at Rough an' Ready," pursued the miner. "Thar's been too much claim-jumpin', in this valley; no-one's property is safe, by thunder. You come along to Rough an' Ready, an' we'll see if 't isn't time for law an' order to take a hand in this game. Yore claim won't peter out while you're gone—not if it's any good; an' whilst I believe in fightin' when you have to, thar's no use sheddin' blood if thar's an easier way 'round to get the same thing."

"What do you say?" invited Mr. Adams, of the two other men. As for Charley, he saw that his father was ready to fight or not; he wasn't afraid, was this tall, soldierly veteran who had served with Scott in Mexico.

"I prefer getting our rights without any blood on them, if we can, of course," answered Mr. Walker. "I hate to start in in a new country with a fight of any kind. But you can count on me, whatever you decide to do."

"Let's try miners' law, first, then," spoke Mr. Grigsby, shortly. "If that doesn't help, we'll have to protect ourselves the next best way, even to shooting. But our rights we'll have, or bust."

"Very well," said Mr. Adams. "Rough and Ready's four miles. I'll take the boys, so they can tell their story, and our friend here; and you and Walker stay with the animals and keep an eye on the ridge. We'll be back as soon as we can. Come on, lads," and away he strode, with the miner, and with Charley and Billy working hard to keep up.

They passed between the Golden West ridge and another, and emerged into a wide pleasant valley which the miner said was called Grass Valley. Down the valley they hastened, and in about an hour the miner, who acted as guide, pointed ahead, with the remark:

"Thar's Rough an' Ready—the best camp in the hills. Now we'll see what's what."

Miners were busily at work, digging and heaping piles of dirt from the ravines and the flats; and before, against a hill slope, partly in the pines and partly in the open, were tents and huts. As they hustled up, the miner was greeted right and left.

"Hello, Eph. What's your hurry?"

"Injuns after you?"

"What's the news from yonder?"

"Thought you'd left the country."

"How are things at your diggin's?"

"Cleaned up your pile already?"

"By the way you're travelin' you must have made a strike, or else you're after grub!"

"Strike!" growled Eph. "You bet thar is, an' somethin' to pay, too. Come on, you fellows. I want everybody in the camp. We're goin' to hold a regular town meetin'."

Rough and Ready was another conglomeration of tents new and old, bough lean-tos, and shacks covered with canvas. In front of a tent labeled, rudely: "New York Generul Store," Eph halted and uttered a resounding whoop. The miners began to gather; there were other whoops, and cheers, and the gay beating of gold pans, like gongs, until it seemed as though the whole camp was on hand. A booted, whiskered, "rough and ready" crowd they made, too.

"Well, Eph, what's the trouble? Somebody got the dead-wood on you?" demanded a strapping big miner in torn red shirt and prodigious boots. He seemed to be a sort of a leader.

"These boys and I——" began Mr. Adams; but Eph interrupted.

"I'll do the talkin', fust. You save yore powder. This gentleman an' these two lads belong to a party I met up with at t'other end the valley. They were prospectin' for a claim they'd heared of. The two boys located it atop a ridge, yon, an' as I understand, they were actually on the ground, sizin' it up, when another party jumped 'em, at the p'int o' guns made 'em vamoose, an' proceeded to hold down the claim themselves. Show yore sample, boys. What do you think o' that, men?"

Charley handed out the sample. As it passed around among the craning heads and hairy fists, it created tremendous excitement.

"Whar'd you get it?"

"Gold quartz, or I'm a sinner!"

"That'll run a thousand dollars to the pan, I bet ye."

"Hooray for the new diggin's! Come on, fellows. I'm off."

"Hold on, thar," bade the red-shirted man, stopping what would have been a stampede. "That doesn't settle the matter. Eph, here, has called a meetin' for a purpose; haven't you, Eph?"

"You're talkin'," assured Eph. "It's time claim-jumpin' 'round these diggin's has got to stop. If this gentleman can prove up for his party that they've fust rights to that discivvery, we ought to go back thar an' show those other fellows that Rough an' Ready is takin' a stand for law an' order."

"Hooray!" cheered the crowd, which seemed ripe for anything new.

"You say you've got fust location on that quartz claim?" inquired the red-shirted man, of Mr. Adams.

"Yes, sir," replied Charley's father, promptly. "By two reasons. It was given us by the former owner, in St. Louis; and these boys, who are partners in our party, found it again on their own hook."

"What might be the name of that claim, then, stranger, if it was given to you?" asked somebody else.

"The Golden West," answered Mr. Adams. "It was given to us by a man whom we befriended in St. Louis. We had the documents to prove it, but they were stolen by the very gang who drove the boys away. Even that doesn't matter, though, for they found it, stake and all, and — —"

"What did you say the name is?" demanded half a score of voices.

"The Golden West."

"Fetch the woman," cried the voices, now; and the demand rose to a clamor: "Fetch the woman."

The crowd laughed and jostled expectantly; and presently they parted, to give passage to a young woman, ceremoniously conducted by two of the miners, their hats off. And who should follow her, but Mr. Motte—the young man who had been left behind at Panama!

"Strangers," announced the red-shirted spokesman for the camp, to Mr. Adams, "if you've found the Golden West, here's the owner of it, an' I reckon she'll thank you for your trouble. The hull camp's' back of her, so you'd better talk peaceable. Ain't that so, boys?"

"You bet!" came the resounding cheer.

"Well, if that's the case, of course — —" said Mr. Adams, uncertainly, removing his hat, while the young woman, in sunbonnet and neat calico dress, appeared much embarrassed. Charley and Billy stood with mouth open at the unexpected turn of events. But Mr. Motte pressed forward, extending glad hand.

"Hello," spoke Mr. Adams. "How'd you get here?" He shook hands with Mr. Motte, and so did Charley, and so did Billy, although he didn't know exactly why.

"Yes, sir, here I am, thanks to your ticket. And here's my wife, too. This is the gentleman who gave me the ticket from Panama, Mary."

"Hooray!" cheered the ready miners.

"How long have you been here?" asked Mr. Adams.

"Two or three days. I've been laid up (and indeed he looked thin), but I'm all right now. The camp's been mighty kind to us. They tell me you've found the Golden West quartz claim. Is that so?"

"Yes, sir. These boys found it; three rascals who have dogged us from New Orleans (one of them clear from St. Louis), have jumped it. Now I understand you or your wife have prior rights to it. How about that, sir?"

"To tell the truth, I think that probably we have," answered Mr. Motte; "but you shan't lose out, anyway. Not after you helped me along the way you did, with that ticket. No, sir. Shall he, Mary?" And the young woman shook her head. Mr. Motte continued, while the camp listened intently. "As I've explained to these men my uncle—or my wife's uncle, rather, whose name was Tom Jones—wrote us a letter last year telling us to come out and giving us the Golden West quartz claim that he had just located in this region, somewhere. He said it was a bonanza, with plenty for all. The letter didn't get to us for six months, and that's the last we heard from him, though we wrote him we were coming as soon as we could. I've the letter, as this camp knows."

"You're talkin'," approved the crowd, emphatically.

"So, thanks to you, sir, we got this far, and then we ran up against the fact that nobody seemed to know anything about a Golden West quartz claim. My uncle was in the diggings early, and he prospected alone, evidently, and nobody knew him, except a few people remembered his name—and one man did recollect something about a quartz claim from which there were samples. My uncle was a queer, quiet sort of a man—never talked much."

"Let the stranger tell his story, now," bade the red-shirt.

So Mr. Adams did, from the beginning in St. Louis, to the apparent end here; and he concluded:

"Your right to the mine evidently is prior to ours, sir, and we wouldn't think of contesting it—especially not with a woman," and he bowed to Mrs. Motte, who flushed, ill at ease among all these men.

"You're O. K.!" approved the crowd. "Especially not with a woman, you say; an' with the only woman in Rough an' Ready. Hooray!"

"But you've made a long trip," protested young Mr. Motte, also flushing. "You've found the claim for us, and if it hadn't have been for you I might have been in Panama yet, either alive or dead. So I don't agree——"

"Let's act fust an' talk afterward," interrupted the red-shirt. "Fust thing is to oust those thar claim-jumpers yonder, for the good of the camp, an' to put the little lady in possession. Get yore tools an' weapons, boys, an' come on."

With a great shout the crowd rushed hither-thither; and away they all went, streaming through the valley, laden with picks and spades and crow-bars and guns, hustling Mr. and Mrs. Motte and Mr. Adams and Charley and Billy along in their midst. They acted like a lot of school-boys on a frolic, but there was an undercurrent of earnestness.

To the three men on the ridge it must have looked as though an army was advancing; and Charley could see Mr. Walker and the Frémonter staring from their posts whence they were keeping watch on the claim. Well, this was pretty tough: to have traveled clear from St. Louis, and spent a lot of money, and acted honestly all the way through; and then only to have put somebody else in possession of the mine.

"Thar's the place—straight ahead on top the ridge," directed the miner Eph, who was leading with the red-shirt. And following these two, up the slope trooped the company.

The heads of the three men in the hollow poked up over the rim, as their owners surveyed, probably in amazement, the onslaught. The muzzles of the guns protruded, also, but the big red-shirt made no account of them.

"Come out o' thar!" he roared, in a voice that might have been heard a mile. "Drop those weapons; they'll do you no good. So come out o' thar, an' come quick. Don't you know enough to make room for a lady?"

Up slowly rose the long-nosed man, and emerged, glowering but weaponless, his hands in the air; and emerged likewise his two partners. The long-nosed man tried to bluff his way.

"What's the meaning of this attack?" he demanded. "Where's your warrant for it? Would you drive three honest men off ground to which they've got rights according to evidence? Won't you consider our documents in this matter?"

"Shot-gun rights don't go any longer in Grass Valley, mister," roared the red-shirt. "If you'd had the right sort o' rights you'd have proved 'em peaceable. Besides, with yore docyments—which you stole—you're barkin' up the wrong tree. Here's the true an' ondisputed owner of this claim—the heiress of the Golden West, not to speak of bein' the only woman in this district an' entitled to the best that goes. See? Get down in thar, lady; Eph, you do yoreself the honor of escortin' her, an' read what it says on that thar stake. If it says Golden West an' is signed Tom Jones, that settles the matter, pronto."

"But the claim was abandoned. It hasn't been worked for a year," spoke up one of the long-nosed man's companions.

"Then you lose out thar, too, stranger," retorted the red-shirt. "'Cause in that case, barrin' better rights, it belongs to these two boys by right o' rediscivvery. So don't argue with me; I'm a reg'lar lawyer in argufyin'."

The miner Eph had very politely helped the little woman to the stake, and stooping had traced with his gnarled finger the words on the notice.

"This is the claim," he announced. "Shore as shootin'."

"Hooray!" cheered the Rough and Ready crowd. Said the red-shirt, to the Jacobs trio: "You git! An' I app'int the camp o' Rough an' Ready, here assembled, as a committee of the whole to see that you do git. Don't you stop till you're so far you'll never come back. But fust shell out those dockyments, and be quick."

"Look here. I——" attempted the long-nosed man; but he was interrupted.

"Shell 'em out!" roared red-shirt, advancing a step.

Without a word Mr. Jacobs looked at his companions; and as if in answer to his unspoken appeal one of them (Charley tried hard to compare him with the stranger aboard the California) extracted from a pocketbook the well-remembered slips, and tossed them aside, to the ground.

Charley daringly darted forward and picked them up. Billy followed and rescued his rifle.

"Are those the same?" queried red-shirt, of Charley.

"Yes, sir."

"All right. Now," repeated red-shirt, to the Jacobs trio, "you git, as aforesaid."

That the long-nosed man and his two cronies had guilty consciences was very plain, for replying by naught (and rather white in the face at the threatening advance of several Rough and Ready-ites) they backed away, down the other side of the ridge; at a little distance they shook their fists and yelped something, but they kept on going, so long as Charley looked. They had left not only Billy's gun, but their own guns also.

Young Mrs. Motte now was speaking, and so was her husband.

"It isn't fair," she declared bravely. "This gentleman and his two boys found the claim, again, and have given it up without a word, after all their trouble; and they took care of my uncle, and it looks as though he intended them to have the claim, as much as us."

"He certainly intended them to have some of it — —" added her husband.

"More likely he thought that you hadn't got his letter, and for that reason gave us a chance," put in Mr. Adams, quickly.

"But I owe you the mine, anyway," insisted Mr. Motte. "Your ticket from Panama was what brought me to San Francisco."

"The whole thing's soon settled," boomed the big red-shirt. "I app'int myself chairman of this here town meetin' of the new camp of Gold Hill (the same which is the name of this ridge) — —"

"Hooray for Gold Hill!" cheered the miners.

"An' I further app'int Eph Saunders clerk, to record the minutes when he gets whar thar's somethin' to record with. I'll make the motions, too, if thar's no objection. I move that it be the sense of this camp that the little woman, here, an' her husband, by name o' Motte, be declared legal owners of the Golden West quartz claim, extendin' 100 feet, both sides of the claim stake, followin' the main lode an' includin' all dips an' angles an' spurs whatsoever; the same bein' really two claims, one by 'heritance an' one for luck."

"I second the motion," yelled everybody.

"Moved an' seconded. All in favor can say 'aye.'"

"Aye."

"Next I move it be the sense of this here camp," continued the chairman, "that in consideration of this gentleman an' party havin' sartin rights o' rediscivvery in the Golden West claim, an' havin' sort o' defeated themselves 'cause they were kind to a young feller down at Panama, an' havin' acted mighty white since they've been in these diggin's, they be allowed next ch'ice o' claims, to the extent o' one hundred an' fifty feet along the main lode, on both side o' the Golden West, bein' 300 feet o' claims in all."

"Second the motion."

"Motion bein' seconded, all in favor say 'aye.' An' I hope no citizen of this camp'll be so dogged mean as to say anything else."

"Aye," pealed the lusty chorus.

Mr. Adams tried to speak; Charley and Billy looked at one another and grinned. And Billy waved at his father and Mr. Grigsby, who had pressed up the hill to learn what was going on.

"The motion bein' carried unanimous, the chair app'ints the indivijools known as Pike and Dutch to pace off the aforesaid distances, as close as they can, an' mark the ends."

While everybody gravely watched, the two miners designated paced off the 100 feet, on either side of the stake, along the ridge, and again the 150 feet, further. They hastily marked the distances and returned.

"There bein' no other bus'ness before the meetin'," shouted red-shirt, "I declare it hereby dissolved—an' every man for himself. Stake yore claims, boys, while thar are any!"

Away he jumped, and away broke all. With shouts and cheers and laughter the whole hill was covered, in an incredibly short time, with men picking and digging and peering and driving their stakes or piling up stones.

XXII

THE BEST OF ALL

Mr. Grigsby and Billy's father had arrived in time to hear as well as to see the outcome of the adventure on the newly-named Gold Hill. Watching the retreat of the Jacobs party, Mr. Grigsby, leaning on his rifle, laughed shortly.

"They got off easy," he said, in grim manner. "Let me see the map, boy."

"That smudgy place does look like a 'G. W.'," asserted Charley, passing the paper over. "Anyway, it looks as much like 'G. W.' as it does like 'G. H.'"

And so it did. However, that mattered little now, and the feebly scrawled assignment of the Golden West claim also was of small importance; for the Golden West had been found at last, and everything had turned out all right. Here on Gold Hill, as at the Shirt-tail Diggin's, "the goose hung high."

Now, with everybody busy, it remained to develop the Golden West lode, which under the hurried operations of the bevy of workers could be traced for a mile.

"I suppose," remarked Charley's father, "that the next thing for us to do is to form a company and to lay plans for development, and to name our property."

"If your party have no objections," spoke young Mr. Motte, hesitantly, coming forward, "my wife and I would be very willing to combine our claim with yours, under the name Golden West, and work all together. We are able to do our part, of course."

Certainly there were no objections. Thus the agreement was drawn up, and the Golden West Mining Company was formed from the two parties.

At the base of the ridge there almost immediately sprang into being the town of Gold Hill, for which Mr. Adams himself was elected alcalde, or mayor, and Mrs. Motte clerk. But the development of the Golden West mine went ahead much more slowly. Paying mines, especially lode mines, do not grow up in a day, or a week, or a month. The surface rock could be loosened with pick and crow-bar, and pulverized and washed, to get some gold, but the hard rock below the surface required special machinery, for treatment.

So pending the arrival of the machinery the work was all development work: picking here and there, digging a few tunnels, and much exploring and planning. Hard work it was, too. However, the weather continued to hold fine and sunny and crisp, in the early fall a light snow fell but soon disappeared, and an Indian summer set in. There was hunting for deer and elk, and fun, evenings, in the camp—but something seemed lacking. What that was, Charley found out, when one morning Billy hailed him excitedly.

"Say! Hurrah! Do you know it?"

"No," admitted Charley.

"My father and yours are going to send for my mother and yours! They might be out here with us as well as not. See? They'll be company for Mrs. Motte. She's having a great time, and loves it. If she can stand it, they can—and besides, we want 'em."

Want 'em? Want his mother! Charley let out a wild whoop, and rushed for his father, who greeted him with a twinkle. Why, that was the very thing lacking—his mother! Of course it was. And now— —!

"Do you think it will be Christmas present enough for you?" queried his father. "They'll have just about time to get here for Christmas, we figure."

Surely nothing, not even another Golden West mine, could be half so good for a Christmas present.

Time fairly dragged, despite the busy days. Development work proceeded, but better far and more interesting were the two cabins that were being put up, in readiness for the great day. And suddenly (for all things come to him who waits!) Charley and Billy found themselves actually delegated to go down to San Francisco—just they two—and meet two Somebodies at the steamer pier!

It seemed great to be sent on such an errand; and it gave one rather an important feeling to be alone and responsible in a city like San Francisco. By way of Sacramento and the river and bay they landed there—two real miners from the hills, clad in their miner costumes.

They had intended to put up at the Parker-house; but at Sacramento rumors of a great fire reached them, and sure enough, they found San Francisco still smouldering. For in the middle of December fire had swept through all the flimsy buildings of down town. The whole of Portsmouth Square lay in ashes. However, already new buildings were going up as fast as hands could work. Nobody seemed discouraged, but toiled with a cheer. The floor beams of another Parker-house had been placed—and this new Parker-house was to be of brick! Good for San Francisco!

That night Charley and Billy slept in a large tent that had been erected by the Parker-house to take care of what patrons it could. Charley had tried to show his partner the "sights," but in only those few months San Francisco had changed amazingly. It had doubled in population since that date when the steamer California had landed the Adams party in the bay, and its people had changed, too. Why, there were as well-dressed men and women on the streets as in St. Louis; and some of the stores which had not burned were like Eastern stores!

A new scheme had been invented. On top of a high hill called Telegraph Hill, overlooking the Golden Gate, a signal had been installed. It consisted of a tall post equipped with wooden paddles, like arms, that flourished in a system of wigwags. The positions of the arms signaled "brig," "bark," "side-wheel steamer," etc. And on "steamer day"—a day when one of the big mail and passenger steamers was expected in—every citizen was gazing at Telegraph Hill to see the arms extend horizontally right and left, wigwagging, at last, "side-wheel steamer."

"The Panama! When was the Panama due?"

"On the nineteenth, bub."

But would she come? Supposing she were late. Then those mothers might be late, too, for Christmas! But she was not late; no, sir; for at sunset of theeighteenth, see, up went the two arms of the signal on Telegraph Hill, extended horizontally to announce: "Side-wheel steamer entering the Golden Gate." And presently there came the Panama, surging majestically through the channel, and rounding to before the city.

That was a long night, intervening before the passengers might land. Charley and Billy slept scarcely a wink. They were at the wharf bright and early—but no earlier than an army of other persons almost as excited as they. The Panama began to unload her passengers; the usual fleet of skiffs and ship's boats put out, filled, from her side.

Charley and Billy peered expectantly. Supposing, after all, those mothers had missed the Panama and had not come. But no! That was they, wasn't it, in the second boat? Yes! Hurrah and hurrah! Forward bolted Charley; forward bolted Billy; and delivered such a series of frantic hugs that their mothers simplyhad to know them, in spite of tan and clothes.

"Why!" gasped Charley's mother, holding him off a moment, to gain breath and to make sure. "How well you look! Where's your father? Is he all right? When do we get to the mine? Are things going well? Oh, Charley, but I'm glad to see you!"

"Everything's splendid," panted Charley. "But this is the best of all."

And from the behavior of Billy and his mother, Charley rather imagined that they agreed with him.

So it proved to be a merry Christmas at Gold Hill and the Golden West mine. And thus the famous year of Forty-nine passed into the busy prosperous year of Fifty, during which California and the Golden West mine grew and prospered together.

9 781836 571872